# "Look," He said, Night Was Just One of Those Things.

We both wanted it, but both of us know it's over. I enjoyed it and so did you, so what are you so upset about?"

What could she say? Because I'm disappointed in myself? Because you don't give a damn about me? "I could ask you the same thing," Randy murmured.

Luke shrugged. "Maybe it comes down to the fact that I'm not interested in a purely physical affair."

"Are you saying that's all it could ever be? That I'm not the type of woman you want to associate with?"

"Yes," he said bluntly, and walked away.

---

## BROOKE HASTINGS

is that rare individual who can combine many careers and excel in all of them. In addition to her writing, she is active in California politics and community affairs and maintains a home for her husband of many years and their two children.

Dear Reader,

Silhouette Special Editions are an exciting new line of contemporary romances from Silhouette Books. Special Editions are written specifically for our readers who want a story with greater romantic detail.

Special Editions have all the elements you've enjoyed in Silhouette Romances and *more*. These stories concentrate on romance in a longer, more realistic and sophisticated way, and they feature greater sensual detail.

I hope you enjoy this book and all the wonderful romances from Silhouette. We welcome any suggestions or comments and invite you to write to us at the address below.

Jane Nicholls
Silhouette Books
PO Box 177
Dunton Green
Sevenoaks
Kent
TN13 2YE

# BROOKE HASTINGS

## An Act of Love

*Silhouette*

*Special Edition*

Published by Silhouette Books

Copyright © 1983 by Deborah Gordon

Map by Ray Lundgren

*First printing 1983*


**British Library C.I.P.**

Hastings, Brooke
    An act of love.—(Silhouette special edition)
    I. Title
    813'.54[F]        PS3515.A82868

    ISBN 0 340 34379 6

Printed and bound in Great Britain for
Hodder and Stoughton Paperbacks, a
division of Hodder and Stoughton Ltd.,
Mill Road, Dunton Green, Sevenoaks,
Kent (Editorial Office: 47 Bedford
Square, London, WC1 3DP) by
Richard Clay (The Chaucer Press) Ltd.,
Bungay, Suffolk

For my father-in-law, Jules Gordon

# An Act
# of Love

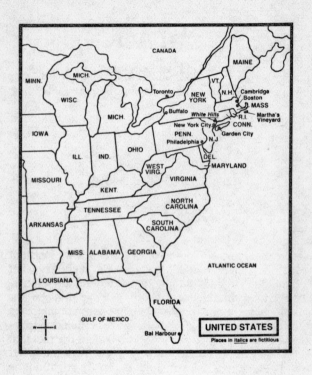

CANADA

MINN.

MICH.

WISC.

MICH.

Toronto

NEW
YORK

VT.

MAINE

N.H.

Cambridge
Boston
R.I. MASS

Buffalo

White Hills

Martha's
Vineyard

IOWA

New York City

CONN.

PENN.

Garden City

ILL.

IND.

OHIO

Philadelphia

N.J.

MISSOURI

WEST
VIRG.

DEL.

MARYLAND

VIRGINIA

KENT.

TENNESSEE

NORTH
CAROLINA

ARKANSAS

SOUTH
CAROLINA

MISS. ALABAMA

GEORGIA

ATLANTIC OCEAN

LOUISIANA

FLORIDA

N
W        E
S

GULF OF MEXICO

Bal Harbour

**UNITED STATES**

Places in *italics* are fictitious

# Chapter One

Miranda Dunne's stomach emitted a low, insistent growl. She had known her father's secretary, Pat O'Donnell, for far too many years to feel any embarrassment; on the contrary, the knowledge that she was actually hungry brought nothing but surprise and then relief. For the past six months her once-healthy appetite had hidden out in parts unknown, and the fact that it had rejoined her on her visit to New York made her think that leaving California permanently might not be a bad idea.

Pat smiled, looking up and down Randy's slender body but making no comment on the twenty-five pounds that had disappeared since her last visit to the office at Christmastime. "Didn't you eat anything this morning?" she asked.

Randy shook her head. "Not really, even though they plied me with food on the plane. There I was, trying to get some sleep, and the flight attendant kept coming around with one meal after another."

She mimicked the motherly first-class stewardess with a piquant accuracy which was too good-natured to be truly cutting. "'Would you like some cheese and crackers, dear? It's imported brie. No? How about some fresh fruit then?'"

Pat lazed back in her chair, enjoying the performance, and Randy went on, "An hour later it was cold cuts. 'Corned beef, roast beef or pastrami, dear. You're so thin. Are you sure you don't want me to fix you a sandwich?' And an hour before we got into New York I woke up to the smell of omelets and sausage. I settled for toast and coffee. I figured Dad would take me to his favorite French restaurant for lunch, and I didn't want to spoil my appetite." Or what's left of it, she thought to herself.

She glanced at her watch. "My stomach says it's five after ten even though the time in New York is five after one, so why am I dying for cream sauces and French pastry?"

"Because you love to eat." Pat hesitated, a look of concern on her face. "At least, you *used* to love to eat. What have you been doing to yourself in Los Angeles? Trying some crazy new diet?"

Randy didn't tell the truth because the truth was much too painful to discuss. "I was up for a part in a movie and I had to lose a lot of weight," she said. Her breezy smile was totally convincing. "I didn't get the part, so I can't *wait* to gain back at least fifteen of the twenty-five pounds I lost. I was a little too heavy, Pat—over one twenty-five."

"You're five-seven. One hundred and twenty-five pounds isn't too heavy except in Hollywood." Pat glanced back over her shoulder at the closed door to her boss' office, then added, "Bill told you to meet him at twelve-thirty?"

Randy nodded. "Right. He's usually prompt to the point of neurosis. What on earth is going on in there?"

*"That,"* Pat answered, "is the sixty-four-thousand-

dollar question." She tossed a report she'd been editing into a file folder and put it to one side of her desk. From her bottom drawer she produced a box of breadsticks, holding it out for Randy's inspection. "Want one?"

"If he's going to be out soon, I probably should wait." Randy eyed the breadsticks covetously. "On the other hand . . . Do you think it would be all right if I knocked on the door and asked him how much longer. . . ."

"I wouldn't," Pat answered firmly. "Take a breadstick, Randy. As you've just pointed out, your father never keeps people waiting, so if he's taking this long, there's a good reason for it."

Her curiosity aroused, Randy tried a different tack. Bill Dunne had a device on his telephone that permitted Pat to listen in on his private conversations. It was powerful enough to pick up anything in his office above a whisper, and Bill left it switched on for all but the most confidential of meetings. He'd installed it so that Pat could take notes without being physically present or, if a meeting was running overlong, listen in and decide whether or not to rescue him. After nineteen years as his secretary she was almost an alter-ego.

Randy winked at her and reached for the phone, but Pat promptly pushed her hand away from the receiver. "It's personal, not business, Randy," she explained. "I couldn't violate your father's privacy." She held up the box of breadsticks again.

With the charming shrug of a con artist who's been caught in the act, Randy accepted the box and rapidly disposed of a pair of breadsticks. Then she cocked an inquiring eyebrow at Pat.

"Well?" Her tone was as teasing as it was eager. "Who's Dad talking to?"

A discreet silence greeted this query. Randy thought privately that Pat O'Donnell would have made a wonderful secret agent. In the intensely competitive world of department store retailing neither the bribes of competitors nor the machinations of the press could induce her to confide even the most minor detail of the company's business. Amused, Randy tried again.

"Remember, Pat," she murmured conspiratorially, "you're talking to the heiress apparent. Come clean. Is the fate of millions being decided behind that closed door? Is Dad buying stolen Paris designs or hatching schemes to take over Neiman-Marcus?"

Randy's melodramatic questions were of less interest to Pat O'Donnell than her mocking reference to herself as "the heiress apparent." Although amused by Randy's cloak-and-dagger tone of voice, she had no intention of satisfying her curiosity. Instead she began to pepper her with questions.

"Heiress apparent? Are you leaving California? Resigning from the repertory company? Does your father know? Or are you going to tell him at lunch today?"

Randy was spared the necessity of answering by the sound of a door being flung open so forcefully that the intricate silver doorknob smashed into the hand-painted wallpaper on the adjacent wall. A tall, powerfully-built man charged out of her father's office like an enraged bull, his head down, so that only his wavy brown hair was visible. Randy wondered if his face matched his beautifully proportioned body, which was as perfect as any professional actor's. He stalked across the oriental carpet, repeated his ungentle ministrations on the outer door and disappeared from view.

Randy had winced with each violent slam. "Who," she asked incredulously, "was *that?*" Not only had the man treated her father's beautifully furnished outer office with careless disdain, never in her life had she witnessed such a display of temper from one of the company's employees. Given Bill Dunne's low-key approach it was surely unnecessary, and given his commanding personality, it was definitely foolhardy.

"*That,*" Pat said, mimicking Randy's tone, "is our

newest vice president, Luke Griffin. He supervises the fifteen branch stores. Incidentally, he's also your competition—at least, *my* money's on him to succeed your father as president of this humble little empire. Although after the scene we just witnessed . . ."

Pat's voice trailed off as her boss emerged from his office. The usually suave William Dunne was looking distinctly harried, his customarily perfect appearance marred by a loosened, off-center tie. His graying blond hair was in disarray, as though an anxious or exasperated hand had recently been run through it.

His expression changed to one of apology when he noticed Randy, who was standing stock-still, clutching the box of breadsticks. He promptly walked over and enfolded her in a lingering hug. Upon her release, she straightened his tie and smoothed his hair, then submitted a bit nervously to his inspection of her appearance.

His eyes traveled from her long blond hair, which fell several inches below her shoulders, to the dark blue eyes that matched his own, down the length of her body. Her silk-blend, printed shirtwaist dress was appraised with a professional eye. "First," he informed her, "I want to know how you manage to look so glamorous when you've been flying half the night. And second"—he looked mildly sheepish—"tell me who designed the dress. It isn't anyone we carry, but we should."

"Always business," Randy teased. "I'll make you a deal, Dad. Take me to lunch before I pass out from starvation and I'll tell you where I bought the dress."

"Agreed." Bill smiled. He reeled off a short list of instructions to Pat and then took Randy's arm. "Your mother called to warn me about how much weight you'd lost," he said as they walked out of the office, "but she didn't mention that you were even skinnier than your sister. What kind of role were you up for? A prisoner of war?"

"A model." They stepped inside a private elevator. "You know how heavy I photograph, Dad. I looked like a blimp in that diaper commercial I did last year."

"You looked like a contented new mother, which was exactly how you were supposed to look," Bill retorted. He added that he'd never understood why Randy was always so worried about her weight, and that he never should have allowed her to leave New York in the first place.

Randy didn't bother to remind him that he'd had no choice in the matter. At twenty-two she'd wanted nothing more than to flee the nest, so after finishing college in New York City she'd enrolled in a master's degree program in theatre arts in Los Angeles. Her father grudgingly paid her way, but if he hadn't she would have used the money she'd inherited on her twenty-first birthday. After the first year of graduate school, however, she was bored with studying and eager to live in the "real world." Her goal was to support herself as an actress without spending any of her inheritance. That she'd succeeded was due more to the diaper commercial than to her job at the Westwood Theatre Company, where she earned a meager salary for doing everything from painting scenery to acting in plays.

Sometimes Randy had wondered if the financial security of having the inheritance money had detracted from the drive and ambition that an actress needed to succeed, but over the last few months she'd come to believe that she was too gentle to reach the top. She couldn't stomach the idea of clawing past the people ahead of her and stepping on the ones beneath. It was part of the reason she'd come to New York.

She and her father took the elevator down to the main floor of Conover-Dunne's flagship store in Manhattan, walking out past a special promotion of merchandise from the People's Republic of China that tied in with the scheduled visit of the Chinese premier later that month. Walking south along Lexington Avenue, Randy paused to admire a competitor's window display, remarking to her father that C & D should try to steal away the person who'd designed them.

They turned east, enjoying the early June sunshine and warm breeze. As they walked, Bill told Randy that her grandparents had called from Paris the day before and sent her their love. Jonathan Conover, who had founded the company forty-four years before and now held the title of chairman, was spending the summer in Europe, on a buying trip with Randy's grandmother.

As soon as they stepped inside the French restaurant an obsequious maître d' greeted them with a broad smile and an accent that Randy decided was either a total fabrication or, at the very least, a considerable exaggeration. Although they were forty-five minutes late it seemed there would be no question of keeping Monsieur Dunne waiting. They were seated immediately at a quiet table to one side of the crowded room; Randy admired the fluid grace with which the maître d' slid the reserved sign from the table with one hand while smoothly relieving William Dunne of a ten-dollar bill with the other.

The sommelier hurried over in response to Bill's subtle beckoning, returning as requested with a bottle of French wine. The ritual of opening and tasting correctly performed and the wine duly approved, the waiter materialized to take their order. Finally, the preliminaries having been attended to, Bill raised his glass and smiled at Randy.

"To my beautiful daughter Miranda, who in twenty-four and a half years has never once precipitated an ulcer attack."

Only because I don't tell you the things that would upset you, Randy thought, then listened with growing amusement as he continued, "May she take into account her father's precarious health, abandon her no-doubt dazzling career in Tinseltown and come back to New York where she belongs, to the bosom of the family that loves and misses her."

Randy shook her head, laughing, and sipped her wine. After accusing her father of emotional blackmail, she reminded him that his health was perfect and that he'd never had an ulcer attack in his life. Then she added coyly, "You forgot the part about coming into the family business, Dad. Although I'll never understand why Linda doesn't get equal nagging time. She's just as smart as I am, with fabulous taste and twice my energy, and—"

"And she's totally incorrigible," Bill interrupted. To Randy's amazement, he proceeded to empty half his glass in a single draught.

"Business must be terrific if you can afford to swill down expensive wine like it cost three seventy-nine and came out of a jug," Randy said. "Or else something's actually flapped the unflappable William Dunne. It wouldn't have anything to do with the reason why you were half an hour late, would it?"

"I think you've figured out that it has everything to do with the reason I was half an hour late. *And* with your older sister Linda." Bill had no sooner reached for his glass again than a waiter darted over to refill it. He made no attempt to hide his irritation from Randy, but instead met her thoughtful look, his mouth curved into a frown.

Although math had never been Randy's strongest subject in school she had learned to add one and one with reasonable proficiency. "Linda—and the man who came storming out of your office. Pat said he was a new vice president. Is something going on between them? " she asked.

Her arithmetic was accurate, but she'd inserted the wrong man into her equation. Bill was quick to correct the error. "Linda and Luke's brother-in-law. His younger sister's husband. Or so he says." He shook his head impatiently. "I shouldn't be discussing this with you—it's not your problem."

Randy knew exactly *why* he thought he shouldn't be discussing it with her—the details were presumably too sordid for her innocent ears—and reacted with a mixture of amusement and exasperation. "I've been hearing about Linda's transgressions from the time I was twelve and she spent the night with that pimply rock musician boyfriend of hers," she reminded her father. "It didn't corrupt me then and it won't corrupt me now. After twelve more years of her escapades I thought you'd stopped being upset about what she does."

"I try to stay out of her life. I understand that it's a waste of time to try to talk any sense into her when she's determined to make a mistake. But that doesn't mean I don't love her, Randy, or feel a sense of responsibility toward her." Bill's explanation reeked of parental tolerance. "Luke's been unusually moody since last Thursday, and that's not like him. He has a temper, but usually he either keeps it under control or says what's on his mind and then puts it behind him. It was obvious to me that something was wrong, so I decided to have it out with him. I called him into the office and forced him to tell me what was eating him. I almost wish I hadn't. He told me that Linda had met his brother-in-law at the company picnic on Memorial Day. Luke wasn't there—he had to work—but his sister and her husband were visiting from Poughkeepsie and he thought they'd enjoy spending the day at the country club. He sent them along. His sister called him the following Wednesday night, hysterical because she suspected her husband had spent the weekend with another woman—Linda."

"So?" Randy didn't find the situation particularly palatable, but it was hardly the stuff of major confrontations either. "Married men have been having affairs ever since marriage was invented, although I admit I'm disappointed in Lin. I thought she stuck to the single ones."

Bill seemed a little startled by his daughter's matter-of-fact response, but agreed with a sigh. "You and me both. The problem is that Luke is incredibly protective of his sister. And he's been with C & D almost a year, which is long enough to hear the gossip about Linda's marriages. Once I got him going he was like one of those Fourth of July firecrackers that won't stop exploding. What was I supposed to do when he called my daughter a tramp and asked me why I couldn't control her? Agree with him and apologize? I told him to come back when he'd raised the perfect daughter and threw him out of my office."

"You actually lost your temper?" Randy was awe-struck. "But you're always so . . . calm. When Linda left Brett for her tennis instructor you never said a word. I assumed . . ." She lifted her shoulders, momentarily speechless.

"You assumed wrong. I don't approve of Linda's private life, you know that, but there's a caring, outgoing side to her that anyone would have to admire. I won't sit there and listen to someone who doesn't even know her condemn her out of hand." Bill shook his head, looking a little rueful. "I overreacted, I suppose, but it could have been worse. He could have been complaining about *you.*"

"I'm glad he wasn't." Randy had never attempted to correct her father's rather unrealistic view of her; Linda's mistakes had caused him more than enough parental guilt without adding her own to the load. "Listen, Dad," she said, "you tried your best with Lin. No daughter could ask for more wonderful parents than you and Mom, but there's something wild in her, something almost self-destructive at times. She's got all that energy, all that restlessness. There's nothing anyone can do about it—except Lin herself."

"Sure, I know that." Bill slowly sipped his wine. "*Rationally* I know that. Most of all I'm probably annoyed with myself for losing my temper over the whole thing. I didn't go to all the trouble to lure Luke Griffin away from Stockman's in California just to have him resign in a rage over some pointless argument that I should have had the tact to avoid."

Randy was intrigued by the statement. Her father preferred to promote from within his organization and rarely resorted to luring executives away from his competitors. He was astute enough in recruiting talent and wise enough in developing it that he seldom needed to go on a corporate raid.

She was forced to contain her curiosity because the waiter was approaching with their first course. Although her father seemed to have little interest in the scallops in wine sauce that were placed on the table in front of him, Randy laid siege to her shrimp. She only succumbed to the urge to question him further when half the plate was clean.

"Aren't you going to tell me more about this paragon of yours?" she asked. "Did you really swipe him away from Stockman's? And is Grandpa thinking of retiring as chairman so you can move up? Because Pat claims he's going to steal the presidency out from under my nose."

Bill Dunne cocked an eyebrow at his daughter, his attention caught by her last statement. "What happened to spending the rest of your life in California? I thought trying to recruit you for C & D was a lost cause."

But Randy was not to be sidetracked. "First you tell me about Luke Griffin, and then I'll tell you what I've decided."

Her father leaned back in his chair, a teasing smile on his face. "As a matter of fact, I had him in mind for you. Intelligent, handsome, charming—and single.

While you're in New York, why not go out to dinner with him? He's . . ."

"Hold it right there," Randy ordered, waving her hand back and forth in protest. "No matchmaking. Just because *you* married the boss' daughter and took over the company doesn't mean you have to marry *me* off to some hotshot vice president who wants to do the same thing."

"And how is your social life these days, Miranda?" her father asked. "Still keeping them all at arm's length?"

The gentle gibe found its target, but not for the reasons that Bill Dunne thought it would. Having grown up with the example of a promiscuous older sister, Randy had consciously set out to avoid the mistakes that Linda had made. For the first twenty-three years of her life she'd succeeded, but then she'd met a fellow actor named Sean Raley who'd made her forget every sensible resolution she'd ever made. As a result of their love affair Randy was considerably less naive and self-righteous than she used to be.

"Would it be the worst thing in the world if I never married?" she asked her father. "Men today don't seem to want to take the time to develop a relationship before they jump all over you. And very few of them are interested in making a commitment."

"If I made that kind of blanket statement about women your feminist sensibilities would be outraged," Bill replied. "Men aren't all the same. Why don't you go out with Luke? I promise you he won't jump all over you."

"I thought you were furious with him, that he was threatening to resign."

"So we'll both apologize and that will be the end of it. I've told him about you, honey. He's looking forward to meeting you."

Randy was not particularly tempestuous; on the contrary, she was unusually good-natured and accommodating. But her father had pushed too hard on the sorest of spots. She wasn't interested in Luke Griffin or anyone else right now.

"One more word about Mr. Griffin and you can find yourself another daughter—or heiress apparent," she said firmly. "Here I've finally decided that I'd like to learn enough about the business to make a decision about the future, and all you want to do is marry me off to some ambitious vice president who'd probably sell his soul to get his hands on C & D. Of course he'd like to meet me! But I don't intend to be the docile little woman behind some insufferably arrogant man." She frowned at her plate, then stabbed a hapless shrimp with her fork.

It irked her no end when her father merely chortled. "I told you, Luke is very charming—most of the time. Once you meet him you won't stand a chance. So when will you start work? Tomorrow?"

"I'm going to Cambridge tomorrow to see Linda," Randy informed him, "and then up to New Hampshire for a while. After that I'll have to straighten out a few things in Los Angeles before I can come back to New York and start work."

Bill lit his pipe, took several puffs and pushed aside his plate. "I'm tempted to ask you if you want a theatre date tonight, but I have the feeling that if I did, the rest of your shrimp would wind up on my head." He winked at her, smiling broadly.

"You're being charming," Randy accused, smiling in spite of herself. "I'm certainly not going to argue with you when I've been looking forward to seeing you and Mom for months. Why don't you tell me your plans for me—besides marrying me off, that is."

Over the rest of lunch Bill did exactly that. Randy listened with growing enthusiasm as he described the company's executive training program, which would begin in September. She even managed to hold on to her temper when he announced that she would spend the summer itself as the executive assistant of his favorite vice president, Luke Griffin. It was obvious that she could learn a lot from the man and she was perfectly willing to do so, just as long as the course of study was confined to retailing.

After lunch Randy toyed with the idea of spending the rest of the afternoon shopping at C & D for clothes befitting an executive trainee, but the combination of jet lag and French wine had made her so sleepy that she decided to hail a taxi to her parents' apartment instead. She walked in to find a note from her mother, Emily, an interior decorator, saying that she was shopping with a client and would be home at dinnertime.

Randy curled up on the canopy bed in the bedroom she had occupied while growing up and fell asleep almost immediately, thinking that her parents had left the room exactly as it had been two years before, when she left for California. Her tastes had become more sophisticated over the years and she would certainly want something other than pink and white ruffles if she stayed in New York permanently. It never occurred to her not to live at home; it was better than spending her salary on some tiny apartment far from the store. As for privacy, thanks to Sean Raley she felt no particular need for it.

Emily and Bill arrived home together, bringing Italian food and a bottle of chianti from Randy's favorite neighborhood hangout. They ate in the dining room, the cardboard pizza box looking incongruous in the company of the Dunnes' inlaid hardwood table and French crystal wine glasses. When the subject of Randy's trip to New Hampshire came up, Bill began a worried catechism.

"You're sure you'll be all right up there?" he asked.

Randy assured him that she would, only to have him continue, "It sounds pretty primitive—no phone, no indoor plumbing. You need to rest and gain some weight, not rough it in the woods. I think you should call us. . . ."

"Good grief, Bill," Emily groaned, "stop treating her like a baby. When she was in California we didn't hear from her for weeks at a time and you didn't carry on this way." She looked at Randy. "You go up there and have yourself a great time, honey. Heaven knows you're going to need to be relaxed when you come to work at the store. We'll be gearing up for fall."

Randy shot her mother a grateful look, saying, "I thought I'd spend a day or two with Linda before I join Sarah and her sister in New Hampshire."

"I know she'd love to see you. She's just settling into the house she bought, although knowing Lin," Emily laughed, "she's probably reacquainted herself with all her old Cambridge pals by now. She stayed with us for a few days on her way up from Texas. Did Dad tell you?"

Randy glanced at her father, who had taken a sudden interest in his pizza. It seemed he had chosen not to acquaint Emily with Linda's recent activities, so Randy assumed that a change of subject was definitely called for. She accomplished this so skillfully that her parents never realized that she was purposely steering the conversation away from Linda and onto her most recent acting job.

She took great delight in convincing her father that she'd played a bedroom scene in the nude, but his shock gave way to chagrin as soon as she admitted she was only teasing. Her mother promptly announced that the stage would lose a superb actress if Randy decided to go to work for C & D.

Randy's body was still on California time, and she had difficulty both in falling asleep that night and getting up the next morning. She managed to stay awake long enough to have breakfast with her parents and kiss them goodbye, then went back to sleep for another two hours before getting up for good.

Her first thought was to contact Linda and let her know she'd be spending the night. Lin had no phone yet; she'd left the number of the downstairs tenant in case the Dunnes wanted to reach her. Randy called, accepting the woman's offer to leave a note on Linda's door saying that Randy would arrive about three. Randy only hoped that Linda would see the message and remember to be in the apartment to let her in. If her sister were running true to form she probably spent very little time at home.

The New Hampshire woods didn't require an extensive wardrobe, so Randy packed only a few pairs of jeans and tee shirts, a nightgown and swimsuit, and some toiletries into her small canvas travel bag. She also borrowed an old ski jacket from her mother's closet in case the weather turned chilly. The trip through Connecticut and Massachusetts wasn't especially scenic or enjoyable, but the radio made the time pass quickly enough. Unfortunately, about halfway to Cambridge the air conditioning on her father's Lincoln turned recalcitrant. The air became less and less cool until it became more comfortable to shut off the system and open the windows. Rather than stop at a service station along the way and risk a possible fleecing, Randy decided to endure the heat and humidity and wait until she arrived in Cambridge to have the car checked out.

She had no problem following her parents' directions to Linda's house, and at two forty-five pulled up to a fairly new two-family house with brown siding and white shutters. She spent the next twenty minutes looking for a parking space because the small driveway belonging to the house was illegally blocked by a beaten-up van. Then a car pulled out around the corner and Randy quickly edged into the space.

The outer door to the building was unlocked so she

went inside. There was a door at the rear of the downstairs hall that opened into the tenant's apartment, while a flight of steps to the left led up to Linda's half of the house.

Randy was two steps from the top of the stairs when she heard the outer door open and then slam shut behind her. She turned just as a breathless Linda came charging up behind her.

"I'm so glad you just got here. I got Mrs. Siskin's note but I had to go run an errand," her sister explained, giving her a hug. "And then I got stuck in the most miserable traffic along the river and now some jerk is blocking my driveway." She fished out her key and opened the door.

The apartment was in total chaos. Wallpaper had been partially removed from four of the five rooms. The only furnishings were a bridge table and two chairs in the dinette and a pair of twin-sized mattresses and box springs in one bedroom. A black and white television set sat on the kitchen counter and cartons were stacked up everywhere. Linda, never terribly interested in housekeeping, had left dirty laundry scattered all over the bathroom floor.

After a quick inspection Randy asked weakly, "What happened to your furniture from Dallas?"

"It reminded me of Brett." Linda wrinkled her nose as she uttered her ex-husband's name. Brett Franck was an oil millionaire twice Linda's age. He had held his beautiful young wife's interest for even less time than her first husband, a Harvard instructor whom she'd married at twenty-one and divorced four years later.

"Besides," Linda went on, "it's been fun shopping for new things. I've had a great time since I got here last week—all I've done is buy, besides seeing my friends, that is. It's terrific to see you again, Randy. I'm glad we'll be spending some time together, even in *this*." Her hand circled the living room where they stood.

It was obvious to Randy that Linda assumed she'd be staying for more than a day or two. "I'm only staying till tomorrow—or Thursday at the latest," she said.

Linda looked totally deflated. "Only two nights? But we haven't seen each other since Christmas, and we barely had a chance to talk then. I thought you would stay a few weeks. We've grown so far apart since I married Brett and you went to California—I thought we could catch up."

Linda seemed so genuinely upset that Randy felt terribly guilty. "I'll come back later in the summer," she promised. "I'm going to move back to New York for at least a few months and try working for C & D. But I made plans to go up to New Hampshire with a friend from college and her sister—their family has a cabin up there."

For the first time since Randy's arrival Linda really looked at her sister, and what she saw distressed her. "I thought you loved acting," she said. "How come you're thinking of giving it up?"

Randy shrugged. "It isn't as much fun as I thought it would be."

"Really?" Linda studied Randy for an additional five seconds. "You've lost a lot of weight."

Randy started to explain about the movie role she'd been dieting for, but her voice trailed off as Linda's dubious look deepened into disbelief. "It's a long story," she finally said, her voice slightly husky.

Linda put a comforting arm around Randy's shoulders. "It always is, with men," she murmured. "You can tell me about it over dinner, but right now I need to go to the supermarket. Keep me company?"

Randy agreed, wondering how her sister had immediately guessed the real reason for the absent twenty-five pounds when the rest of her family had so easily swallowed her story about the movie role. Experience, she supposed, and the fact that up until two years ago the two sisters had been unusually close.

Although Linda was four years older than Randy, she'd almost never complained when Randy tried on her makeup or barged in on her and her friends or borrowed her clothing. Every crush and dream and hope had been confided in her older sister, even though the reverse was certainly not true. As for their recent estrangement, it was Randy's doing, not Linda's.

As they shopped for groceries, Randy was reminded of just how much fun her sister could be. Linda entertained her with stories of Dallas society, mimicking the southern belles and Texas oilmen almost as perfectly as Randy might have. By the time they got home and Randy started cooking dinner she was in a much better mood and no longer anxious to run up to New Hampshire.

Linda was still on the subject of her marriage when they sat down to eat. "I really thought I was in love with Brett," she explained as she helped herself to a piece of fish, "and I admit he spoiled me rotten when it came to material things. But after six months the marriage was a disaster. His children hated me. I was bored and restless—he wouldn't hear of me taking a job—so I filled my days with charity work and tennis. Everyone was twice my age, except for the tennis pro." She made a helpless little gesture with her right hand. "After the first few months Brett and I might as well have had separate bedrooms, Randy. The tennis pro—Andy—kept chasing me, and eventually I let him catch me. He even proposed, but at least I had the sense not to plunge into another marriage. I came back to Cambridge because I was happier here than anywhere else, even though my marriage to Jerry didn't work out."

"What are you going to do up here?" Randy asked.

"I've thought about putting my fine arts degree to use by opening a gallery or antique shop." Linda was only pushing her fish around now, a wistful look on her face. "What I'd like most of all is to be a buyer for

C & D, traveling around the way Grandma and Grandpa do, looking for one-of-a-kind items for the boutique in the Manhattan store. But I know Dad would never give me the chance—not given his opinion of me."

"You'd be surprised at his opinion of you," Randy told her sister. "He got into a huge argument with one of his executives over you."

Linda laid down her fork, totally baffled, and Randy proceeded to explain what had happened between Bill Dunne and Luke Griffin. Lin was both surprised and pleased that her father had defended her so staunchly, murmuring when Randy finished the story, "Tom Havemeyer. I'll be darned. I didn't realize he was related to anyone at C & D—he told me he worked for one of our suppliers. The funny thing is, I never go out with married men. I don't need that kind of trouble. You have to sneak around, and all they want to do is tell you their troubles. But Tom begged me to meet him, and he was so sweet that I broke my rule and made an exception for him."

"I think you'd better unmake it," Randy said. "That brother-in-law of his is liable to come up here and strangle you if you don't."

Randy didn't miss the calculating look in Linda's eyes. "I was supposed to see him again this weekend. I really am fond of him." She shrugged a trifle too dramatically. "But it looks like I'd better end it. I'll make you a deal, Randy. I'll try to talk some sense into Tom and send him back to his no-doubt loving wife if you'll stay with me for a week or two and keep me company." She flashed an engaging smile at her sister. "What do you say?"

"You were going to stop seeing him anyway, I could tell," Randy protested.

"And you were going to agree to stay here with me anyway, *I* could tell," Linda shot back.

Randy, knowing when she was beaten, admitted that Linda was right. "The truth is, I need someone to talk to," she said. "And not just anyone. You. But first of all, I owe you an apology, Lin. I was upset after your first divorce, because I really loved Jerry, but when you married Brett, I was . . . shocked, I suppose. I told myself you wanted his money, even though I know that's ridiculous. Neither of us will ever have to worry about where our next designer dress is coming from. Anyway, I've sort of cut you out of my life for the last few years and I'm sorry. I was very childish."

Linda found some paper cups in a half-unpacked box and took a bottle of wine out of the refrigerator. "Let's go sit in the bedroom," she said. As they walked across the living room, she added, "I understood what you felt. You needed to be on your own, away from the family, to grow up. You also needed to learn a little about life to stop judging me so harshly. But you got hurt along the way, didn't you?"

Randy nodded, suddenly unable to speak, and sprawled out on the bed.

Linda sat down beside her. "Randy?" she prompted softly.

She shook her head. "I just—I've never talked about it." She hadn't even told her apartment-mate, preferring to put up a false front of sophisticated acceptance.

A moment later Linda's arms were around her and she was sobbing on her sister's shoulder, choking out half-coherent phrases. "I was crazy about him—when he'd touch me—and then he went to Italy—and all the gossip—people kept telling me. . . ."

It took a long time for Randy to control herself, and Linda patiently waited, murmuring gentle words of sympathy. Eventually, of course, the story came pouring out. Sean Raley was handsome and smooth and Randy had fallen like the proverbial ton of bricks. He'd left for Italy in the middle of their blazing love affair for a minor role in a film, but it wasn't very long before stories in the local tabloids appeared, speculating on his relationship with the daughter of his director.

"I guess it's an old story," Randy said in a flat tone of voice. "His letters came less and less often, and when people would ask about him I'd shrug and say that of course all men played around. But it was tearing me apart. He used to tell me he loved me. I thought he wanted to marry me, but obviously he didn't, because he married the director's daughter four months ago. She'll help his career a lot more than I ever could."

"I'd like to kill the man," Linda muttered.

"He's not worth it." Despite the bitter overtone, Randy knew it was the truth. Now that she was calmer she could face the most shattering part of the whole experience. "I don't think I really ever loved him, Lin. I was crazy about him, and wildly infatuated, but I never bothered to look beneath the surface and see the selfishness and egotism there. When I think about how bad my judgment was, about how stupid I was. . . ." She paused. "Sean hurt me, but I hurt myself more. And I always prided myself on being so level-headed, and—and moral."

"Welcome to liberation," Linda drawled.

There was something about Linda's expression, so world-weary yet indomitable, that made Randy smile. "I suppose I'm over Sean," she said, "and I'm even getting my appetite back. For the first time in my life I don't have to worry about what I eat, so I guess I should thank him for that. But I don't have any interest in other men. Dad's trying to match me up with that insane vice president of his, Luke Griffin, and I almost wish I could tell him about Sean just so he'd drop the subject. But I can't."

"Knowing Dad, I agree. But you need to get back into circulation," Linda said. "Take it from a veteran, Randy, the best way to get over an unhappy love affair is with a new man. And you might even *like* Luke Griffin."

Randy straightened up, a little irritated. "Do you think I want to go out with someone who knows that ten thousand shares of Dunne Industries stock will be part of the package? Not to mention the presidency of the company? The man will probably ooze charm and try to convince me he's madly in love with me. And with my track record, I'll probably be stupid enough to believe him!"

"All men are liars and cheats," Linda said solemnly.

Randy quickly understood Linda's point; she flushed and looked into her lap. "Are you telling me they're not?" she asked.

"That's exactly what I'm telling you," Linda answered.

# Chapter Two

$\mathcal{L}$ inda left the house at ten the next morning to go into Boston to look at oriental carpets for the living room. Randy decided to stay at home, telling Linda that she felt the need to do something more physical than shop, and teasing that one look at the kitchen suggested an outlet for her excess energy. It was the only room on which any progress had been made. The wallpaper had been stripped from the walls, new cabinets installed and vinyl flooring laid down, but the appliances needed cleaning and Linda's housewares were only half-unpacked. It was typical of Linda that she owned every culinary contrivance ever manufactured, even though her talents lay more in the direction of promoting dinner dates than cooking. Fortunately for her and Randy, Randy enjoyed cooking almost as much as she enjoyed eating.

Linda returned a few hours later, inspected the now-spotless kitchen, and insisted on buying Randy a thank-you present. In the end they dropped in on half a dozen local boutiques, buying an array of businesslike but feminine outfits that Randy only hoped would fit properly once she'd regained some weight.

After stopping at a phone booth so Randy could call her friend Sarah, who hadn't yet headed north, to beg off the New Hampshire vacation, the two sisters drove home. Randy tossed her shopping bags into the trunk of her father's Lincoln—she'd have no occasion to wear the clothing in Cambridge—and then drove the car to a service station a few blocks away. Not only did she arrange to have it repaired, a sweet smile and soft plea persuaded the owner to let her leave it in his parking lot until she was ready to go home. It would spare her the hassle of finding another parking space.

Over the next few days an assortment of ponytailed young men and strong young women arrived at the apartment to hang wallpaper, sand and stain the floors, and paint the ceilings and doors. Linda trusted these people far more than Randy would have, letting them in in the morning and telling them to lock up when they were finished. The two sisters spent their days browsing in bookstores and art galleries, shopping for furniture or clothing, or simply driving around the countryside, enjoying the early summer weather. Only when Linda went out to visit friends or dropped in on evening parties did Randy decline to accompany her. She explained that getting back into circulation wasn't her way of coping with disappointment, and Linda seemed to accept that.

Late Friday afternoon, however, Linda returned to the apartment and looked at Randy with a downright wicked gleam in her eye. She was carrying a hat box and opened it up with a flourish to reveal a brunette wig and several packages with cosmetics inside. Ignoring Randy's wary expression, she began to affix the wig to her sister's head, emitting a gleeful chortle when she was through.

"May I present . . . Her Royal Highness, Princess Elizabeth of Yugoslavia," she announced.

"They don't have princesses anymore, Lin," Randy pointed out.

"I know that. You're a deposed princess," Linda informed her.

"A deposed princess," Randy slowly repeated. "May I ask why?"

"Because the Communists are in power and your family was booted off the throne, of course. You grew up in Paris," Linda explained.

"In Paris. A deposed Yugoslavian princess," Randy said. "What am I doing here? And why with you?"

"You're twenty years old and you're going to Harvard in the fall. You're with me because your Mama adores C & D and she's like this"—Linda held her thumb and index finger a quarter of an inch apart—"with Mom. I volunteered to look after you while you get settled in."

"And I'm *most* grateful for your help," Randy said, adopting a French accent colored with the slightly British lilt of cultured Europeans. Then she reverted to her usual speech, which was free of regional intonation. "Who's the joke on, Lin?"

"I'm going to a party with a bunch of people who think they're the social and intellectual elite of the world. I can't *wait*," Linda said with relish, "to produce *you!*"

Randy accepted the explanation, but not completely. "Would it be paranoid to think that you're also determined to drag me out with you?" she asked.

Linda smiled, but didn't attempt to deny it. "It will be the best thing for you," she said. "Will you do it?"

Randy fingered the long hair of her wig, then smiled back. "When could I ever resist getting up on a stage?" she asked.

It took her a good forty-five minutes with the make-up Linda had purchased before she looked like a twenty-year old brunette, but a last-minute check in the bathroom mirror still failed to satisfy her. She looked demure enough in Linda's long-sleeved, round-necked blue silk dress, but something was missing. "Jewelry," she finally told Linda. "Pearls, I think."

Twenty minutes of searching turned up a pearl necklace and earrings which Linda had packed at the bottom of a box of towels. When Randy put them on, Linda nodded her approval. "High class and innocent, but sexy," she said. "You're perfect."

The party was being held in the home of the president of a Boston electronics firm, given by the son of the house, who was a graduate student at M.I.T. The guests included a Big Ten football hero whose parents lived nearby, miscellaneous local media types, political staffers with an exaggerated sense of their personal power and young professors with inflated opinions of their intellectual powers.

Randy and Linda arrived at seven, just in time for the buffet supper, but Linda asked to speak with the host as soon as they stepped inside, explaining casually, "I'd like to introduce him to the princess."

The young woman who'd answered the door darted a startled look at Randy, who smiled regally and inclined her head a fraction. Then she hurried off. When their host appeared a minute later Linda pecked him on the cheek and made the introductions. He looked a little skeptical as his eyes flickered over Randy's body, but when she extended her hand as though he should feel honored to take it, he quickly shook hands and mumbled that he was very pleased to meet her.

"I do hope I'm not . . . crashing your party," Randy said, her smile both teasing and self-possessed. "You must believe me when I tell you how difficult it was to persuade Mama and Papa to allow me to attend school here. One hears that Cambridge is rather wild, but surely no more so than Paris, where I grew up."

Their host was thoroughly captivated. He offered

Randy his arm, asking her permission to introduce her to the other guests. The next two hours provided more entertainment than she'd enjoyed in months as those present fell all over themselves to meet her, to say the right things and find out about her. In the manner of royalty everywhere, she put them at ease by encouraging them to talk about themselves, doing so with such skill that none of them realized that she was evading all their questions.

She had just excused herself to go outside for a breath of air when she was joined on the terrace by a rather handsome man whom she'd noticed staring at her earlier. "It *is* hot in there, isn't it?" he said, not in the least intimidated to be talking to a princess.

"Very hot," Randy murmured. "The breeze feels lovely."

"Would you care to take a walk with me?" he asked. "Our host's mother is an avid gardener. Some of her specimens are so perfect they hardly seem real."

"Then I must accept your kind invitation," Randy said with a formal smile. The man gestured to indicate the way, but didn't take her arm or speak to her.

The full moon provided just enough light to let them appreciate the beauty of the garden. Randy examined one of the roses with genuine pleasure, gracefully bending down to catch the scent. As she straightened, she was startled to feel the man's hand on the back of her neck.

She gave no sign of surprise, knowing that good breeding dictated that she simply withdraw, putting the man in his place. "Shall we return to the house?" she asked with just the right note of disapproval in her voice.

"Not yet," he said, laughing at her. He bent down to whisper something in her ear. It was in a foreign language and Randy didn't understand him.

"I beg your pardon?" she said coolly.

"I told you that I love you in Serbo-Croatian. Surely Mama and Papa"—he mimicked Randy's use of the terms—"must have told you that too, at some point?"

"I was born long after the war's end and was raised in Paris. I never learned my native tongue." Randy hoped that the explanation was convincing. "Perhaps I shall study it at Harvard."

"Nice try," the man said with a grin. "My name is Aaron Gregov and I teach Eastern European history at Harvard. Princess Elizabeth of Yugoslavia is old enough to be your mother. So who are you?"

Randy sighed and peeked up at him, her eyes full of laughter. "Oh, dear," she said in her normal unaccented English. "Are you going to blow my cover?"

"That depends on what my silence buys," he teased. "Tell me your name."

"Randy Dunne. Linda Franck is my older sister."

"You're a very good actress," Aaron told her. "If I weren't an expert you would probably have fooled me. Do you live in Cambridge?"

"California. I'm only visiting here." Randy sensed that Aaron was attracted to her and since she didn't want any involvement she added, "I'm going up to New Hampshire tomorrow, and then moving to New York. I've had a lot of fun tonight, though. Thanks for not spoiling things."

"I've been waiting to get you alone for the past two hours," Aaron said. "And as far as thanking me goes, there are more suitable ways than with words."

With a smile, Randy twined her arms around his neck and brushed her lips over his mouth. The kiss was something of an experiment for her, a way of finding out whether she could touch a man without instinctively recoiling. The answer turned out to be yes, and when Aaron deepened the kiss, turning a superficial caress into a possessive discovery of her mouth, she was surprised by how pleasurable it was. She supposed that

Aaron was appealing to her without being *too* appealing; she could enjoy the kiss without worrying that she'd be tempted to go too far.

After several seconds she gently pulled away, saying she wanted to go inside, but Aaron didn't seem discouraged by her withdrawal. "Can I have your New York address and phone number before we leave?" he asked. "I'm down in the city every month or two and I'd like to take you to dinner." When Randy agreed he took her arm to escort her back to the house, well-pleased with himself.

Later, driving home, the two sisters laughingly discussed the evening. Randy told Linda what had happened in the garden, admitting, "I have to thank you twice, once for all the fun I had tonight, and the second time for helping me find out that Sean Raley didn't warp me for life."

"Are you going to see Aaron again?" Linda asked.

Randy shrugged. "I will if he calls. It's the least I owe him. Besides, I really did like him. I guess your theory about how to get over an unhappy love affair makes sense."

"Just don't overdo it," Linda quickly answered. "Too much of a good thing can be a mistake. Take it from me, I know."

On Saturday morning Linda drove out to western Massachusetts, to the inn where she'd arranged to meet Tom Havemeyer. Although Randy wondered why Linda was keeping the date at all, she told herself that her sister was far more knowledgeable about breaking off a love affair than she would ever be. In the meantime, she enjoyed being alone, especially at night. The twin mattresses and box springs were now attached to frames and a king-sized headboard, all of which had arrived on Friday, and although there was plenty of room in the bed Linda was a restless sleeper whose tossing and turning had kept Randy up at night.

Randy spent a couple of hours on Saturday morning catching up on her sleep, and then, her energy restored, decided to tackle the house. Although the walls were papered and the floors refinished, the workers had left sawdust, strips of paper and other miscellaneous debris scattered everywhere. Since Randy was accustomed to daily dance and exercise classes she enjoyed the physical labor involved in sweeping and washing and polishing. She felt a real sense of accomplishment when she was finished, but had enough of a sense of humor to realize that if she wanted the place to stay as clean as she'd made it, she would have to hire her sister a housekeeper.

Linda returned on Monday morning, looked around at the spotless apartment and rewarded Randy with a huge hug. "This is fantastic," she said. "I was going to hire a cleaning service, but now I don't need to bother."

The phones had been installed earlier that morning, prompting Linda to continue, "Let me make a few calls. I'll bet if I coax hard enough I can get the carpets here tomorrow and the furniture delivered on Wednesday and Thursday. Which means that I can go away with Roger on Friday. Do you mind?"

*Roger?* Randy thought. *Who's he?* But all she said was, "Of course not. In fact, I was thinking of driving up to New Hampshire in a few days. I don't have any way to reach Sarah, but as far as I know she's still at the cabin."

"Perfect," Linda said. Ninety minutes later, after the most dazzling display of pleading and flattery that Randy had ever witnessed, she managed to schedule every item of furniture except for the dinette set.

"They won't bring it till Friday," she told Randy. "Can you wait around for it? If not, I could talk to Mrs. Siskin downstairs and—"

"No problem," Randy interrupted. "All I really

want to do is hear about your weekend. I'm dying of curiosity."

They sat down at the cardtable in the dinette, Linda bringing in a couple of cans of soda from the kitchen. "You would have been proud of me," she began. "I spent all of Saturday listening to Tom's problems and convincing him to try again with his wife. He went off to the room to sulk and I went into dinner. They serve it family-style, at long tables. And the most gorgeous male just happened to sit down next to me." She winked at Randy. "By this morning we were the best of friends."

"That would be Roger," Randy guessed, thinking that she needed a scorecard to keep track of Linda's male friends.

"Right. But you can relax because he's divorced. He's a producer and he lives in New York. He's terribly high-powered—he went to Massachusetts to relax for a couple of days. He needs to scout locations along the New England coast for a movie he's doing, and he asked me to come along. Naturally I said yes."

"So what did Tom do? Leave?" Randy wondered if her sister had any feelings at all for the man. She'd liked him enough to meet him twice, so she must have.

Linda shrugged. "To tell you the truth, Randy, it was never much of an affair. That first weekend I could tell how ambivalent he was, so I put him off. We didn't even share a room. He has a lot of problems and I think having an affair was a way of making himself feel more masculine, or of getting back at his wife. It wasn't really *me* he wanted. I only agreed to meet him this weekend because it was easier than arguing, but I wouldn't have gone if you hadn't told me about his brother-in-law. Anyway, he stayed around till Sunday and then left. I hope the owner didn't notice that I was still there with Roger—heaven only knows what she would have thought."

"Ah, yes, Roger," Randy teased. "How long is *he* going to last?"

She was surprised when Linda avoided a direct answer. "I want you to meet him, to find out what you think. Why don't I call to see if he can come up Thursday and take us both out to dinner?"

Linda had never before solicited anyone's opinion of her boyfriends, and Randy was flattered to be asked. She was also pleased that her sister was showing some caution for a change. "I'd enjoy that," she said. "And when you're finished talking to Roger, can I phone Dad? He's probably convinced himself that I've either drowned in the lake or been eaten by a bear by now." She hesitated a moment. "Since I'm going up to New Hampshire in a few days anyway, do you think it would be dishonest of me to let him think I'm already there and that everything's been fine? Just so he won't worry?"

"Knowing Dad, I would say that it's not only not dishonest, it's simple self-preservation," Linda joked. She winked at Randy and headed for the phone.

Luke Griffin and William Dunne had managed to get through an hour-long meeting without either of them alluding to the subject that was on both their minds, but Luke supposed it couldn't continue much longer. He'd received a second hysterical phone call from his sister around lunchtime, and every protective instinct told him to do whatever was necessary to get Linda Franck out of his brother-in-law's life. But he wasn't fool enough to tackle the woman without first asking her father's permission.

"I understand your reluctance to move on the problem in our Philadelphia store," Bill was saying, "but the profits aren't getting any better in the meantime."

Luke realized that. "Let me wait till the six-month figures come in," he said. "I'll be on firmer ground

41

then. I've shaken things up enough without starting to fire people, and the resentment. . . ."

"Right. I'm only offering advice, Luke, not giving you an order." Bill took a cigar out of a humidor on his desk, a signal to Luke that the formal part of their meeting was over. Luke knew what was coming next, even before Bill lit his cigar and leaned back in his chair. "How's your sister doing?" he asked.

"Upset," Luke answered. First and foremost he wanted to avoid another argument. He'd behaved totally gracelessly the week before and was only grateful that Bill Dunne hadn't done anything more than throw him out of the office. "Her husband had to 'work' again last weekend," he explained, "but he left his coat at the inn where he stayed with your daughter and the owner called his house a few hours ago to say she'd mail it back." He shook his head. "I can't believe he was stupid enough to give them his home number."

"Terrific." Bill muttered a curse underneath his breath as his eyes lit on the photograph on his desk. The picture showed the Dunne family at the beach, and Luke guessed it was about ten years old. The bikini-clad young woman on the right of Bill and Emily was obviously Linda, and Luke had to admit that she was delectable with her long blond hair and slender curves. Randy, in a one-piece suit to her parents' left, still had braces on her teeth and a bit too much baby fat. Luke knew she'd improved with age because he'd seen her diaper commercial on television, and he figured that if she lost ten or fifteen pounds she wouldn't be half-bad.

"Listen to me, Luke," Bill continued. "I wish I could promise you that it would solve matters if I talked to Linda, but I can't be sure it would. If she's really infatuated with your brother-in-law she might not listen. But in all fairness to Lin, you have to admit that your brother-in-law wasn't exactly dragged kicking and screaming into this business."

Bill was only partially right, but Luke had more sense

than to point out that Tom had no track record as an adulterer whereas Linda was an old pro. "Would you mind if I went up to Cambridge to talk to her?" he asked.

"In person?" Bill smiled, looking as though he thought it would be a waste of time. "You're welcome to try. In fact, I wish you luck." He paused, then drawled, "But I should warn you that more than one man has found my daughter rather irresistible, Luke."

"I'll keep it in mind." Luke looked at the picture again, thinking that he could well believe it. Perhaps talking to the woman was the wrong approach, a thought that suggested an alternate plan. After a few moments of thought he said casually, "I may need to take a couple of days off."

Whatever comment Bill Dunne might have made was lost in the buzz of his intercom. Pat put through only the most important calls when Bill was in a meeting, so Luke automatically started to get up to leave. But before he was halfway out of his chair Bill waved him back down.

"Speak up, honey," he said into the phone. "It's a bad connection."

Bill's next few questions—"How's the weather up there? When are you coming home? Are you sure you're okay?"—told Luke that he was talking to his daughter Miranda. He'd heard via the secretarial grapevine that Miranda Dunne was in New Hampshire for a couple of weeks. He'd also heard that she was sorely displeased with her father for suggesting that Luke would be a suitable husband. Luke himself didn't take Bill's efforts in that direction seriously; the girl was much too young for him, in terms of both years and experience.

Bill, having satisfied himself that Randy was alive and well, held out the phone to Luke. "Why don't you say hello?" he suggested.

Luke, unable to resist milking the moment for all it

was worth, asked Bill to switch on the speaker so that both of them could listen in. Then, in the most suavely charming tone he could muster, he drawled, "Miranda, this is Luke Griffin. I hope you're enjoying yourself in New Hampshire. I'm looking forward to meeting you when you get back."

He wondered if she would freeze up the line from New Hampshire to New York, but all that came back was a girlish simper. "Luke who? I'm sorry, but do I know who you are?"

Luke choked back laughter. "You know exactly who I am, but I'll tell you anyway," he said. "I'm the new vice president for Branch Operations, and I'll be your boss when you start work at C & D." He couldn't stop himself from adding, "Which I hope will be very soon, Miranda. Your father's told me all about you and I plan to work very closely with you."

The explosion he half-anticipated never came. Instead Randy gushed back, "How exciting! I'm sure you'll teach me everything you know."

Luke glanced at Bill, who looked mildly disapproving, and said outrageously, "You can count on it, sweetheart."

Several seconds of silence followed this statement. Finally Randy answered curtly, "Please say goodbye to my father for me, Mr. Griffin. My three minutes are almost up." She hung up before either man could get out a word.

"You shouldn't have teased her that way," Bill said, replacing the receiver. "She obviously took you seriously and she's annoyed with you."

The pang of guilt Luke felt didn't last very long. "Don't worry, Bill," he said with a wink. "I can handle your daughter without any problems." But as he got up to leave he wondered whether his claim applied to the older daughter as well as the younger one.

* * *

Three days later, much to Linda's amusement, Randy was still muttering about how pompous and arrogant Luke Griffin was. Part of the problem was that she'd had too much time to think about the man. By the time the first day of waiting for deliveries drew to a close, Linda was restless to the point of insanity— Randy's insanity. Randy finally ordered her sister out to shop or visit friends while she herself stayed in the apartment. For the next two days Linda had flitted in and out of the house while Randy spent her time reading or unpacking cartons. She was truly awed by the number of stores Linda had ordered from, and by now was nodding weakly whenever a trucker asked for Mrs. Franck, signing Linda's name to the delivery slips quite automatically.

Late Thursday afternoon Linda came tearing into the apartment at twice her normal speed and handed Randy a small velvet box. "This is for helping with the apartment," she said. "I don't know what I would have done without you."

Randy opened up the box. Inside, nestled in navy satin, was a delicately filigreed gold cross. "It's beautiful, Lin," she said. "But you didn't have to. . . ."

"I wanted to. Do you like it?"

"I love it." Randy, deeply touched, hooked the chain around her neck. "Is it an antique?"

Linda nodded. "I found it in a shop in Boston. I spent most of the day looking." She gave Randy a quick hug and then ran off to the bathroom, calling over her shoulder, "Roger will be here in less than an hour. I need to wash my hair. I can't keep him waiting."

Up till now, keeping a date waiting had never troubled Linda in the least. Randy went off to the bedroom to change, thinking that her sister must be totally smitten with the man.

When the doorbell rang Linda and Randy were

standing in the kitchen, sharing a glass of wine. Randy waited while Linda answered the door, but apparently there was no lingering hello kiss, because Linda came back almost immediately with a smiling, dark-haired man in tow. He was about average height and a little stocky, but extremely attractive in a tough, New York City sort of way. Only the lines around his eyes and mouth revealed his age, which Randy guessed was close to forty. Unlike Linda's first two husbands, he didn't look like the type of man anyone could push around.

They shook hands, silently taking each other's measure. "The likeness is incredible," Roger finally stated, "considering the four-year age difference." He frowned, looking a bit puzzled. "Are you sure we haven't run into each other, Randy? Lin mentioned that you're an actress. Maybe you tried out for one of my films?"

Randy hadn't, but she knew why Roger thought so. "You probably recognize me from the commercial I did—Sweetheart Diapers. Except I was twenty pounds heavier then and looked like a whale."

Linda rolled her eyes. "You looked a *little* plump." Turning to Roger, she added, "Randy's appetite is a family legend. That *might* be the reason why she's been on a diet for fourteen years." She held up her hand to forestall the obvious comment. "Don't even ask why she's so thin now. It's personal."

The comment made Randy uncomfortable, but Roger tactfully changed the subject to his latest movie and started to usher them out to the car. They had dinner at a Boston restaurant, and with each course Randy was more impressed with the man. As Linda had mentioned, Roger Bennett was divorced, and his two teenaged children lived with their mother during the summer and stayed with him during the school year. Randy liked his steady, confident style and the way that he gently put Linda in her place when she tried to wheedle him into making a change in his itinerary to suit some sudden whim of hers. He was perfectly charming to Randy, asking about her acting experience and telling her that if she ever changed her mind about working for C & D all she had to do was knock on his door and he'd introduce her to all the right people. Of whom he was one, of course.

She felt so thoroughly at ease with him that later, over after-dinner drinks in the living room, she found herself asking him if he knew Sean Raley.

He was quicker than she'd expected him to be. "I've met him," he said. "Is he the one who cost you those twenty-odd pounds?"

Randy admitted that he was, and could have hugged Roger for his tactful, matter-of-fact response. "You aren't the first and you won't be the last, Randy. Raley has enough charm and sex appeal to have turned some of the most sensible heads in Hollywood, so don't let it bother you. I hear he's up for the lead in a new series, by the way. But no big loss to you—he's too busy loving himself to love anyone else."

Roger spent the night on the sofabed in the guest room. He and Linda planned to get an early start the next morning because Roger had several appointments to keep, but unfortunately for Linda she overslept. While Randy made Roger breakfast Linda hurriedly dressed and packed, dumping out her purse to exchange it for a chic imported handbag, throwing clothing into her suitcase, grabbing her cosmetics and toiletries and dumping them into a carry-all. When Randy came into the bedroom and noticed her harried sister surrounded by total chaos she shook her head in amazement.

"I told you, I can't keep Roger waiting," Linda said breathlessly. "He'll leave without me."

She finished packing just as Roger poked his head in the door. Linda gave Randy a quick kiss and then picked up her cases. "Thanks again, Randy. Call me when you're back in New York." To Randy's surprise,

Roger ignored her outstretched hand in favor of her cheek. "I've enjoyed meeting you," he said as he kissed her goodbye. "When you get back to New York I may give your father some competition for your services."

With Linda gone, Randy showered and then dressed, putting on shorts and a tee shirt. She was still wearing the gold cross, which she slipped inside the shirt. She spent the morning straightening up the house, especially the disaster-hit bedroom. Discarded clothing was strewn all over and Linda's everyday purse was still on the floor, its former contents scattered beneath clothing or under the bed. As Randy picked up the pieces, she noticed that Linda had taken her change purse but left behind her leather credit card case, which also contained her driver's license. Randy tossed the case and Linda's brush into the purse along with an extra pair of sunglasses, two pens, miscellaneous cosmetics and some loose money, and left it on the bed.

At lunchtime she fixed herself a sandwich and iced tea and was putting the dishes into the dishwasher when the doorbell rang. Obviously the dinette set, she thought.

She opened the door to see a tall, solidly-built man with wavy brown hair and dark brown eyes standing before her. He was dressed in dark gray slacks and a striped charcoal and white shirt, and carried a clipboard. He didn't look like a furniture mover to Randy, but she nonetheless asked politely, "You've come with the table and chairs?"

Something about him made her uncomfortable. Perhaps it was the fine scar running down his right cheek, or the hard look in his eyes, but his answer was ordinary enough. "No. I have a telegram for Mrs. Linda Franck." He held out the clipboard.

Randy knew only that Linda was on her way up the coast of Massachusetts, but told herself that the sensible thing to do was to sign for the telegram, open it up and see if it were urgent enough to bother tracking down her sister. No doubt Roger's office would have some idea of his whereabouts.

She took the pen the man held out, only half-aware that he'd entered the apartment and closed the door behind him. She was absorbed in wondering about the telegram as she scrawled Linda's name in the space provided and then reached for the envelope the man was holding. The last thing she remembered thinking was that he looked no more like a messenger than a furniture mover. A hand came up, held something over her face, and she collapsed onto the floor.

# Chapter Three

Randy woke up feeling dry-mouthed and confused. It took her a few moments to realize that someone had strapped her into a seat on a small airplane, but then she jerked her head up and looked to her left at the pilot—the man with the alleged "telegram." Although she was frightened, she was not so panicked that she didn't notice how attractive he was. He had a cleft chin, moody brown eyes and blond streaks in his brown hair. The scar on his cheek didn't detract from his looks; on the contrary, when taken together with his slightly irregular nose, it gave his handsome face an intimidating, macho overtone. Randy wondered how many fights he'd gotten into in his time, and shuddered.

Any thoughts she might have had about doing something foolish vanished with her quick inspection of him. Not only did he look as tough as reinforced concrete, he was big—several inches over six feet and probably close to two hundred pounds. At the moment he was smiling a thin-lipped, amused smile at Randy, as if he found her frightened scrutiny of him highly satisfying.

She remembered collapsing near the front door of the apartment. Obviously the man thought she was Linda, but it made no difference. If he'd kidnapped her for ransom one sister was as good as the other. The smooth operation had all the earmarks of a professional job, and Randy tried to find something positive about that. If he did this kind of thing for a living, he wouldn't be stupid enough to risk a murder charge.

Some small part of her was detached enough to admire her acting ability when she forced down her fear and said coolly, "How long is it going to take you to reach my father and get your money?"

He lazed back in his seat. "I'm in no particular hurry, Mrs. Franck." His gaze dropped to her sandaled feet and traveled up her body, lingering on her breasts before continuing to her pale face and tangled hair, where it remained. She'd been wearing shorts and a tee shirt when she answered the door, but now she was dressed in blue jeans and a knit blouse. The blouse was Linda's, and clingingly revealing, especially since Randy hadn't bothered with a bra that morning.

The longer he stared at her the more uncomfortable she became. She swallowed to moisten her throat, but it really didn't help. "Please," she said, "may I have some water?"

"Sure. What do I get in return?"

There was no mistaking his meaning. The top three buttons of Randy's blouse were unbuttoned and she protectively fastened two of them, her eyes focused on her lap.

"If you want something from me you should try taking the blouse off, not the other way around," the man drawled. "You're a little flat-chested for my taste, but even so, I liked it the way I fixed it. Unbutton it, Linda."

51

Randy looked out the window at the wooded terrain below. Her throat was parched, her lips dry. She coughed a few times, only too aware that the man was not going to give her a drink unless she did what he wanted. Her hand was trembling as she unbuttoned the two buttons.

Apparently satisfied, the man took a thermos out of a leather satchel, opened it up and handed it to her. Randy took a long drink, unhooking the confining shoulder harness in an effort to get more comfortable, and then drank again. Her thirst quenched, she silently held out the thermos to return it to him, but he ignored her outstretched arm and got out of his seat to stand beside her. When he reached out a hand to touch her hair she flinched, terrified. Every vestige of self-control abruptly vanished. She dropped the thermos onto the floor as she flung herself at him, kicking and clawing. Her medium-long nails raked the side of his face, leaving three bloody scratches in their wake.

Up until that point he'd merely defended himself against Randy's attack, but when he lifted a hand to touch his face and looked at the blood on his fingers his expression turned icy. Randy reeled backward from the quick shove he gave her, lost her footing and fell onto the floor. Cowering away from him, she put her hands over her face and began to sob softly.

"Okay, just take it easy. If you kill me who's going to land the plane?" Randy realized that he sounded rattled. "Are you okay?" he asked.

Unable to answer, Randy took a deep breath, trying to stop crying. The man took a few steps toward her, causing her to shrink back and look up at him. "I'll knock you out if I have to," he said. "I'd rather give you an injection than let you get hysterical."

Injections conjured up only one image in Randy's mind: heroin addiction. Why else would he have a syringe, or know how to use it? That was obviously why he needed money. "My father—he can get you treatment," she said urgently. "I promise—nothing will happen to you if you let me go."

He shifted his weight from one foot to the other, a handkerchief against his bleeding cheek, a puzzled look on his face. "What are you talking about?" he asked.

"You're an addict. That's why you need the money. That's how you know how to inject. . . ."

Whatever reaction she might have anticipated, it certainly didn't include an indulgently reproving grin. "I wouldn't shoot you up with dope," he said. "I brought along a tranquilizer. I was in the Peace Corps for eight months in Africa, as a medical technician."

Randy, now more confused than frightened, thought to herself, *the Peace Corps?* It didn't make sense. How did someone who was idealistic enough to serve in the Peace Corps wind up kidnapping the daughter of a wealthy businessman?

He held out his hand to help her up, but she couldn't bring herself to let him touch her. "Obviously I frightened you a lot more than I meant to," he murmured. "I'm sorry about that." He reached down to grasp her hand and, reassured by his apology, Randy allowed him to help her up.

He nodded toward her seat. "Go sit down. I'm not going to hurt you—not unless you try to scratch me again, that is."

Randy did as she was told, wondering if she could believe him. He didn't seem at all menacing anymore, but someone who went around kidnapping people was obviously very dangerous.

Water had spilled all over the floor when Randy dropped the thermos, and now she watched in silence as the man took a soiled rag out of a box in the back of the plane and began to mop things up. When he was finished he sat back down in the pilot's seat and then fished out a foil-wrapped towelette from his satchel. As he dabbed at his face, wincing at the sting of the alcohol, she felt a stab of remorse. She had to remind

herself that he'd fully deserved the scratches she'd
given him.

The minutes dragged on. The man went back to
flying the plane, and there was nothing to do but watch
the ground. The cities and towns of what Randy
assumed was Massachusetts slowly gave way to rolling
countryside covered with evergreen and broadleaf
trees. Randy decided that when they landed she would
run up to the first person she saw at the airport and beg
for help. She replayed this scene over and over in her
mind, refining it until she'd convinced herself that she
would succeed in getting away.

More than an hour later he finally looked at her
again. "Get your seat belt back on," he said. "We're
landing."

Randy buckled it up and stared out the window. She
saw no airport, only a large field surrounded by wooded hills. He circled, landing the plane quite smoothly
despite the absence of a paved strip.

She had a million questions but asked none of them.
She checked her watch—it was just past six o'clock.
The man handed her Linda's purse and two suitcases,
one of them Linda's, the second presumably his own,
and told her to get out of the plane. There was nothing
to do but obey. He followed a moment later, carrying a
large carton of groceries.

Their destination was a small cabin, invisible from
the air because it was set back into the woods. A metal
shed stood adjacent to it. As the man led her inside the
unlocked wooden building Randy nervously inspected
the interior. It wasn't the Ritz, but it was hardly a
shack, either.

The plank floor was covered by several hooked rugs;
an old-fashioned couch and two overstuffed chairs
surrounded a maple coffee table and faced a fireplace,
where someone had laid a fire. An alcove at the right
rear half of the cabin housed a simple kitchen, with a
table and four chairs nearby. Several doors opened off

the living room, but they were closed. Randy devoutly hoped that at least two of the three led to bedrooms.

The man noticed her looking toward the left, at the closed doors, but made no comment. Amazingly, now that they were inside and it appeared that she wouldn't be locked in some ghastly underground chamber, she was much less frightened.

The feeling didn't last. The moment he told her to sit down on the couch her heart began to pound heavily and she started to feel a little sick. She watched warily as he lit the fire, then sat down uncomfortably close to her on the couch. She didn't suppose it mattered to him whether he'd grabbed Linda Franck or Miranda Dunne, but she felt that she had to make the effort to identify herself.

"I'm not Linda Franck," she said, concentrating on the hands that were clenched together tightly in her lap. "I'm her sister Randy."

"Really." Plainly he didn't believe her. "Tell me, what happened to Linda?"

Randy tried to sound confident and convincing. "She left this morning with a friend on a trip up the coast. I've been visiting for the last week or so, keeping her company and helping her with her apartment."

"I see. Does she always leave her purse sitting on the bed when she goes out of town? With her driver's license and credit cards inside?"

Randy shook her head, admitting to herself that the explanation would sound implausible. Nonetheless she continued, "Lin's kind of sloppy. She was in a hurry to leave and when she changed purses she just dumped everything onto the floor and took what she wanted. She must have forgotten the credit card case."

The man shot her a skeptical look. "I had a look around when I changed your clothing and packed up. I didn't see any indication that anyone else was around. But I'll accept what you say if you can enlighten me on a few points."

Randy sensed that he was toying with her, not viciously perhaps, but not without a certain pleasure, either. She nodded.

"First," he said, "there's the car. Bill Dunne's blue Lincoln. I didn't see it parked on the street."

"The air conditioning broke down," Randy explained. "I took it in to be repaired and arranged to leave it at the service station till I was ready to leave Cambridge."

Randy couldn't tell whether or not he accepted her story—his expression was poker-faced. "Second, the fact that Randy is in New Hampshire," he went on.

He seemed to know a lot about her family, but maybe that wasn't surprising if he made a habit of this sort of thing. Naturally he'd take the time to check out his targets. "She never—I mean, *I* never went." Randy could have kicked herself for the slip. The man had her thinking about herself in the third person by now. "I decided to stay with Linda for a while instead."

"So you told me." He was allowing his disbelief to show again, but the smile on his face bespoke enjoyment, not cynicism. "And did you go on a crash diet, also? Maybe *we've* never met, Linda, but I *have* seen your sister on television. You look very much alike, but she's obviously quite a bit younger. She's also about thirty pounds heavier."

*That blasted diaper commercial,* Randy thought, defeated. *Blimp city.* It was pointless to spin stories about nonexistent movie roles or deliver urgent explanations about unhappy love affairs if the man had seen that commerical. When taken together with everything else the fact that she'd lost weight would seem totally unbelievable. In truth, of course, it made absolutely no difference.

"Okay," she sighed. "What happens now?" The question reminded her that despite his occasional smiles the man was a professional criminal. "Do you want me to write a note to my father?"

He put his feet up on the coffee table and lazed against the back of the couch. "I haven't kidnapped you for money, Linda. I have much more interesting plans for you than that." He was looking at her through half-lidded eyes, still smiling.

Randy had been focusing exclusively on the idea of kidnapping, but no one but an innocent girl could have failed to understand what he meant. She felt as though she was caught in a nightmare. Why was this happening to her?

The man twisted sideways on the couch and reached out to touch her cheek. Randy went rigid, afraid to fight him after what had happened on the plane, but momentarily too frightened to move. She could only stare into the fire and try not to panic.

He stroked her hair and then dropped his hand. "What's the matter?" he murmured. "Don't I appeal to you as much as all the other lovers you've had? Because you certainly appeal to me."

Randy couldn't manage an answer. She saw the man move away out of the corner of her eye, but felt very little relief that he'd decided to leave her alone. She knew it was only temporary.

"I'll lay out the ground rules for you," he said. "For the next few days, or week, or maybe longer, you're going to do exactly what I tell you to. You're as spoiled and selfish as you are beautiful, Linda, and it's about time someone did something about it. Just keep in mind that I'm not one of the ex-husbands or lovers who you've wrapped around your little finger all your life and we'll do fine together."

Randy darted him a confused glance, trying to make sense of what he'd said. Was revenge the man's motive, rather than money? If so, she had to make him believe that she wasn't her sister.

She took a deep breath and slowly exhaled, trying to relax enough to sound convincing. "You're not entirely wrong about my sister—she can be impossible when it comes to men. But she's also loving and caring and a lot of fun. It's not just her looks that attracts them."

As soon as she finished this speech she realized that the man was seriously irritated with her. "You tell the most creative lies of any woman I've ever met," he said, "but credit me with at least a minimal IQ. I'm tired of the 'I'm not Linda' routine, so drop it. You can start work by unpacking the two suitcases and the carton of groceries. I'm going outside to crank up the generator and then into the bedroom to lie down for a few minutes."

Randy followed his progress with her eyes as he got up and walked to the door. The tasks he'd assigned weren't at all onerous, although she supposed that Linda might have thought so. She tried to imagine her sister's probable reaction and decided that Lin would either have spit fire and fury or else laughed her head off, then promptly tried to seduce the man. The situation was so incredibly absurd that Randy refused to believe that the man wouldn't figure out she was telling the truth and return her to Cambridge. All she wanted to do was forget the incident. The reference to ex-husbands and lovers told her that he was connected in some way to someone in one of those two categories, perhaps to Linda's ex-husband Brett. Brett had taken the divorce very hard.

At the moment, however, there was no point in refusing to do as she was told. She opened each of the doors off the living room in turn, discovering a bathroom and then two bedrooms. One had twin beds, the other a double, so she carried her suitcase into the first and the man's suitcase into the second.

When she started to unpack she noticed that most of the clothing he'd taken was Linda's. Ordinarily Randy couldn't wear her sister's clothes, but she'd lost so much weight that she'd dropped a few sizes. The man had taken all the necessities, including her own flannel nightgown, which Linda wouldn't have been caught dead in. Her sister's tastes ran more to silk and lace.

Randy also noticed that he'd folded each garment quite neatly, as though he'd had all the time in the world. If nothing else she had to admire the fellow's audacity. She found herself thinking that it was a thorough shame he *hadn't* snatched her sister. The two of them would have made an interesting pair.

As for herself, it was peaceful here, though she wondered where in God's green earth they were, and she had no objection to a little work. After putting everything away she made her way next door. The man was sprawled diagonally on the bed, apparently fast asleep. Randy had gone flying with a cousin a few times and he'd taught her a little bit about how to pilot a plane. Although she wasn't fool enough to try to take off she could at least use the radio to call for help. For a few moments she stood there, indecisive, and then casually strolled out of the room and out of the cabin. Once outside, however, she broke into a brisk run. She was only a few yards from the aircraft when she was hit from behind by a flying tackle that sent her tumbling to the ground. The man landed beside her.

The next instant she was flat on her back, pinned beneath his body. She was winded, but at least he was keeping most of his substantial weight on his elbows. She tried a sheepish smile. "You can't blame me for trying," she said.

The way he was looking at her put an end to her attempt at humor. His eyes were moodily intent, as though he couldn't decide whether to chew her out or make love to her. Randy wasn't frightened that he would hurt her, but she *was* annoyed that he'd put an end to her escape attempt. She tried to wriggle away, failed completely and promptly ordered him to let her go.

He shook his head. "I don't think so."

She didn't waste her time arguing. Instead she relaxed for a few moments, hoping to catch him off-guard, and then started to fight him in earnest. But he simply caught at her wrists and forced them up over her head, holding them with a single, firm hand.

Breathing hard now, Randy stared up at him. He didn't look at all angry anymore, only aroused. She could feel his hard contours pressing against her body and was shocked at her awakening response to him. His eyes dropped to her mouth for several long seconds, and then he eased himself against her, obviously intending to kiss her.

Randy quickly turned her head to the side, confused by the rush of heat that suddenly shimmered through her, but the man simply released her wrists and started to nuzzle her neck. His lips were firm, cool and gentle on her skin. Randy didn't want to respond, but his murmured, "You're beautiful," had an alarming effect on her common sense.

His hand feathered lightly up her side, trailing fire through her thighs, her stomach and then her breasts. When he stretched over to reach her mouth and began to nibble at her lower lip she closed her eyes and thought to herself that the situation was impossible. She didn't even know his name, so why was her body aching this way?

The longer he played with her mouth the lower her defenses dropped. Ultimately she abandoned her efforts at resistance, gave a little moan of concession and allowed her lips to part.

She'd dated more than one actor acclaimed for his on-screen technique, but nothing had prepared her for this man's expert conquest of her mouth. He alternated deep, satisfying kisses with tantalizing nips and caresses, so that each time he withdrew to tease her she became more excited and submissive, more eager for him to take her mouth again. Her arms found their way around his neck and she arched her body to meet his demanding movements, too aroused to stop him when his hand wandered underneath her blouse to stroke a swollen breast.

When he slowly pulled away Randy could only stare up at him, at first confused that he'd stopped, and then embarrassed by the wildness of her own response. His breathing was far more regular than her own, his expression much calmer. "The ground isn't very comfortable," he said with a complacent smile. "If you ask me nicely I'll take you inside to bed now."

Randy was mortified. Hadn't she learned *anything* from Sean Raley? She felt cheap and used and thoroughly disgusted with herself. The man rolled off her, waiting for her answer, but she maintained a tight-lipped silence and started to get up.

"Oh no you don't," he said, pulling her firmly down again. "You aren't ready to ask me yet, is that it?"

When Randy didn't answer he went on rather cheerfully, "That's okay, though. I can be patient when I have to be." He winked at her, grinning broadly. "But not *too* patient, Linda. Let's go eat."

The moment he released her Randy scrambled to her feet and began walking rapidly back to the cabin. Her emotions were a chaotic jumble of annoyance, humiliation and, much against her will, growing bewitchment. She was beginning to suspect that her opponent could be dangerously charming if he put his mind to it.

Back in the cabin, he gestured toward the kitchen, prompting Randy to say irritably, "I suppose you expect me to make you dinner."

"Very perceptive," he drawled.

Her temper heated up a fraction more—she didn't appreciate being ordered around—but then she gave a mental shrug. The fact was, she was hungry, and she'd lay odds that she was a darn sight better cook than he was. He left her to go back outside and she started to unpack the carton of groceries, adding staples and canned goods to the items already in the cupboards. A few minutes later he returned with a large cooler, which he set on the counter. Randy checked the refrigerator, found that it was still quite warm, and decided that unloading the cooler should wait.

She took out some chicken breasts, boned and cut them up, and assembled the ingredients for sweet and sour chicken. The stove was gas and the nearest thing to a wok was a cast iron frying pan, but it worked well enough. She also cooked some rice and heated some peas to go along with the main course. As she worked the man who'd abducted her sat in a chair by the dining area table and watched, his expression giving no hint of his feelings. He opened his mouth exactly once, to inform her that he'd taken the precaution of disabling the plane's radio.

Randy had plenty of time to think as she cooked and was honest enough to admit that she found her captor much too attractive. The situation was even rather romantic—being alone in an isolated cabin with a man who obviously wanted to make love to her and just as obviously knew all there was to know about pleasing a woman in bed. Linda would have loved every minute of it.

The problem was, she wasn't like Linda. Physical infatuation had already led her into one disastrous love affair, and she didn't want it to happen a second time. Her self-esteem, already shaken by Sean Raley, would wind up shattered if she tumbled into bed with some half-crazy stranger.

They ate their meal in silence, but there was nothing hostile or uncomfortable about the lack of conversation. Randy felt relaxed enough to help herself to seconds, and by the end of the meal had decided to find out just what she was doing up here.

"Are you a friend of Brett's?" she asked.

He looked up from his plate. "Your ex-husband? No."

She tried a different approach. "Then what's your name?"

"You could call me 'sir.' Or 'my lord'—that has a nice ring to it. Although," he said, lazing back in his chair, "I'd hardly want you to whisper that in my ear if I decide to make love to you later."

Randy contemplated her empty plate, grateful that she'd waited till now to question him because she suddenly felt sick to her stomach. She was almost sure he wouldn't force the issue, but the way he was looking at her told her he wanted to touch her, and it bothered her very much that she might permit him to do so.

She started to clear away the dishes, putting them into the sink, and was about to begin washing up when he ordered, "Make some coffee first. I take it black."

There was nothing to gain by refusing. Randy quickly located a drip coffee-maker and an unopened can of coffee in one of the cabinets. She'd had trouble with the can opener when opening the peas, and had no more success with the coffee. After she'd fumbled with the recalcitrant utensil for fifteen seconds the man got up and took it away from her. "I'd resigned myself to the worst meals of my life up here," he said as he opened the coffee and set it on the counter. "How come you can cook like an angel but can't work a simple can opener?"

Randy turned her back to him and measured out the coffee. "That thing must be an antique," she said. "I've never seen anything like it." Actually she was pleased by his compliment, and had to smile when she imagined Linda in these circumstances. Her sister probably would have poisoned the man—unintentionally!

As they drank their coffee she continued to study him. Something about him seemed familiar—his hair, perhaps, or the masculine way he carried himself. At last it bothered her so much that she asked him if he were sure they'd never met. "I know I've seen you somewhere," she added.

"I doubt it," he answered, "although I do happen to work for your father."

Randy almost choked on her coffee. "You mean he *knows* about this?" she sputtered.

"You don't suppose I'd go around snatching up my boss' daughter without his permission!" he said. "I'm not crazy."

Randy's head was spinning. She'd just placed the wavy brown hair and masculine stride. The last time she'd seen him he'd been storming out of her father's office. And the last time she'd heard his voice he'd been smoothly and odiously charming to her. If the phone connection when she'd called her father from Cambridge hadn't been so poor she would have placed the drawl immediately.

"You're Luke Griffin," she stated. "I don't believe this." His action had a certain logic considering the hotness of his temper, but Randy was amazed that her father had gone along with it. It wasn't like Bill Dunne at all.

"I'm also Anne Havemeyer's brother-in-law," Luke reminded her. "You do remember Tom? The guy you've played house with for two weekends? Better to stick with me, Linda. At least I'm single."

Now that Randy was recovering from the initial shock of discovering the man's identity, her annoyance was beginning to get the better of her. So this was the man her father was so eager to marry her off to! What had he said? That once she'd met Luke she wouldn't stand a chance? Then she remembered Luke Griffin's comments on the phone and rolled her eyes in exasperation.

"Linda," she informed him in her most withering tone, "was with a man named Roger Bennett for most of last weekend. And she never 'played house' with your brother-in-law. Mostly she just listened to his problems."

"Roger Bennett, the New York producer?" Luke asked.

"You know him?"

"Sure I know him. I took his girlfriend away from him, for a month or so anyway. Or didn't Roger tell you that he lives with someone?"

Having met Roger Bennett and liked him very much, Randy didn't want to believe that he was involved with anyone else. "He must have broken up with her," she said. "He wouldn't do something like that."

"You seem to know a lot about him," Luke replied, "considering that you're not Linda."

"I told you, I've spent the last ten days with my sister," Randy said clearly and slowly, as if talking to a mental incompetent. "I met Roger in Cambridge."

"Your sister's been in New Hampshire for the last week," Luke contradicted. "Cut the song and dance about Miranda. I was in your father's office when she called. I even spoke to her."

"And do you want me to recite the conversation?" Randy asked impatiently. She mimicked Luke's final comment to her with devastating accuracy. " 'You can count on it, sweetheart.' Honestly, Luke! If your ego gets any bigger it'll outgrow Manhattan Island! I made that call from Cambridge. I didn't want Dad to worry. . . ."

"You mean Miranda called you up and told you about it," he interrupted. "We've been through your list of explanations too many times already." He smiled engagingly. "When your sister gets back from New Hampshire she's coming to work for me. Your father has the idea that I would make a perfect husband for her. But I think I'll pass."

"Really!" Randy decided that Luke Griffin was

conceited enough to give even Sean Raley a run for his money. "May I ask what's wrong with her?"

"Sure. She's too young for me, unlike you. And rumor has it that she's one of the few actresses in Hollywood who could give an authentic portrayal of a vestal virgin—assuming she lost a few pounds. I'm not in the market for a chubby child bride."

Randy was so aggravated with the man that she felt like throwing her coffee at him. "So who are *you?*" she asked. "God's gift to the female sex?"

"A few women have thought so," Luke laughed. "I kind of thought you agreed. You have a lot to look forward to if you behave yourself and do as you're told."

"In that case I'll be sure not to," Randy retorted. She knew by the sparkle in his eyes that he was only needling her, but couldn't help snapping at the bait. To be called a vestal virgin was bad enough, but *chubby?* And a *child?*

"When my father finds out that you've got me instead of Lin he'll have your head," she warned him. "He's very protective. . . ."

"Come off it, Linda. I've seen your sister and I've spoken to her on the phone. There's a picture on your father's desk of the two of you and I've seen that, also. One more word about being Miranda and I swear I'll turn you over my knee. . . ." He cut himself off, grinning at her. "But don't worry. I'll make sure you enjoy it as much as I do."

By now Randy didn't trust herself to speak. The man was totally impossible. He wouldn't listen to a word she said, he was the worst tease she'd ever had the misfortune to encounter, and his self-confidence was so great that it approached epic proportions. It took her a few minutes to calm down enough to realize that she was handling him all wrong. She wasn't sure just what he wanted from Linda, but the simplest way to resolve the situation was to find out and give it to him. She could afford to be charitable—after all, she'd have the last laugh when they met again in New York.

She finished up her coffee and started to toy with the cup, asking ingenuously, "Where are we, Luke?"

"It's enough for you to know that we're somewhere in Maine, at a cabin my great-uncle left me. It's a long story—I'll tell you about it sometime. But right now you need to clean up the kitchen and get to bed. Tomorrow will be a long day."

Randy didn't bother to ask what he meant. As she worked in the kitchen Luke brought in more wood from outside, stacking it on the hearth. Randy quickly realized that there was no heat in the cabin beyond what was provided by the fire.

Luke brushed off his pants, yawned and stretched. "Unless you want to freeze your beautiful backside off, leave your bedroom door open. It gets cold here at night. And if you want a shower do it now, because I turn the water heater onto pilot at night to save gas. Everything has to be flown in."

There was no lock on the bathroom door and Randy was half-afraid that Luke would try to stroll in and watch her, but he apparently had more finesse than that. The long-sleeved, high-necked flannel nightgown wasn't the kind of sleepwear that drove men mad, so she wasn't particularly concerned when she opened the door to find him standing just outside—until he dropped a hand onto her shoulder. No man, she told herself, had the right to be so sexy, especially not Luke Griffin. His closeness made her pulses race, but she forced a boredom into her voice that she was far from feeling.

"Did you want something?" she asked coolly.

He studied her detached expression for an uncomfortably long moment, then removed his hand. Since Randy was trapped between the wall and his body there was no need for him to actually touch her in order to detain her. "Yes, I want something," he murmured.

He twined a large hand through her hair to gently pull her head up and placed his other hand on her neck, the thumb lightly caressing her jaw. Randy met his gaze with a level stare, resolutely ignoring the fact that his hands were scorching her face. He kissed her softly on the mouth, rubbing his lips back and forth over her own, but she refused to respond. Fortunately he didn't persist, but straightened up and shook his head, smiling. "But it doesn't look like I'll get it tonight." Then he walked into the bathroom, closing the door just a little too hard.

Back in her own room Randy snuggled under the goosedown covers and curled up into a tight ball, trying to warm up. She'd won a minor victory just now and permitted herself the luxury of relishing it. Luke was obviously annoyed that she hadn't tumbled straight into his bed, and her rejection must have been all the more galling since he thought it had come from a woman who'd allegedly had more lovers than she could count.

But as pleasant as it was to put Luke in his place for once, it hadn't solved anything. She was still in Maine with a man who thought she was her sister. She only prayed that her father never got wind of Luke's mistake, because despite her previous threat, that was actually the last thing she wanted. Knowing William Dunne, he would either fire Luke Griffin, in which case C & D would lose a highly talented executive, or else he'd get out his figurative shotgun, which would be highly embarrassing for everyone concerned.

At least, Randy thought with a yawn, Luke wasn't the ambitious fortune hunter she'd taken him for. She wasn't flattered by his inaccurate view of her, or by the realization that he'd only been teasing her on the phone, but it was nice to know that the man had some integrity.

She stretched and yawned again, suddenly terrifically sleepy. It was so peaceful and lovely here—wherever in Maine "here" was. As isolated and restful as New

Hampshire would have been, but with some very lovely modern conveniences.

The wind had come up a bit and was rustling gently through the trees. Randy thought she heard the sound of running water, and the soft tones of an owl hooting filled the night. She pulled up the quilt a little higher and closed her eyes.

# Chapter Four

"Linda!" Randy jerked awake at the sound of her sister's name. For a moment, disoriented, she couldn't remember where she was. Then she noticed Luke Griffin and the events of the day before came flooding back.

He was standing in the doorway wearing a knee-length terrycloth robe, looking anything but cheerful. It was so cozy in bed that Randy said beseechingly, "Luke, it's so cold. Why on earth do I have to get up?"

"Because I'm hungry and I want some breakfast, and because you're going to make it for me." He paused. "Unless you want me to join you in bed, that is," he added.

Yesterday when he'd made those kind of comments he'd kept a smile on his face and a teasing note in his voice. This morning, however, he was as irritable as a child who'd lost his favorite toy. Randy figured that he was either one of those people who are cranky until they've had their second cup of coffee in the morning, or else he was still annoyed about spending the night alone.

She reluctantly pulled herself up. With her tousled hair and flannel nightgown she looked like the child Luke had labeled her the night before. They stared at each other for several long seconds before he turned on his heel and strode out of the room. Randy soon heard him poking viciously at the fire, then throwing on a couple of extra logs.

Amused by his sour mood, she put on Linda's bathrobe and slippers and trotted into the living room. Given the fact that Luke refused to believe her explanations, it seemed logical to attempt to change his mind with her behavior. He considered Linda spoiled and selfish, so she'd confront him with someone who was solicitous and accommodating. Given her basic nature, it wouldn't be too difficult.

"What do you feel like eating?" she asked him.

He gave the fire a final poke and turned around. "Bacon and eggs. Two, over easy. Coffee and toast. And step on it, Linda. I'm starving," he said grumpily.

Heat from the fire and the smell of frying bacon soon filled the cabin. As soon as the coffee was brewed Randy filled a mug and brought it over to Luke, who was now sitting at the table. He didn't bother to thank her when she set it down in front of him.

There was at least one positive note to this whole insane experience, Randy decided—her appetite was again as healthy as it had been six months ago. She made herself a breakfast almost as large as Luke's and ate it just as quickly as he did.

"I can't figure out where you put it," he muttered.

Randy suspected that she'd only be wasting her time to tell him, but answered with a smile, "Sure you can. You've seen the diaper commerical, although it *did* make me look heavier than I really was at the time."

71

She paid no attention to his frown, but went on blithely, "I've lost a lot of weight over the last six months, but I'm going to enjoy gaining some of it back. I love to eat, but usually I have to watch the scale with a microscope."

Luke tipped his chair onto the two back legs, looking down his nose at her. "What did I tell you would happen if you brought that up again?" he asked.

Randy could tell that his mood had improved, presumably the result of a full stomach, but decided not to press her luck. Her apology was very meek, but then her sense of humor took over, prompting her to add in a vexed undertone, "It's just so hard to remember that I'm supposed to be Linda."

He began to get up, a determined look on his face, and Randy bolted out of her seat and fetched the coffee pot to top off his mug. Her attentiveness seemed to placate him.

She washed up the dishes as Luke dressed. She'd just finished wiping the counters when he emerged from his bedroom dressed in worn jeans, work boots, a wool shirt and a vee-neck sweater. "I'm going out to cut some wood," he told her. "Get dressed and come help me."

Randy did so, wishing that Luke had packed something other than Linda's expensive leather jacket. It was lined with fur and quite warm, but hardly suitable for dragging wood around in. Luke Griffin, she decided, could darn well pay for a new jacket if this one got scratched.

At first Randy enjoyed the exercise involved in helping Luke with the wood, especially since the air was crisp and clear and the wooded hills a joy to the senses. But after forty minutes of holding up branches while he cut them with a gas-powered saw she started to feel muscles she never knew she had. Twenty minutes later she removed her coat, sweaty and a little achy.

"Isn't this enough wood?" she asked. "We aren't going to stay here all summer, are we?"

Luke put down the saw. "Okay. Get busy carrying it." To Randy's utter astonishment he sat down at the base of a large tree, took out a pack of cigarettes, and lit one up. The message was clear enough. He expected her to carry the logs to the woodpile near the cabin while he sat there and supervised.

She was an affable woman, but her affability didn't extend quite that far. "I could use some help," she pointed out.

"Maybe." Luke took a few drags on his cigarette before he went on. "But it seems to me that all your life you've had men running in circles trying to please you. You need to learn that you can't walk all over me."

Randy had never met a man who could spark her temper so easily. It was all she could do to count to five before answering, "I wouldn't *dream* of walking all over you, but I'm not going to carry the logs while you sit there like the Maharajah of Ranchipoor, Luke."

"I don't recall giving you a choice," he said.

There was no point stalking away; Luke would only bolt up and stop her. "And if I refuse?" Randy asked.

"I'm not giving you that option."

By now Randy was ready to pray for divine intercession to prevent her from trying to strangle the man. She folded her arms across her chest, shot him a look that oozed exasperation and announced firmly, "Yesterday you laid out *your* ground rules and today I'm laying out *mine*. I assume my father must have seen some dim glimmer of intelligence and common sense in you in order to have hired you away from Stockman's, and I will further assume that eventually either one quality or the other will manifest itself and you'll take me home. Until that happy hour arrives, however, I'm willing to do only so much. I'll do the cooking in the interest of assuring myself decent meals and I'll do the cleaning up because watching me work seems to bring you an inordinate amount of satisfaction." She saw a smile tugging at Luke's mouth but couldn't be sure whether he was laughing at her clipped little speech or at his own overbearing behavior. "I'm an active person and I like to keep busy," she continued, "so I'll even help with whatever needs to be done at your cabin. You'll notice, Mr. Griffin, that I used the word 'help.' I won't play the slave to your taskmaster, and I promise you that if you so much as lay a finger on me to try to force me to do so, my father will skin you alive." Recalling his words of the day before she concluded briskly, "Just keep all that in mind and we'll do fine together."

He was smiling openly by now, his expression a little rueful. "The minute you figured out who I was the whole game plan was probably shot to hell," he admitted. "I can't threaten to beat you and you won't let me make love to you, which just about eliminates the traditional methods of handling a difficult woman." He stubbed out his cigarette, then stood up. "You win. I'll help with the wood."

Randy was charmed by his concession speech and couldn't pretend otherwise. The logs were heavier than she'd expected and it was very hard work to haul them the fifty or so feet to the house, but she really didn't mind. Eventually, however, her arms were simply too sore to continue. Luke didn't look too pleased when she told him she was going inside to lie down, but he didn't argue with her, either.

She slipped under the covers and waited a little tensely, wondering whether he'd come in after her, but when five minutes went by with no sign of him she relaxed and closed her eyes. After all, he'd just admitted that there was nothing he could do to enforce his wishes.

Eventually she dozed off, only to be awakened by the slam of the front door. She was wonderfully comfortable and hated to get up, but the sound of Luke's footsteps in the room started to change her mind. She opened her eyes to see him leaning against the door-jamb, watching her.

"Am I going to have to wake you up every time I want a meal?" he asked lazily.

Randy was still half-asleep. "It isn't very nice to be woken up by somebody nagging at me for meals all the time," she complained.

"You agreed to do the cooking. Besides, I get very moody if I'm not well-fed."

Just like the bears in the zoo, Randy thought as he left the room. She took a minute to brush out her hair and walked into the living room to find him sitting on the couch, his feet up on the coffee table, holding a paperback book. Randy had read that particular novel earlier in the year and remembered it well. The hero and heroine were caught up in a series of incidents that ultimately had them confusing illusion with reality.

Some perversely impish streak got the better of her, and she sat down beside him on the couch and said ingenuously, "Is that your inspiration for this crazy abduction of yours? By the time you get through with me I'm likely to wind up thinking that I really *am* my sister."

He snapped the book shut and tossed it on the table. Randy knew she'd made a serious error even before she found herself flat on her stomach, helplessly pinned over his thighs. She tried to squirm away, laughing, but Luke obviously had no intention of releasing her. His hand explored the curve of her bottom much too thoroughly, then lifted. What followed was a playful little slap that was far too gentle to punish—unless one considered an erotic game a form of punishment.

Randy didn't. Even before the first gentle slap her heart was racing, and by the time he got around to the second the blood seemed to be tearing through her veins. By the third she was ready to admit that this so-called spanking was in fact a very expert sort of seduction, and just as enjoyable as Luke had claimed it would be. She was still trying to wriggle away—it was clearly part of the game—when he wrapped his hands around her waist and turned her over.

"That's enough of that," he said, pulling her into a sitting position on his lap. His eyes glowed with hunger, but not for food.

Randy looked at his mouth, wanting him to kiss her, but aware that it would lead straight into the bedroom. His hand slipped under her turtleneck to cover her breast, teasing the nipple to hardness and sending a spasm of sensual awareness to her loins. If she didn't stop him now she wouldn't stop him at all.

"I'd better go make—" she began, but her words were cut off by his lips, possessively claiming her own.

She thought of her affair with Sean and started to pull away, but Luke snaked an arm around her shoulders to keep her close and held her chin in his hand so she couldn't turn her head. Randy didn't try to prevent him from deepening the kiss, but she certainly didn't respond to it, either.

His tongue probed her mouth for several fruitless seconds before he broke the kiss and released her, saying hoarsely, "What are you trying to do to me? Drive me crazy?"

Randy quickly stood up and backed away from him, putting several yards in between them. "I don't want to sleep with you," she said. "Regardless of what you think, I'm not my sister and I don't—"

"You sat down next to me," Luke interrupted coldly. "You teased me into reacting and loved every minute of what I did to you, but now you're suddenly saying no." The longer he spoke the more angry he seemed to become. "I don't know what your game is, Linda, but try it again and I'm not going to play. And if you want to cry rape to Daddy you go right ahead and do it."

Randy was thoroughly shaken by the time he was finished yelling at her. The fact was, he was right. Although teasing him had been the furthest thing from her mind, she *had* provoked him. Her behavior reflected her deep ambivalence about him: she was extremely attracted to him, yet determined not to plunge into another reckless love affair. Since she hadn't asked the blasted man to haul her up to Maine in the first place she couldn't quite bring herself to apologize, so she simply walked over to the kitchen and started to fix lunch.

Once she'd placed two cheese sandwiches in a buttered frying pan to grill them she began to struggle with the can opener in order to open a can of soup. She succeeded in getting the can partially open but when she tried to pull the lid away she slashed an angry-looking cut near the base of her right thumb with the jagged edge. Her muttered curse gained Luke's attention; he looked up from his book just as Randy shoved her hand under the running faucet in the hope that the cold water would relieve the sting. It was bleeding heavily, turning the water in the sink red.

Luke put down his book, got up and walked over to her. "Let me see how bad it is," he ordered.

Randy silently held out her hand. Luke inspected the cut, then took a first-aid kit out of one of the cabinets and fished out a box of gauze pads. For a moment he pressed a pad against her injured thumb, and then told Randy to hold it there. "It should stop bleeding in a moment," he said. "When was the last time you had a tetanus shot?"

"Two years ago, after I finished . . ." Randy choked back the last word, "college." This wasn't the time to argue about who she was. Luke removed a roll of gauze and some adhesive tape from the first-aid kit and waited another minute before checking the cut.

If Randy had doubted his story about being a medic

in the Peace Corps she would have believed it now. He carefully washed his hands before applying an antibiotic ointment to the wound with his finger, then wrapped her thumb in gauze up to the first knuckle and added a layer of adhesive tape.

"Isn't that a little elaborate?" Randy asked, not displeased by his efforts.

"I'm a frustrated doctor." Luke grabbed the can of soup and opened it up. "Besides, it's in a bad spot. A Band-Aid wouldn't have stayed on or protected the cut very well."

"Luke?" Randy's voice was so uncertain that Luke cocked a puzzled eyebrow at her. "Would you mind opening the cans from now on?"

He smiled. "Sure. Just ask me."

At first Randy was baffled by how quickly Luke's anger had left him, but then she remembered her father's comment about him—that Luke Griffin had a temper, but either controlled it or said what was on his mind and put it behind him. In this instance, obviously, the second rule applied.

Whatever tension remained between them slowly dissipated as they ate. By the time Randy got up to make the coffee she felt thoroughly confident about asking a few questions.

"Where did you get the scar, Luke?" she began.

"Oh, that was put there by my first kidnap victim," he said, eyes twinkling.

Randy shook her head, smiling. "No, really."

"I grew up in a tough neighborhood in Brooklyn," he explained. "When I was twenty and my sister was twelve, one of the local thugs started to bother her. I told him to lay off. The next day he and a group of his friends picked a fight with me and my friends. Somewhere along the line he flipped out a knife and I was dumb enough to get in the way. Then a squad car showed up and we all ran like hell. But he left her alone after that."

Randy had grown up sheltered in a high security building and had attended exclusive private schools. Although she'd gone to college in New York City, just as Luke apparently had, she'd traveled back and forth to the campus in a chauffeured limousine, not on the bus or subway. Luke Griffin's childhood was as foreign to her experience as an Iowa farm boy's would have been.

"Your nose is a little crooked," she said. "Did you break it in a fight, too?"

"You think I'm a physical wreck, hmm?" he drawled.

"Obviously not," Randy said, refusing to be teased. "Your nose?"

"Was broken during a game of street football," he said. "I'm still hungry, Lin. What's for dessert?"

"You know what you brought up here as well as I do," Randy reminded him. "Exactly nothing."

"I was thinking Spartan. Obviously a major error. Why don't you make me something? Chocolate chip cookies, brownies . . ."

Since his doctoring deserved something in the way of a reward, Randy got up and rummaged around in the cabinets. "No chocolate chips or baking chocolate," she informed him. "What did you have in mind after lunch?"

"The floor in the living room could use cleaning and waxing." He held out his mug for some coffee. "Why?"

"I could probably manage to bake a cake," Randy said, pouring the coffee. "Given the ingredients you've got around it would have to be plain vanilla. That might not serve your purpose as well as having me scrub floors, but I'll remind you that I'd expect you to help." She shrugged, then added, "But it's *your* stomach."

"You're on. The floors can wait." He sat and drank a second cup of coffee after they'd finished the first, watching as Randy cleared the table and began to wash the dishes. The soapy water quickly penetrated Luke's bandage, however, causing her to wince with pain and pull her hand away.

"Go sit down, Linda." Randy hadn't heard him get up over the sound of the running water and she started slightly. "I'll do the dishes for you," he added.

She thanked him and went over to the couch, thumbing through an old magazine she found sitting on an end table. Luke Griffin could be very sweet when he wanted to be, she decided. When he was through with the dishes he strolled over to her, holding out one of the most dog-eared cookbooks she'd ever seen in her life.

It was no problem to find a recipe for vanilla cake, and in a creative moment Randy even decided to try using some hot chocolate mix for frosting, an experiment that succeeded admirably. Luke was so absorbed in his book that he paid absolutely no attention to Randy while she worked, but the moment the cake was cooled and frosted some sixth sense seemed to tell him that food was in the offing, and he promptly appeared at the table.

Randy cut two pieces, a large one for Luke and a smaller one for herself. His was gone amazingly quickly, but then, the cake was actually quite good.

"This deserves a reward, Mrs. Franck," he said. "A reprieve for both of us—no floors till tomorrow. Want to come for a walk?"

Randy immediately agreed. She was beginning to wonder if her father's assessment—that once she'd met Luke Griffin she wouldn't stand a chance—could be correct. She wanted to get to know him better, and felt that everything would be okay as long as she kept him at arm's length. She'd learned her lesson with Sean and wasn't about to make another mistake.

They doubled around to the back of the cabin and entered the evergreen and maple woods, reaching a trail of sorts after a hike of about twenty feet. The trail led to a gurgling, pristine stream, obviously the water that Randy had heard the night before. A few little fish darted past as they watched.

"I pump my water from here," Luke told her, taking her hand to help her across the rocks that provided convenient stepping stones to the other bank. "When I first inherited this place there was nothing but the cabin. The generator and pre-fab shed had to be flown in piece by piece. The same with the plumbing. Only somebody as eccentric as my father's uncle would have built the cabin in the first place."

"Tell me about him," Randy said.

The path continued on the other side of the stream and they started to follow it further into the woods as it meandered up the gently sloping hill. The tangy scent of pines and spruce was intoxicating, and the maples would be spectacular in autumn.

"My father was a salesman who hit the road permanently when I was twelve and my sister was four," Luke told her. "At first he sent my mother money, but after about a year the checks stopped coming and we lost track of him. My mother is a nurse—she used to work the three-to-eleven shift so she could get us off to school in the morning but still be home to sleep. I looked after my sister in the afternoons."

Randy had never met anyone with a background like Luke's. She couldn't imagine what it would do to a child to be abandoned by a father at age twelve and take major responsibility for a younger sibling at the same time. It was little wonder that Luke was protective of Anne—he was more father than older brother to her.

"My mother remarried when I was nineteen, but she didn't quit her job," he continued. "I was going to City College at the time and when I graduated I decided to try the Peace Corps. I only stayed eight months, though, and when I got back—" He cut himself off, saying, "Look to your left, Linda."

She did so, and was rewarded by the sight of a

graceful doe and her spotted fawn, standing stock-still
only ten feet away, watchfully sniffing the air. They
soon bounded out of view, to Randy's acute disappointment.

"They're enchanting," she said. "Do you see many
animals up here?"

"I'm not tremendously observant when it comes to
wildlife," he admitted. "I once saw a moose feeding on
plants in the streambed, and a few miles downstream
there used to be a beaver lodge, but that's about all,
unless you count birds. I'm not too interested in birds,
except"—he winked at her—"certain species."

Randy smiled but didn't answer, and they continued
on in silence for a time, companionably enjoying the
beauty of the lovely old hill. But after a few minutes
she prompted, "You were saying, when you got back
from the Peace Corps . . . ?"

"Right. A few months later some lawyer got in touch
with me. It was the first anyone had heard of Arthur
Griffin, my father's uncle. Apparently he'd settled in
Maine near Portland and made a pile of money with a
string of inventions. He was a bachelor and must have
had a thing about solitude, because he bought this land
and had the cabin built—"

"Where?" Randy interrupted.

Luke's mouth quirked a fraction but he answered the
question. "In northern Maine, about twenty miles from
the Canadian border. According to his will his money
was supposed to go to his oldest male relative. My
father was his only nephew and the lawyers traced him
to Las Vegas through his employment history. One of
them told us he'd been killed in a fire about two years
before. They located me through his second wife. I
eventually met her—she's a very nice lady—and naturally I paid her well for her help."

"So there was more than just the cabin and land?"

"Right. The minute I laid eyes on this place I loved

it, but I'm too much of a city slicker to live with outdoor plumbing and gaslight. It cost a lot of money to fix up, but thanks to Arthur Griffin money wasn't a problem."

"If money wasn't a problem, and if you were serious before about being a frustrated doctor, why didn't you go to medical school?" Randy's question suggested a second one. "And why did you leave Africa after only eight months? Isn't two years the usual tour of duty?"

"Personal reasons," Luke said. Randy knew she'd hit a very raw nerve by the curtness of his tone. They walked on, side by side, for another few minutes before he picked up the story. "I would have liked to be a doctor, but I knew it would take too much of my time and I had other obligations to think about. I wound up at the Business School at Stanford instead. It was valuable in more ways than one. I got a first-rate business education and I learned how to invest my money. There are trust funds for my two nieces and even income to pay for little amenities, like the plane."

Randy hadn't realized that Tom Havemeyer had children, and found Linda's dalliance with the man all the more dismaying because of that. But even more than disappointment with Linda, she felt intensely curious about Luke. What had he meant by *personal reasons?* And what was the nature of his *other obligations?* Since he clearly didn't want to talk about it, however, she didn't bother to ask.

They were walking through thicker woods now; the ground was covered with a blanket of brown evergreen needles and the path had petered out. Every now and then Randy heard the sound of a small creature scurrying out of their way.

"Why did you decide to work for my father?" she eventually asked him.

"I'd started working at Stockman's during the summer after my first year of business school. I never expected to make a career out of retailing but I found I had a talent for it and enjoyed it. I joined the store full-time after I graduated. By the time I was thirty I was managing the flagship store in San Francisco, and then there was a promotion to a company vice president."

A small stone had rolled down in front of them, perhaps dislodged by a raccoon or deer, and Luke began absentmindedly to kick it along as they walked. "Last year your father came through California on his way to mainland China," he went on. Randy didn't bother to mention that her parents had stopped in Los Angeles to see her en route back to New York. "He called me up and asked me to consider working for him. At first I said no, I was happy where I was. Then he offered me the vice presidency of Branch Operations." Luke glanced over at her. "It was an offer I couldn't refuse. Especially since Annie was married to a friend's younger brother and had moved to Poughkeepsie the year before. I missed her after she left—" He cut himself off, frowning.

"After she left where?" Randy asked.

"Nothing. Forget it."

There was no way Randy could forget it. She started to fit puzzle pieces together, beginning with the fact that Luke couldn't have missed his sister unless she'd once lived nearby. That meant she'd been in California with him, but for how long? Had she gone to college there and stayed? Or was she perhaps the "obligation" he'd mentioned earlier? She mentally picked up another piece of the puzzle—the reason he'd left the Peace Corps. What had made him rush away from Africa? His mother's death, perhaps?

"Is your mother still alive?" she asked.

"My mother?" He seemed surprised by the question, but not offended. "She lives in Florida with my stepfather. He's retired now."

There was a coldness in his voice when he referred to

his stepfather that told Randy he didn't like the man. She tried to fit that in with everything she'd learned. Perhaps Luke hadn't rushed *away* from Africa, but *back* to New York. It sounded very much like he'd taken his fifteen-year-old sister with him when he'd gone to California, and his mother had obviously permitted it. Add the fact that he disliked his stepfather. . . .

Randy started to feel a little sick. Maybe she was miles off-base, but she had to find out if she was right. "Did you leave the Peace Corps because you found out that your stepfather was . . . bothering your sister?"

Luke stopped dead in his tracks. Randy looked at him, then took a step or two backward at the icy expression on his face. "You're very quick," he said. "For some reason I didn't expect you to be."

He seemed to debate whether or not to fill in the details before finally continuing, "My mother was still working evenings and that left Annie at home with my stepfather. After he tried to touch her a few times she wrote to me. She was afraid to tell my mother and didn't know what else to do. I was on the next plane home. Fortunately things hadn't gone too far, or I would have . . ." He didn't bother to finish the sentence, but Randy shuddered to think what he might have done.

"Well, these are enlightened times," he went on sarcastically. "The man was obviously sick and he got himself some help. Maybe it's to my mother's credit that she stood by him, but you'd damn well better believe that I wanted my sister out of that house. Arthur Griffin couldn't have bought the farm at a better time."

"So you took Annie to California with you," Randy murmured. "No wonder you're so close."

Perhaps it was the wrong comment to make, since it reminded Luke Griffin of where that closeness had eventually led him. Randy could see him stiffen up next to her; even his stride took on an angry cast. "That's exactly right," he said, "and I'll tell you something else. Annie met Tom when he was seventeen and she was sixteen. From the day they first set eyes on each other there was never anyone else for either of them—until you got in the way." He stopped, catching Randy by the shoulders and turning her to face him. "They have two little kids at home, four and two. Their relationship isn't some game that you can wander in and out of, Linda. Or don't you even care how much damage you've done by picking on a guy who's scarcely even heard of the league you play in, and then making him so damn crazy about you that he—"

"Just a blasted minute," Randy interrupted. "Tom was the one who picked up the phone in the first place. No one forced him to do it. Did it ever occur to you that maybe your sister and brother-in-law have some real problems, problems Annie hasn't told you about, and that—"

"If they do, you certainly haven't helped matters," Luke snapped.

"On the contrary, Linda sat and talked to Tom—"

Luke cut her off with an angry curse. "Linda sat and talked . . . ! When are you going to stop that garbage and start to take responsibility for what you've done?" He gave Randy a little shake and then yanked his hands away, as though tempted to do far more.

Her temper aroused, Randy turned her back to Luke and marched on ahead of him, no longer even noticing the scenery. His totally exaggerated characterization of Linda was bad enough, but his refusal to believe that she was who she said she was even worse. Luke followed behind her, making no attempt to match her pace. They were hiking up a moderate incline now and the combination of Randy's rapid strides and the pitch of the hill soon had her gasping for breath. She slowed down and then, suddenly dizzy, wrapped her arms around the trunk of a small pine tree to keep from falling down.

Several moments later Luke was beside her. He detached her arms from the tree and pulled her gently to the ground. "Sit down for a few minutes," he said. "You're probably not used to the altitude yet."

Randy, still breathing heavily, made no attempt to get up again. Luke sat back against a tree a few feet away, his legs sprawled out in front of him, apparently in full control of himself. "You know," he said, "I've been impossible to work with ever since my sister called to tell me Tom was having an affair. Your father called me in to find out what the problem was, and I told him. I had some pretty harsh words for both of you; he cursed right back at me and finally threw me out of his office. Even though I knew I'd gone too far I still couldn't figure out why he'd bother to defend you. But now I can. You're captivating, Linda. No wonder Tom couldn't resist you. You could make a saint succumb to temptation if you put your mind to it."

Randy might have been flattered if Luke had sounded the least bit tempted, but his tone was accusing rather than admiring. As for Randy, having witnessed the outcome of that violent session in her father's office and having heard her father's account of it, she was beginning to doubt that Luke had actually persuaded her father to agree to something so outrageous as hauling Linda off to Maine to curb her wanton ways.

"So you were lying when you said he knew about this," she said. "But I suppose you think you can get away with anything. Future president and all that."

Her irritation only amused him. "If you knew me better you'd know that I always get what I want. And after the second time Annie called me, hysterical because Tom had spent another weekend with you, I knew I wanted you out of the picture."

"Why are you so sure it was me?" Randy knew that Luke and his sister were correct in assigning Linda the scarlet woman role, but she wanted to find out how they'd guessed.

"Come off it, Linda! After the way you threw yourself at Tom at the picnic Annie didn't need to be psychic to figure out who he was with. To make matters worse, Tom is so naive that he doesn't even know how to manage an affair. He left his coat in that cozy little inn you shacked up in together. On Monday the owner called his home to say they would send it back. Naturally Annie took the call. Tom had told her he was in Buffalo on business during those weekends, not playing games with you in Massachusetts." Luke shook his head in utter incredulity. "I couldn't believe it. Not only does he leave his clothes scattered all over the East Coast, he gives his home address and phone instead of his office phone."

"Whereas you," Randy said irritably, "would have made none of those mistakes."

"I told you, I'm single. And I don't take out married women," Luke answered.

Of course not, Randy thought, picking up a stick to occupy her hands lest she be tempted to throw a rock at him. You're perfect. You never do anything hurtful or stupid. But aloud she merely remarked, "You never told me how you got my father to go along with all this."

"It wasn't hard," Luke said with a shrug. "He told me it would probably be hopeless to talk to you if you were infatuated with Tom, and I asked him if he minded whether I tried. He didn't do anything more than wish me luck. Around C & D rumor has it that he gave up trying to talk common sense into you years ago. I think he knows that somebody needs to take you in hand and if I can do it, he's not about to object. Your father has a great deal of affection for you, that's obvious. But how does it feel to know that he has almost no respect?"

As usual, Randy thought, Luke's assessment was only part of the truth. There were certainly things about Linda that gave Bill Dunne fits of parental anguish, but there were other things that he genuinely admired. Randy didn't bother to contradict Luke because she saw little point in arguing with a man who was sure he knew everything. She was only inches from losing her temper as it was, something Luke might have recognized had he noticed the vicious way that Randy was stripping the bark off her stick. One more word, she thought silently, staring at the denuded stick.

Suddenly Luke was no longer sprawled against the tree, but was striding over to Randy, glaring down at her. "Okay, so you don't care what anybody thinks of you," he growled, "even your own father. He even warned me how irresistible you are, and I could well believe it—I'd seen your picture. At the time I had no objections to taking you to bed, but now—I find your morals almost as contemptible as your lack of regret. You may look like an angel, but I wouldn't touch you if you begged me to."

His arrogant rejection was the last straw. Randy was either going to slap him or taunt him, and the second was definitely safer. She pulled herself up and faced Luke, who was standing only inches away, then nonchalantly trailed a finger down the bare, blond-haired arm revealed by his rolled-up sleeve. "Wouldn't you, Luke?" she mocked. Her fingers reached up to play with his mouth. "You'll forgive me if I don't believe you."

His response was to angrily push her away from him. "Believe it, lady. I intend to see to it that by the time I'm through with you you'll think twice about hurting an innocent, decent woman like my sister." Without another word he turned away and started back to the cabin.

For a long time Randy made no attempt to follow. At

first anger kept her standing alone in the Maine woods, and then fear. Up till now she hadn't had any problem standing up to Luke Griffin, but he'd made the kind of threat that made her shiver. For a long time she was simply too frightened to go back to the cabin, but then the sun dropped lower in the sky and the air turned cooler, and she knew she couldn't continue to stay on the mountain indefinitely.

As she started back down she reminded herself that Luke had a hot temper that fortunately cooled down quite quickly. She recognized the pattern by now. By the time she got back to the cabin the worst of his anger would have passed.

She slowly made her way through the trees, but lost her bearings in the unfamiliar terrain and never managed to find the trail. When she finally spotted the edge of the woods she realized that she was several hundred yards from where she'd started. Her face and arms were covered with scratches by now, the result of too many unfriendly brambles. And to make matters worse she either had to cross the stream at a point where it was far wider and deeper than before, or else fight her way upstream through the underbrush. Tired and a little depressed, she elected the first option, removing her shoes and rolling up her jeans before she waded in. Halfway across she lost her balance on the algae-covered rocks along the stream bed, tumbling into the water. She had to fight her way to shore against the current, and emerged soaked and shivering from the icy water.

If Luke were worried about her or concerned about the condition she arrived in he gave absolutely no sign of it. When Randy opened the door he merely looked over his shoulder and then ordered, "Get out of that wet clothing and fix dinner." He stuck his head back into his book.

If nothing else, cooking kept Randy busy and took

her mind off her troubles. She prepared what she considered to be an excellent lamb curry, but for once a good meal failed to improve Luke's mood. And this time he left Randy to wash the dishes. Both the cut on her thumb and the scratches left by the underbrush stung uncomfortably, so by the time she was through her mood was considerably more resentful than subdued.

Dinnertime conversation had consisted of Luke's "Very good" when he finished eating. When he stuck his nose back into his book Randy walked over to a bookcase that stood in the corner of the living room and started to inspect the ancient magazines and bestsellers it held. But the moment Luke realized what she was doing he stood up and said firmly, "No."

Randy looked back at him. "No *what?*"

"No reading. This isn't a vacation. You can either do some work or go to sleep."

Her patience frazzled, Randy threw the book on the floor and stalked off to the bathroom. She showered and washed her hair, taking care to keep the hot water away from her scratches and on her sore muscles. It felt marvelous. It wasn't only cutting and carrying the wood that had tired her out; the long walk in the woods had left her legs aching and feet sore. Daily dance classes had never been like this.

She emerged from the bathroom wrapped in a large bath sheet, a smaller towel covering her wet hair. A little more relaxed now, she was determined not to lose her temper. For a minute she stood in the doorway, indecisive, but then Luke sensed her presence and glanced over at her.

"Is there—do you have a blow dryer?" she asked in what she felt was an entirely reasonable tone of voice.

He looked disgusted. "This is the middle of nowhere, Linda, not some damn penthouse. Get to bed!"

His sarcasm was her undoing. Sorely provoked, she

marched into her room, grabbed her brush and stalked back out to the living room to kneel down in front of the fire, her back to Luke. She could feel his eyes on her bare skin as she brushed the tangles out of her hair and let the heat from the fire start to dry it.

When she was finished she shot Luke an exasperated look that accelerated into anger when he smiled rather smugly at her. "You're really angry," he said.

"Yes. Also tired," she agreed. "So far today I've been a lumberjack, a packhorse, a cook, a maid, a hiker and, much against my will, a diver. Frankly, the company around here is a drag and I'm going to sleep."

As she got to her feet she was suddenly aware that she'd gone too far. Luke was no longer amused—he was flat-out aroused. She'd issued a challenge and he meant to accept it.

"Oh no you're not," he told her. "Not yet. So I'm a drag? Well then, let's see if I can't find something to entertain you. I'm going to tell you exactly what's going to happen. I'm going to carry you into my bedroom. I'm going to take a good look at what's under that towel. And then I'm going to make love to you, and I'm not going to stop until you're so turned on that you'll beg me to change my mind when I throw you out. *Then* you can leave."

Randy started to run away, but before she'd taken three steps Luke had scooped her up and was carrying her into the bedroom. He ignored her struggles and tossed her onto the bed like a battered old duffel bag. Her attempts at escape succeeded only in exhausting her and she lay there, unable to move, trying to catch her breath.

When Luke yanked off the towel and threw it on the floor Randy stiffened and stared at him in alarm. He was inspecting her with aggressive eyes, drinking in her narrow waist, small, high breasts and rounded hips. Her mouth went dry and her heart started pounding double-time. She slid off the bed just as Luke began to remove his shirt.

She grabbed for the towel but Luke simply put one large foot on it to prevent her from picking it up. He shrugged out of his shirt, which joined the towel on the floor, and started on his belt. Randy bolted toward the door, but Luke got there first, standing in front of it to prevent her from leaving.

She backed slowly away as Luke removed the rest of his clothing. He was even more intimidating stripped-down than fully dressed. His legs were firm and power-ful, his arms sleekly muscled, his chest broad and covered with a light hazing of hair. Randy wasn't immune to sheer male appeal, but she'd made herself a promise and she intended to keep it. She picked up the towel and held it protectively in front of her. "I don't want you," she said coldly. "Let me out of here."

"We'll see," Luke replied. He strolled over to her, pulled the towel from her clenched fingers and picked her up.

As he tossed her onto the bed he yanked the string of the bedside lamp to turn it off, then lay down beside her and pinned her down. "You don't seem to be fighting me anymore," he murmured, nuzzling Randy's neck.

Randy was glad that the light was out so he couldn't see her face turn red. The weight of his leg across her thighs and the feel of his mouth nipping at her ear lobe were enough to make her forget her efforts at escape. "It's called passive resistance," she lied, wondering how she could possibly not respond when even a hand accidentally brushed across her breast had the power to scorch her down to her toes.

Luke proceeded to explore every inch of her body, his touch both deft and gentle. He began by running his fingers lightly over her breasts and she was powerless to keep the nipples from hardening with pleasure. She choked back a moan as he massaged each one in turn with his thumb and index finger, but her enjoyment must have been perfectly obvious to him. For a moment his mouth stroked her lips, rubbing softly back and forth, but when she kept her mouth tightly closed he simply returned to her ear, his tongue tracing the intricate curves outside and the sensitive area within.

In the meantime his hands went on with their exploration, fondling the soft curve of her stomach, caressing the bones of her hips and brushing up and down her thighs. Periodically he would return to tease her mouth with his lips, as if he knew perfectly well that sooner or later she would welcome his kiss.

Randy didn't suppose that she was fooling him. She was trying not to move but her body insisted on arching hungrily and her heart beat wildly. Her skin was covered with a thin film of perspiration by now. At one point Luke picked up her wrist, stroked the back of her hand and then placed his thumb over her pulse. "Is it getting any more tolerable yet?" he murmured.

"No," she lied, the word sounding admirably forceful considering the fact that she felt as though she were lying in the middle of a raging fire.

"I'll have to try harder, then," he said. His hand began to caress her intimately, stroking and arousing until she couldn't think straight. And this time when his mouth returned to toy with her lips she parted them to invite his kiss. His tongue skillfully probed her mouth even as his fingers gently probed her body. With a moan of surrender Randy's arms went around Luke's waist and she kissed him back, her tongue tasting and exploring in response to his.

Luke turned her onto her side, one hand splayed firmly against her lower back to hold her close against his hardened length, and continued to kiss her. The feel of his body destroyed her little remaining control. She clutched him almost frantically, her nails digging into his skin, and eagerly followed the dominating thrusts of his body. When he pushed her onto her back again and gently eased himself on top of her, she murmured his name and sought his lips.

A hard leg slid between her thighs, parting them, and Luke whispered into her ear, "Should we finish what we started?"

Randy wanted nothing more. "Yes—Luke . . ." she moaned softly, seeking his mouth again.

"You're sure?"

How could he even ask? "Yes—please . . ." she whispered.

"Good." The word was clipped and self-satisfied. The next moment Luke was pulling away, rolling off and sitting on the edge of the bed. He stretched and yawned, saying to a stunned Randy, "You're right, Linda. It's been a long day and my company bores you. So go to bed."

"You—you can't really want me to go," Randy protested. She'd felt the hunger in him, perhaps not as great as her own, but urgent nonetheless. "You still want me. Don't tell me you don't."

"Physically, yes," Luke admitted coldly. "But emotionally, never. Why should I bother with a tramp like you? Get out of here."

A chill ran through Randy's body and she shivered convulsively. Without another word she got up from the bed, walked out of the room and returned to her own room, closing her door gently behind her. Although rationally she understood that Luke's contempt was reserved for Linda, emotionally she felt horribly rejected. Still naked, huddled under the covers, she shut her eyes tightly and refused to let herself cry. Deep inside she felt that she'd acted like the tramp Luke had labeled her. She'd wanted him and there was no use pretending that she hadn't; she'd knelt in front of that fire, well aware that her actions would provoke him.

By now Randy had a pounding, one-sided headache

and a bad case of self-flagellation. Why did she want to go to bed with men who didn't love her?

When she heard Luke's door open she went rigid with alarm, but he passed by her room and continued out of the cabin. Alone now, she started to cry. A slightly ridiculous adventure was becoming increasingly traumatic for her. If venturing into the virgin forest of Maine hadn't been virtual suicide, she would even have tried to walk her way out.

Despite his highly charged emotional state, Luke Griffin was not so totally irrational that he couldn't recognize that he'd been acting like a bloody maniac for the last two days. If he'd behaved anything like this in the office Bill Dunne would have handed him a one-way ticket back to California and breathed a sigh of relief. Who but a dyed-in-the-wool masochist, for example, would throw a passionate, desirable woman out of bed, and all for the sake of proving a point?

So she'd teased him earlier in the day and aroused his temper . . . so he was angry over her affair with Tom and baffled by a lifestyle that exceeded liberation by a substantial degree . . . so he'd pompously threatened to leave her aching for him and would have looked like a fool if he hadn't carried out the threat. Did any of that compensate for the fact that *he* was one big frustrated ache by now?

Luke zipped up his jacket and headed for his plane, lighting a cigarette as he walked. He smoked very little, but another few days in Maine and he'd be going through a pack a day. Admit you've wanted her almost from the beginning, he told himself—and maybe even since the first time you laid eyes on a ten-year-old photograph of her. You could have talked to her in Cambridge but you didn't. Instead you came up with this half-witted scheme to haul her off to Maine.

He'd told himself that he'd wanted to make her forget Tom. He'd figured that the right combination of bullying and charm would accomplish that. A woman like Linda Franck, he reasoned, equated gentleness and concern with weakness. First he had to make it clear that he was the boss, and then he could concentrate on seducing her. He'd expected more of a fight about the cooking and the wood and had purposely provoked her about carrying the latter, but he hadn't expected her to stand there with her arms crossed, calmly and firmly standing up to him. She'd looked so desirable that he'd wanted to pull her down to the ground and make love to her on the spot.

All in all, he thought as he swung himself into the pilot's seat, it just didn't add up. He'd expected her to be hard-boiled and instead she showed flashes of vulnerability. He'd felt like a complete heel when she'd staggered in before dinner, looking like a half-drowned rat. He'd expected her to be spoiled and instead she was cooperative. She was a quick, interested listener who had him telling her the story of his life without his intending to, and fresh and eager in bed rather than jaded, as he'd expected. If he hadn't known better he might even have believed that he'd kidnapped the wrong sister.

But that, of course, was impossible. To believe she was Miranda would have been to believe an incredibly convoluted series of explanations. But even more than that, the one thing company gossip had told him about Miranda Dunne was that she'd never had a lover and, in fact, was rather young for her age. The woman he'd held and caressed was a confident seductress who had wanted him and shown it.

So where did that leave him? He was infatuated with a woman he couldn't really respect and half-crazy to make love to a woman he could never cherish. After spending a restless night on Friday he'd been downright grumpy the next morning, but he had the feeling that after tonight he'd be totally impossible. He was tempted to go back inside and make love to her, but he knew that she wouldn't let him near her until he apologized. And he wasn't about to do that.

# *Chapter Five*

*I*f there had been any way to avoid getting out of bed on Sunday morning Randy would have taken advantage of it. Though her headache was a bit better and her energy level was higher, her opinion of herself was just about the same and her embarrassment had increased. The only new emotion she felt was a healthy anger with Luke Griffin. She didn't really care *what* he thought of Linda Franck—a gentleman didn't call a woman names and then sadistically leave her hanging. But then, she admitted to herself, given Luke's background there was no reason to expect him to behave like a gentleman.

She'd lain in bed for what seemed like hours waiting for him to come in and order her to make him breakfast when it finally occurred to her that the cabin was strangely quiet. Footsteps, doors slamming, running water, Luke stoking the fire—all of these familiar sounds were absent. Shivering, she pulled on a robe and peeked out the door, but saw only a dying fire. The living room was almost as cold as her bedroom.

Panic rose in her throat, sending her dashing into Luke's room. His suitcase was sitting reassuringly on the dresser and he'd left a pair of running shoes on the floor near the foot of his bed. The irony of her feelings quickly struck her—she didn't want to face him but the thought that he might have abandoned her had terrified her. Shaking her head, she went into the living room and stoked the fire, adding two more logs.

Randy wasn't particularly hungry, but knew that some toast and tea would probably settle her stomach, which felt a little queasy. A couple of aspirin tablets might even deal with the headache. As she approached the kitchen area she noticed a note held to the refrigerator by means of a magnet shaped like an ice cream cone.

Judging from the scrawled handwriting, Luke Griffin had either repeatedly flunked penmanship or else had left the cabin rather hurriedly. Randy took it off and stared at it, trying to decipher the words.

"Gone for a ride," it read. "Back in a few hours. L. P.S. Removed all the knives from the cabin just in case. Figure if you used one on me it would be justifiable homicide."

There was no way Randy could stay angry with a man who left her a note like that. In two brief sentences he'd managed to convey not only regret, but also the notion that he'd acted like a total cad. While the note didn't alter Randy's opinion of her own behavior it somehow made her feel better. And a check of the drawers revealed that he hadn't taken the knives at all.

She picked up a magazine after she finished eating, but six-month-old accounts of football games and golf tournaments failed to hold her interest. She supposed that she was just too restless to read and thought about taking a walk instead, but yesterday's battle with the woods had left her less than eager for a rematch. That left the floor. At least, she decided, it would keep her busy.

An hour and a half later she was beginning to wonder if cleaning the floor wasn't a way of punishing herself for her sins of the night before. The combination cleaner/wax that she'd found under the sink had a chemical odor thinly disguised by lemon that made her stomach rebel still further. Crawling around on hands and knees with a bunch of rags wasn't the wisest activity in the world when one was tired to begin with, and moving around bulky furniture and heavy rugs was a job for either a two-hundred-pound man or an Amazon, but not for Randy Dunne.

She only finished because there wasn't that much of the floor left to do, but paid a heavy price for her compulsiveness. By the time she went into the bedroom to lie down her head was throbbing all over again and her nausea was even worse. The wax she'd applied was the type that had to be buffed, but she certainly couldn't do that now.

It was obvious, however, that she'd have plenty of time to do it later. If Luke hadn't taken her home this morning, he clearly meant to keep her at least another night. Lying on the bed, Randy tried to figure out just why he was delaying. Did he want to keep her away from Tom? Teach her some kind of lesson? Take her to bed despite the rejection of last night?

At least, she thought with a grimace, she didn't have to worry about being tempted by the third possibility. Her headache and upset stomach had been joined by a strange kind of dizziness, making her feel about as sick as she'd ever felt in her life. She wished she could fall asleep—it would provide escape from the pain.

It was the unusual noise that woke Randy up, a soft, rhythmic sound that she eventually identified as cloth rubbing against wood—Luke buffing the floor. She automatically started to sit up, but a wave of nausea hit her with such force that she had to lie back down again. She waited for it to ease, then gingerly tried again. This time she succeeded, propping herself against a pillow, not knowing what to do and consequently doing nothing.

The obvious course of action was to talk to Luke about her symptoms. After all, he *did* have some medical experience. Randy remembered how he'd bandaged her thumb, then later, in the woods, helped her when she'd become breathless and dizzy. Someone else's suffering seemed to bring out the best in him, which made the thought of approaching him less embarrassing.

He was sitting in a chair drinking a soda when she slowly walked out of the bedroom. About half the floor was finished and it looked very nice. "Luke," she said hoarsely, "I don't feel very well. My stomach . . ."

He stood up. "Lie down on the couch. Let me take a look."

Randy nodded, easing herself onto her back. When Luke sat down by her waist and reached out to unsnap her jeans she instinctively flinched, thinking of the way he'd touched her the night before. His jaw clenched as he quickly glanced at her, but neither of them said a word.

He slid down the zipper and started to examine her, his fingers firm yet gentle on her abdomen and stomach. For once, however, his touch was anything but arousing. Before he'd even finished Randy knew she couldn't lie there a moment longer. She tore off the couch and ran into the bathroom, to be followed by a tight-lipped Luke. He stood and waited without comment until she was through.

His hand dropped onto her shoulder as she rinsed her mouth, but she sensed that the gesture was meant only to comfort, as a parent would comfort a child. In fact, Randy felt slightly better now. "Into the bedroom," he said. "I want to figure out whether I need to fly you to a hospital."

When Randy was settled on the bed he suggested, "Maybe it was the floor cleaner. That stuff could make a skunk run in the opposite direction. What made you decide to do the floor?"

Randy shrugged. "I had nothing to do. I was bored."

"I can't win," he answered with a smile. "Last night you told me that my company was a drag and now you're saying that my absence is a drag. Any suggestions on how to proceed?"

Ordinarily Randy might have blushed at his remarks, but now she was too sick to bother. When she failed to respond in any way at all Luke went on, "I can see that my teasing bedside manner is a total failure, Lin. Did I hit any tender spots before?"

Randy shook her head. "It's more queasy than painful."

"Any other problems?"

"A little dizziness. And also a headache. I've had it since last night but aspirin didn't help very much."

"One-sided and throbbing?"

She wondered how he'd known. "Yes."

"Sounds like a classic migraine. Bill once mentioned that your mother gets them, but obviously you never have. Let's get you comfortable and quiet and see if it helps. I think I have an icebag around here somewhere for your head."

Luke had started to unbutton her blouse even before he finished talking, but Randy didn't protest as he undressed her and helped her under the covers. She only knew that she felt awful. On his way out of the bedroom Luke pulled down the shades; he returned a few minutes later with the icebag.

The ice and the darkness helped a little, but Luke's reassuring presence helped even more. He certainly had his faults, but he was the kind of man you could count on. He was buffing the floor again, the sound too gentle to be disturbing. To take her mind off her head

Randy started to mentally recite a scene from her most recent play, and found that it worked.

Eventually Luke tiptoed back in and stood by the foot of the bed, looking at her. "It's okay," Randy said, taking the icebag away from her eyes. "I'm not asleep."

"How's your head?" he asked quietly.

"It still hurts, but not as much."

"Your stomach?"

"A little better."

Luke studied the paleness of her cheeks and the tiredness around her eyes and then walked over to sit beside her on the bed. He lifted a hand to stroke her hair, but dropped it when she suddenly tensed up. "I wasn't going to make a pass at you," he said. "You're tired and you can't sleep, right?"

A little embarrassed, Randy agreed.

"So I'll take care of it." Without further explanation he again reached out to touch her, but only to begin a firm, gentle massage of her temples. Randy felt tension she hadn't been aware of begin to slip away as he continued to knead her scalp and the back of her neck. As the pain receded and pleasure took its place she gave a little moan of relief and stifled a yawn. Eventually she dropped off to sleep again.

She was amazed by how much better she felt when she woke up. She stretched languidly and sniffed, then sniffed again. Luke was cooking something and it smelled wonderful. By the time Randy had brushed her hair and washed up, Luke was in the process of removing a batch of garlic bread from the oven. A pot of bubbling minestrone soup was sitting on top of the stove.

"Italian food!" Randy said, suddenly hungry. "I love Italian food. When do we eat?"

"Your timing is perfect." Luke grabbed plates and cutlery from the drainboard and began to set the table. "Go on, sit down. I'll take care of everything."

"Why, Luke," Randy said, "how thoughtful of you. Now I know how to get around that temper of yours. You're a born doctor who can't resist taking care of people. So all I have to do is stay sick."

"That wouldn't serve my purpose at all," he shot back.

The remark effectively shut Randy up. She snatched a piece of garlic bread from the cookie sheet and took a few bites, licking her lips in contentment. "Umm. This is delicious, Luke. You're a great cook. If I'd known that before I would have made you do your share."

He didn't answer, apparently preferring to concentrate on his soup, which contained thick chunks of meat and sliced vegetables and obviously hadn't come from a can. It wasn't until they were having coffee that the urge to talk seemed to hit him. He tipped back his chair, regarding Randy with a bland expression, and announced, "I think it's time I took you home. If I do, are you going to see Tom again?"

Randy was relieved that he'd decided to leave but not really surprised. He probably had to get back to work and had already made his opinion of Linda quite clear. Still, with her release in the offing, she wasn't about to risk her freedom by getting into yet another argument about who she was. She knew it didn't matter—it would be cleared up soon enough.

"No," she said. "That's all over with."

"And Roger? Will you see him?"

"I hope so," Randy answered, wondering what difference it could make to Luke. "I liked him very much."

"So what are you going to do with your life? Go to work? Look for another husband?"

She repeated the answer that Linda had given her in Cambridge. "Maybe open my own business—an antique shop or art gallery. I'm not in the market for a third husband," she added, "at least, not yet." Randy hoped it was the truth, but with Lin one never knew. Although her sister seemed more cautious it might be only temporary.

"Do you regret any of it?" Luke persisted.

Randy didn't bother to ask what "it" consisted of. "If you mean, do I regret meeting Tom, I suppose I do. I didn't know he had children and I'm sorry that your sister was hurt. But in the end all we did was talk. Ask him yourself if you don't believe me."

"I will." The words were a little clipped. "You don't like to talk about yourself, do you?"

"Sometimes I do, but right now"—Randy shrugged —"I feel better than before, but not terrific. Sorry." Actually she felt fine. She just didn't want to keep role-playing the part of Linda Franck.

Even if Luke's frown hadn't conveyed his disbelief, the tinge of sarcasm in his voice when he answered would have. "I forgot," he said. "Go sit down by the fire, Linda. I'll clean up."

In the end they did the washing up together, Randy feeling a little guilty for pretending that she was still sick. If she'd been able to think up any other way to stop him from cross-examining her she would have tried it, but she couldn't. Afterward they sat down together in the living room to read, Luke in a chair with his book and Randy on the couch with a magazine.

She found that her eyes kept wandering to his face, her thoughts on what would happen when they met again in New York. Surely he would apologize, but would he also ask her out? Or would he keep things strictly business?

He only had about fifty pages left to read and was too absorbed to notice Randy's frequent glances. The complexity of his personality had left her deeply ambivalent about him despite the strong physical attraction she felt. She knew he could be charming as well as caring, but he could also be arrogant and tough, even ruthless. Sitting here alone with him, all the old feelings of excitement and desire came flooding back, and yet she was very relieved that he'd never actually taken her. Considering how much she'd permitted perhaps it was academic, but the fact that they hadn't become lovers would make it easier to start off fresh in New York. After all, one unfortunate night didn't prove that she was promiscuous, only that she'd gotten carried away after a day that had left her emotions battered and her quota of common sense a little low.

When Luke snapped his book shut and tossed it on the table he caught her in the middle of a furtive glance. She quickly dropped her eyes to her magazine, blushing.

"Lin?" he murmured.

It wasn't hard to interpret that husky tone. Randy could feel his eyes on her face and reddened still more. "I'm going to shower and go to bed," she said, standing up. "Maybe I'll fill up the icebag. My head is bothering me again."

"Sure." Luke stood up also, grabbing his sweater from the coffee table. "I'm going for a walk. I'll see you in the morning."

He was out the door before Randy even reached the bathroom.

Luke shoved his hands into his pockets, walking briskly but with no particular goal in mind. He bent down and scooped up a few rocks, then threw them angrily across the field.

What was the woman's game, anyway, repeatedly glancing at him only to coolly reject him? Was she taunting him again? Inviting him to seduce her? Certainly she didn't feel sick—he didn't need a medical degree to see that her color was good and her appetite healthy. He thought he understood women, but he certainly didn't understand *this* one.

For a long time he walked around aimlessly, trying to figure out what he wanted—besides Linda Franck's body, that was. He was both attracted to her and repelled. He wasn't stupid enough to think he could change her and knew for a fact that he could never introduce her to his sister, so any real relationship was out of the question. Still, certain facets of her personality drew him to her. In the end he admitted that he'd been warned. A woman didn't attract millionaires like Brett Franck and successful producers like Roger Bennett without something more than a pretty face and body to offer.

By the time he turned back to the cabin he was very well aware that he was headed straight for her bedroom. He told himself that after all the lovers she'd had there was no reason why she shouldn't have one more. He believed that she wanted him and knew he wanted her. It might be only for one night, but he meant to enjoy it. Tomorrow could take care of itself.

Randy muttered an incoherent protest and rolled over onto her side, swatting her hand against her hair when she felt something touch her. She'd been sleeping so deeply—it couldn't be time to get up already.

At first when Luke pulled back the covers and lifted her out of bed she was too disoriented to realize what was happening. They were inside his room before she finally figured it out.

She started to squirm in his arms, only to be laid gently on the bed—his bed. Her nightgown was up around her thighs by now and she suddenly realized that Luke was wearing nothing at all. She tried to get up, moaning, "No . . ." but Luke slid on top of her, his body hard with desire, pinning her to the firm mattress.

When he moved against her the feel of his masculinity tore through her body like a bolt of lightning, leaving her short of breath. She reached up to push him away, but when her hands made contact with his muscled arms she somehow longed to explore, not reject. His body was so sexy, so male. Her hands moved higher, stroking his shoulders and then tangling into his crisp, thick hair.

His lips were against her neck now, nuzzling and nibbling, overcoming her few remaining objections. That little spot below her ear was one of her weaknesses. How could he have found it so quickly? He was setting her on fire, making her ache for him. She turned her head, needing much, much more than this gentle teasing.

His mouth had barely tasted her lips before they submissively parted to receive his tongue, which mounted an impatient invasion, his kiss deep and a little rough with desire. His urgency was contagious. She moaned, arching against him, her tongue mingling with his own before seeking the soft recesses of his mouth.

His fingers deftly dealt with the buttons down the front of her nightgown, pushing the flannel aside when he was through, exposing her breasts to his dominating hands. Randy was floating in a world of pure, intense sensation now, where Luke's body was the only reality. He caressed her hungrily, as though barely able to restrain himself, and she responded with a mindless passion that broke the bonds of his self-control.

She clung to him, her pleasure only too apparent from the little noises she made when Luke took her. They moved together slowly at first, then faster and faster until Randy could barely manage to breathe. When the explosion finally came she repeatedly cried out. Nothing like that had ever happened to her before.

The second time Luke woke her up he was gentler, more tender. Now there was no nightgown to remove, no barrier at all to his lips. She felt them on her breasts first, sucking the nipples till they hardened, tracing the circumference of each dusky circle with his tongue, nipping gently with his teeth as she stirred and murmured his name. When his mouth moved lower she stiffened slightly, but he was insistent about what he intended to do and she couldn't stop him. After a moment or two of his expert probing she no longer wanted to.

Sean had never aroused her this way—no one had. She couldn't control her response or the wild hunger of her movements. She thought she would die of frustration when he stopped for a moment, and was plunged into a mind-shattering ecstasy when he continued again. When the waves of pleasure finally tore through her body she knew she was utterly spent.

Twice more during the night she would learn that she wasn't. After the third time, exhausted, she fell asleep yet again, only to have Luke awaken her and seduce her all over again. The whole experience was surreal, like a dream—a dream with a passion she'd never known existed. The final time she was as wild as a tigress, exploring Luke's body as he'd explored hers, showing a boldness that would have shocked her had the night not been so full of magic. Afterward even Luke was sated.

Randy had never truly understood the phrase "the morning after the night before" until the morning sun woke her up and she realized she was in Luke's bed. She also realized what had happened there—*repeatedly* happened there—during the night. It still seemed like a dream, but Randy knew perfectly well that it hadn't been.

There was barely enough time to start feeling mortified before Luke stirred and opened his eyes. He looked at her, frowned and muttered, "That was one hell of a night."

It wasn't the reaction Randy had expected and it stabbed her like a dull knife. He almost sounded regretful. Where were last night's passion and tenderness? Hadn't it meant anything at all to him?

"Yes," she agreed. "It was."

He stretched and pulled himself up, then asked her if something was wrong. "You seem upset," he added, as though there was no possible reason why this might be so.

"Are we going to see each other again?" Randy blurted out the question even though she knew it was absurd. They'd be seeing each other in only a few weeks.

"Maybe. I'll call you." He trailed a finger down her cheek. "It's a long flight home and we need to get moving. Why don't you make some breakfast while I shut things down?"

Randy returned to her room and pulled on her clothes, then went into the kitchen to fix Luke some eggs. She wasn't at all hungry herself, because she knew exactly what "I'll call you" meant. It wasn't "How soon can I see you again?" but "See you around, honey." She was forced to confront the fact that what had happened last night meant absolutely nothing to Luke and neither did she. The thought made her sick with self-reproach. When would she ever learn?

Luke was just as preoccupied as she was over breakfast. Randy endured half a cup of coffee in his silent presence and then went into her room to pack. She'd never felt like this before—utterly wrung-out, too beaten even to cry.

The plane ride home was just as bad as breakfast had been. Luke went from preoccupied to irritable while Randy spent most of the flight staring out the window but seeing almost nothing. The thoughts that chased around her mind all seemed to begin, If only. If only she'd gone to New Hampshire. If only she hadn't been so attracted to Luke. If only she'd said no. If only . . .

Would he want her when he found out who she really was? And equally important, did *she* want a man who could treat a woman as callously as Luke had treated her today? She didn't have the answers.

In the middle of the afternoon they landed at a small suburban airport outside Boston. Luke walked Randy off the plane, carrying her suitcase for her. "I'll call us a taxi," he said.

She shook her head, holding out her hand. "I'll get home on my own. Just give me some money." She was afraid her precarious composure would buckle.

Luke handed her a couple of twenty-dollar bills, but when she took her suitcase and started to walk away, he reached out a hand to restrain her. Randy gave him a pointed stare and he removed it, running it through his hair instead. He looked annoyed with her.

"Look, Linda," he said, "last night was one of those things that just happens. We both wanted it and it wasn't the first time for either of us, but both of us know it's over. I enjoyed it and so did you, so what are you so upset about?"

What could she say? Because I'm disappointed in myself? Because you don't give a damn about me? "I could ask you the same thing," she murmured.

He shrugged. "It's complicated. Maybe it comes down to the fact that I'm not the kind of guy who's interested in a purely physical affair."

Randy was beginning to get the message. "Are you saying that that's all it could ever be? Because I'm not the type of woman you want to associate with?"

"Linda . . ."

"Are you?" she demanded.

"Yes," he said bluntly, and walked away from her.

On the ride back to Cambridge Randy was alternately furious and close to tears. Praying that Linda was home by now, she had the cab driver drop her off in front of the house. As usual the bottom door was open so she went inside, but the top was locked and there was no answer to her hard knock.

After everything that had happened since Friday this

minor setback was enough to trigger frustrated tears. Randy quickly wiped them away with the back of her hand and told herself to stop acting like a child. Her next move was to try Mrs. Siskin, the downstairs neighbor, but there was no one home there, either. The only other alternative was to leave Linda a note and walk the fifteen or so blocks to Harvard Square, where she could check into a motel. After all, she had Linda's credit cards with her.

Taking a pen from her purse, she rummaged around for something to write on, but couldn't even find a tissue or a piece of scrap paper. It was the final blow.

She was crying as she walked out of the building, barely aware of the silver Porsche coming up the street. Linda spotted her almost at once and bolted out of the car, running into the driveway to intercept her. After one look at her sister's rumpled clothing, defeated stance and scratched, tear-stained face, she asked anxiously, "What on earth happened to you, Randy?"

Randy didn't intend to start keening like a distraught mourner. She thought she could control herself better than that. But when Linda took her into her arms she clung like a small child and began to sob inconsolably. Linda half carried, half led her upstairs and into the apartment while Roger went back for their luggage.

Seated on the couch a little later, settled with a glass of water Linda had fetched, Randy sniffled and said, "I'm okay, really." Roger was standing by the front door, trying to stay out of the way, so she added with an embarrassed flush, "I don't usually carry on this way."

"I'll leave you two to talk," he said. "Lin, can I pick up something for dinner?"

"No, wait." Randy took a quick drink of water. "Sometimes, a man can understand—can *explain* things a woman can't. Lin's just going to tell you everything anyway, so . . ." She shrugged instead of finishing the sentence.

She could see that her sister was pleased by her high opinion of Roger Bennett, but before she could really trust him she needed to clear something up. "Do you live with someone?" she asked as he sat down in the living room.

"Only with my kids, in the winter," he answered. "What gave you that idea?"

"Luke said—"

"Luke?" Linda interrupted. "Luke who?"

"Luke Griffin. He said . . ."

"You were with *Luke Griffin* this weekend? *He* did this to you?"

"Yes, but he didn't . . ."

"Does Daddy know . . . ?"

"For God's sake, Linda, give the girl a chance," Roger interrupted. Looking sheepish, Linda did as she was told. "To answer your question, Randy, Luke was probably talking about Katrina Sorensen. We were together for about four months, but she never actually lived with me. I met Luke when I produced a charity fashion show that C & D did the clothing for. Katrina was one of the models and I introduced her to him. For a time she dated him instead of me, but he lost interest before I did. We broke up a few months ago."

"Who," Linda asked, "is Katrina Sorensen?"

Randy knew exactly who she was. "That blond-haired, green-eyed model who looks like a Scandinavian Amazon," she said. "She does the Dominique perfume ads and also the Kaylar Hotel commercial."

Linda wasn't too pleased by this piece of information. "You never mentioned *her*," she said to Roger.

He grinned at her. "It slipped my mind." Seeing that his answer was something short of satisfactory, he added, "Katie Sorensen is a beautiful woman and a hard-working professional, but she's also very insecure and incredibly self-centered. After a while I just couldn't deal with it. Does that answer your question?"

Linda said it did, then turned her attention back to

Randy. "Now what's all this about Luke Griffin? Didn't you go to New Hampshire?"

Randy poured out the whole story. At first she was afraid she might start crying again, but Linda and Roger kept interjecting the kinds of funny little asides that lightened the mood and kept her going. The most difficult part of the account concerned their final night together, but the gist of what had happened came through very clearly despite her censoring of the details.

"I obviously missed a lot when he got *you* instead of me," Linda drawled, making Randy smile. She darted a sly look at Roger.

"I'll make it up to you," he promised with a laugh. He looked at Randy. "I think I can fill in the rest. This morning Griffin gave you the brush-off. Told you it had been fun, but it was time to get back to the real world."

Randy nodded and filled in the details of their conversation. She wasn't surprised that Roger had guessed, given the state he and Linda had found her in.

When she was finished Linda muttered a very unflattering epithet to describe Luke Griffin and gave her a hug. "A lot of this is my fault," she said, "but who would have thought that someone who works for Dad would turn out to be a lunatic?"

"You're missing the whole point of what happened," Roger said impatiently. "Griffin admitted that he'd enjoyed it, and take it from me, a man doesn't keep a woman up half the night unless he's half-crazy for her. Forget what he told you—did you bother to ask yourself why any normal man wouldn't jump at the chance to repeat an experience like that?"

On the contrary, Randy had taken his explanation at face value. "His opinion of Lin . . ." she began, then stopped. She didn't want to hurt Lin or shock Roger, so she couldn't very well spell things out.

But Linda had no problem interpreting her reticence. "Roger knows all about my wicked past," she said, "although it seems to me that Luke's impression is a little exaggerated. There just haven't been that many men, Randy."

"Not according to him," she muttered.

"All that's beside the point," Roger said. "Luke Griffin is no saint. I know enough about him to know that he's dated women who make Linda look like a convent graduate, among them Katie Sorensen. What he told you is a bunch of garbage. He obviously couldn't get enough of you, Randy, so why wouldn't he want to see you again?"

"My father . . ."

"Stays out of Linda's life," Roger finished for her. His tone said he couldn't understand why women were so dense. "He was close-mouthed and irritable. His problem isn't sleeping with you, it's getting involved with you. If nothing else, he probably wonders what he could possibly tell his sister. It was easier for him to break it off *now,* before things went too far. So what's your problem? You can straighten it out in New York, and . . ."

"Men!" Now it was Linda's turn to hold forth on the stupidity of the *male* sex. "Couldn't you hear how ambivalent my sister is? One moment she was complaining that Luke was conceited and the next telling us how caring he could be. Judgmental and arrogant, thoughtful and gentle, ambitious and manipulative, sweet and protective. She doesn't know *what* she feels. She's been hurt badly once and she's running scared."

"Luke is a decent guy," Roger pointed out, "and once he finds out she's *Randy,* he's not going to start anything unless he's serious. Your father would kill him."

"Do you think I want a man to take me seriously because of *that?*" Randy asked. "Besides, Lin is right. I don't know what I feel. Suppose Luke wants to pick up where we left off. . . ."

"Of course he will," Roger said with a grin. "He's not *stupid.*"

"Well I don't know if *I* do. I'll agree because— because he happens to affect me that way, but . . ." Randy looked into her lap. "And maybe not just him. Maybe a lot of men. I was a late starter, but at the rate I'm going—"

"I refuse to listen to another word of this," Linda interrupted, pounding the table for emphasis. "You've got to stop punishing yourself for a perfectly human, perfectly understandable mistake, Randy."

"And Luke? Was he a perfectly human, perfectly—"

"No. Because I don't think he'll turn out to be a mistake. If Sean Raley hadn't shaken your confidence and left you so distrustful of your feelings I think you'd be taking this a lot differently. I think you'd realize that Luke *liked* the woman he met. It's the one he's only heard about who he *doesn't* like."

As far as Randy was concerned the discussion was pointless. She only knew that she was confused and upset, and that the thought of seeing Luke again left her trembling with anxiety. "Maybe I should just pack up and go back to California," she muttered.

Linda curled her feet up underneath her and stared at the opposite wall for several moments. She had a very odd look on her face that slowly—very slowly— turned into a smile. "California?" she repeated. "Why would you change your mind? After all, you had a *very* relaxing time in New Hampshire. You should be looking forward to working at C & D."

"New Hampshire?" Randy looked at Linda as if her sister were playing with half a deck. "I was never in New Hampshire."

"Dad doesn't think so. Luke doesn't think so. Luke thinks you're—what was the phrase? A chubby vestal virgin? You've already gained back some weight, and by the time you see him again . . ." Linda studied her sister thoughtfully. "A new hairstyle, a few inches taller with heels on, glamorous clothing and sophisticated makeup—you know how alike we look. Luke wasn't the first person to confuse us, especially when they haven't seen us for a while. He's never met me—all he's seen is that photo on Dad's desk, which looks as much like you do *now* as it does like I do. So the next time you meet he's going to think it's for the first time."

"You're in the wrong business," Roger drawled. "I'm going to hire you to do a script for me."

Randy was gazing at her sister in amazement. What kind of mind could dream up something so devious? "Do you think it could work? Really?"

"With your talent as an actress? Are you kidding?" Linda winked at Randy. "If you can convince people that you're a Yugoslavian princess you can convince Luke that you've never met. After all, he had incontrovertible proof of it. He made love to 'Linda,' but Miranda is the only twenty-four-year-old virgin in Hollywood."

Randy knew her sister had a point. "And how am I supposed to act?"

"Innocent, of course. Younger and still annoyed over that phone call. Also unattainable, unimpressed and strictly business. Where's your spirit, Randy? You aren't going to turn down the best role of your life, are you?"

"I just don't know. When he finds out what I've done he'll be furious. And suppose I really fall in love with him? I don't want to lose him by playing games. He may never speak to me again."

"Randy, darling, from what you've told us Luke Griffin is probably half in love with you already. Take care of the present and the future will take care of itself."

Randy had her doubts about Linda's analysis of the situation, but the actress in her couldn't resist the challenge of pretending to Luke that they'd never met.

And the woman in her grabbed at the chance to create some time in which to discover her feelings, to get to know Luke under more normal circumstances, to find out whether he could love her without exposing her own emotions so totally.

As soon as Randy agreed Linda called up her favorite hairdresser, flattering and cajoling for a full five minutes before he agreed to squeeze Randy into his schedule. Later, as she watched six inches of beautiful blond hair waft gently to the floor, she felt total dismay. But by the time she left she was actually rather pleased. Her shoulder-length hair fell in deep waves now, with the bangs and sides gently feathered back from her face. Looking in the mirror she even believed she could pull things off.

When they returned to the house Roger took one look and agreed. With the right clothing and makeup and some skillful acting it could work. Then he suggested to the two sisters that the three of them go to Martha's Vineyard for a few days. "You need some R & R after your supposed vacation," he said to Randy when she hesitated. "I have a cousin with a summer place near Edgartown who we can sponge off of. I have to work this weekend, so on Friday I'll drive you back to New York in the Lincoln and leave Lin the Porsche. I can pick it up next time I come up to see her."

It didn't take too much longer for Randy to admit that she loved the beach and could use a few days to get her equilibrium back. They left after a quick dinner, Linda and Roger in the Porsche and Randy in the Lincoln. Roger Bennett, it seemed, had friends everywhere. They spent the night at the home of a show business acquaintance of his who was not at all surprised that Roger would appear on his doorstep late at night accompanied by two beautiful women. "I would have called, Hal," he apologized, "but I didn't have your number with me. And since it's unlisted . . ."

"No problem." Hal—Roger's introduction didn't

include a last name—immediately ushered them toward some vacant bedrooms, pausing only to ascertain the sleeping arrangements. "Do you sleep with both of them at the same time, Rog? Or will you need two rooms?"

Roger laughed and answered, "No, no, Hal. Those were the Green twins, Jade and Emerald. I go out with Linda, but her sister Randy is involved with someone else, so leave her alone."

This exchange left Randy a little puzzled and mildly shocked. The look on her face must have been transparent, because Roger hastened to assure her, "It's an old joke, Randy. Years ago I dated twin sisters, but never at the same time."

Hal's home was only a fifteen-minute drive from the Woods Hole ferry to Martha's Vineyard. They took the morning boat, leaving the Lincoln in Hal's driveway and taking the Porsche onto the island with them. They arrived at his cousin's cottage to find the place deserted and the doors locked up. Roger simply walked off toward some bushes at the side of the house, fished around in the dirt and returned with the key.

"Are you sure your cousin won't mind?" Randy asked.

"Why should she? She uses my place on Fire Island all the time. Once she nearly burned it down."

They passed through a screened-in porch containing battered deck chairs and several cots before entering the cottage itself. Although the bedrooms and living room were furnished in early garage sale the place looked spotless and comfortable. Randy immediately staked a claim to one of the cots on the porch; she loved to sleep in the open air as long as she had enough blankets.

She lost no time in slithering into a bikini, grabbing a towel, book and suntan lotion and trotting down to a sparsely-populated beach some twenty feet from the house. The day was sunlit and sparkling. While she sunbathed Roger and Linda went into town to shop for groceries; they joined her on the beach a few hours later with a picnic lunch for three.

Over the next few days Randy braved the chilly water for frequent swims, lazed on the beach for hours, took long walks along the shore, went sailing with Roger and consumed an inordinate amount of shellfish. By Friday morning, due in no small measure to Linda and Roger's sympathetic, upbeat company, she was far more relaxed, more accepting of the past and optimistic about the future.

They took the morning ferry to the mainland and drove straight to Hal's house to pick up the Lincoln. The goodbyes between the two sisters were full of warmth and teasing. "I want to hear a blow-by-blow description of everything that happens with that Luke of yours," Linda instructed as she and Randy embraced. "Call me—or I'll call you."

Randy agreed, then waited in the car while Roger and Linda said goodbye. Their kiss was so passionate that she half expected them to send her back to New York on her own, but Roger laughingly disentangled Linda's wandering hands from his body, gave her a sharp slap on her bottom and sent her off toward the Porsche.

At Roger's midtown office Randy took the wheel, leaning out the window to thank him and kiss him goodbye. When she showed up at her parents' door laden with shopping bags Emily wondered aloud just how her daughter had found the time to buy so much, but accepted Randy's answer that in a few hours with Linda one could accomplish more than in a few days on one's own.

It was just about the only true statement that the Dunnes would hear about their daughter's vacation. That night, while watching a display of Fourth of July fireworks with them, Randy fabricated a complete account of her stay in New Hampshire, including appropriate minor misadventures to explain away a lingering scratch or two. Even her father had to admit that she looked wonderful with her suntan, new hair-style and extra ten pounds, although he still believed that anyone who would voluntarily spend two weeks without indoor plumbing was daft.

On Monday morning Randy flew back to Los Angeles and stayed through the following weekend. She had absolutely no problem finding someone to take her place in the apartment—reasonable housing was a scarce commodity. She spent the rest of her time saying goodbye to friends and going to a party or two. In the process she ran into Sean Raley. She couldn't deny that she experienced a little pang of hurt when they said hello, or that she still found him attractive, but her feelings were tepid and easily dismissed. She could hardly fail to notice that the woman he left with wasn't his wife, and decided that she was lucky. It wasn't much fun to be dumped, but it ultimately would have been far worse not to be.

## Chapter Six

Luke Griffin didn't care for surprises. The more he thought about it, however, the more he wondered whether he was in for one of the most unpleasant surprises of his life when Miranda Dunne walked into the executive offices of C & D on Tuesday afternoon. Could the woman in Maine possibly have been Miranda? True, she'd been anything but a neophyte in the bedroom, but then, the gossip he'd heard about Miranda's exemplary virtue could have been much mistaken. The personality of the woman he'd known in Maine hadn't meshed with his image of Linda Franck, but it hadn't meshed with his image of her sister, either.

The week after Luke got back he was summoned into Bill Dunne's office to discuss a routine piece of business and he stayed to answer a vague but nonetheless crystal-clear question about how "things" were going.

"I talked to Linda the weekend before last," he replied. "I don't think there'll be any further problems." He didn't add that a brief conversation with his

123

brother-in-law had confirmed Linda's version of their "affair." Tom had sounded almost petulant about it, complaining that Linda Franck had only been interested in "acting like a damn therapist."

"I suggested to my sister that she and Tom see a marriage counselor," he continued, "but she wasn't too receptive. Right now she's blaming Tom for everything, but in time. . . ." He shrugged. "If she has any sense she'll reconsider."

Bill nodded, saying that he hoped things would work out, and reached for a folder in his "in" basket. Luke could see that he was busy, but decided to stick around for one more question.

"By the way, Bill, I've been giving some thought to where to begin with Randy, and I don't intend to be easy on her. I want her to be challenged. I'm assuming," he drawled with a smile, "that she's well rested after a couple of weeks in New Hampshire?"

"So it would seem," Bill answered. "She gained back some of the weight she lost—she was dieting for some blasted movie role—and she got herself a healthy-looking suntan. She'll be back from L.A. next Monday. . . ."

"And in the office Tuesday afternoon," Luke finished. "I'll see you then, if not before."

*She'd lost weight?* he thought uneasily as he walked out the door. He didn't like the sound of that. As he passed by Pat O'Donnell's desk it occurred to him that Bill's secretary might be able to provide enough information to help him figure out just who he'd been with in Maine. Pat was surprised by his invitation to join him for lunch the following afternoon, but accepted nonetheless.

Luke was aware that Pat O'Donnell was a no-nonsense, straightforward lady with total loyalty to her boss. Obviously he couldn't tell her what was *really* on his mind, so he'd need to come up with a plausible substitute.

As soon as they'd ordered their meals the next day he came straight to the supposed point. "You've known Randy Dunne for a long time," he remarked.

"Nineteen years," Pat agreed.

"I'll be frank with you, Pat," Luke said. "I want to know what I'm going to have to deal with for the next month or two, and Bill is obviously the wrong person to ask. He thinks his younger daughter is a total angel."

Pat took a sip of her cocktail, regarding Luke with a measured gaze. "What gives you the idea she's not?" she asked.

"Other than the fact that nobody could be that perfect?" Luke contrived to sound charmingly nonchalant about the whole topic. "Nobody could be around C & D for very long without being aware that a lot of employees of this company were disappointed when Randy Dunne ran off to California two years ago. Now she's apparently changed her mind about what she wants to do with her life, and common sense tells me that she'll resent the fact that in the meantime someone from outside the family has moved in and gotten himself the inside track on the presidency."

Pat shook her head. "Not Randy. She's not the type of person who expects to have things handed to her on a silver platter. If she's interested in running the company some day she'll expect to earn the right to be considered." She paused. "Frankly, Luke, I find almost nothing to criticize about—"

"*Almost* nothing?" Luke interrupted. "Why *almost?*"

"She's learned too well from her sister's mistakes." Pat hesitated, trying to decide whether to explain, and apparently came up with a negative answer. "It's really none of your business, Luke."

He used his most persuasive smile on her. "But you're going to tell me anyway?" he suggested.

"Don't try that with me, Luke Griffin. Unless you have a personal interest. . . ."

"I might." Luke winked at her, determined to get around her scruples. *"Bill* thinks I should."

"Bill trusts you too far. Randy is too young for you—not in your league at all," Pat said firmly.

"After two years in Hollywood? I find that impossible to believe."

His skepticism succeeded where charm had not. "All right then. Obviously you asked me to lunch to pump me on exactly this subject, and I suppose there's no real reason why I can't satisfy some of your curiosity. People wonder why Linda and Randy are so different, and I think there are some very important reasons beyond their basic personality differences. Linda . . ."

"Basic personality differences?" Luke repeated.

"Yes. Linda is restless and adventuresome. She needs novelty and excitement to be happy. Randy is much calmer, sunny and easygoing and much too likely to let people push her around."

Pat's description only confused Luke more. The woman in Maine didn't fit either of those thumbnail sketches. He wondered whimsically whether there were a third sister hiding out somewhere.

"Before you interrupted," Pat continued, leaning forward slightly, "I was about to explain that Linda was the quintessential Manhattan princess as a girl—rich, adorable and spoiled. Maybe Randy would have turned out the same way but two things happened in the meantime. Emily found out she couldn't have any more children and the feminist movement started to gain ground and affect Bill Dunne's thinking. Linda was twelve by then, and already a little reckless and much too sophisticated for her age, but Randy was only eight. I'd been working for Bill for about three years and I remember how surprised I was when he started to involve Randy in the store. After all, we had exactly no women executives back then and even Emily—the boss's daughter—had almost nothing to do with running C & D. At first it was only taking Randy to lunch every month in the store restaurant or having her model children's clothing in fashion shows, but as she grew up her involvement grew also. I think that since Bill didn't have a son and considered Linda a lost cause, he consciously began to groom Randy for a role in the business. You're obviously aware of how many hearts she won. I'm not sure just why she went to California, but maybe it was because Bill pushed too hard. I don't think she was dying for a career in films. Now she seems to have decided that a career at C & D is the right future for her, and personally, I'm delighted by her decision. In my opinion Randy's major problem is that she's put her private life on hold. She would probably die before she'd hurt Bill and Emily by making the kinds of mistakes that Linda's made. Unfortunately, of course, you can't grow up and have real relationships without risking a little pain. Randy is a wonderful young woman but she has a lot to learn about people and about life in general." Pat sat back in her chair. "I've already said far more than I should have, Luke. You're not getting another word out of me."

As far as Luke was concerned there was no need to keep probing. The person Pat had described was little more than a charming girl and couldn't possibly have been the woman he'd known in Maine. Only one thing continued to bother him, and that was Linda Franck herself. He found himself wanting to see her again, wanting to make love to her. Eventually he even tried to call, but her Cambridge number was unlisted.

Luke wasn't sure why he picked up the phone again five minutes later and called Roger Bennett, but guilt probably played a role. He'd already swiped one of Roger's girlfriends and doing it a second time when he wasn't really serious about the woman in question would have been hitting below the belt.

Luke didn't want Roger to know that he was calling about Linda so he opened the conversation by asking a favor—two house seats to Roger's newest Broadway show, which was red-hot despite the summer lull. The two men traded small talk for several more minutes before Luke actually got to the point.

"By the way," he said, as if the thought had just entered his head, "I hear you're dating my boss' daughter."

A gust of laughter came across the line. "I saw her first, Griffin. I happen to be crazy about her, so keep your hands off."

There was no way Luke could tell him that it was far too late to honor such an order. "I suppose I'd better do that, if I want any more tickets from you. Her sister is coming to work for me," he added. "Have you ever met her?"

"Randy? As a matter of fact, I have. She stopped in Cambridge on her way back from New Hampshire last week—I was visiting Lin at the time. I'll tell you, Luke, if she didn't wear her hair so differently I might have found myself making love to the wrong woman. The resemblance is pretty striking."

"So what did you think of her?"

"I liked her very much. She's a real charmer. If you're worried about having to cope with a spoiled brat of a boss' daughter, don't be. Anything else I can do for you?"

Luke said there wasn't and wrapped up the conversation. He was disappointed by what he'd learned, but somehow relieved, as well. As much as he'd known that it was foolhardy to become involved with Linda Franck the memories of that night in Maine might have gotten the better of him. Now Roger Bennett had given him an additional reason to stay away—his conscience—and he knew it was all for the best.

Tuesday morning was one of the longest mornings that Randy had ever spent. The prospect of seeing Luke Griffin again had twisted her inside out, and the only thing that was preventing an out-and-out anxiety attack was the fact that he wouldn't know who she was—or so she hoped. She changed three times, finally selecting a feminine print dress in shades of green and ivory. The neckline was a gentle U-shape that accentuated her tan; the short sleeves and skirt were cut full to flutter gracefully over the upper arm and down from the waist. She applied her makeup carefully, using the skills she'd learned as an actress to subtly change the contours of her face. When two-inch heels and a new hair style were added, she looked substantially different from the woman Luke had known in Maine. As she stood before a full-length mirror for a final check of her appearance her eyes darted to the cross Linda had given her in Cambridge. She hurriedly removed it and stuffed it into her purse.

Her desire not to be late caused her to arrive at her father's office almost fifteen minutes early. Pat O'Donnell was away from her desk, probably at lunch, and the sound of male voices was filtering out from behind the closed door. After only a moment's hesitation Randy walked over to Pat's desk and picked up the phone. With any luck at all the microphone device would be switched on. In fact, as soon as she pressed down the appropriate button the sound of Luke's voice came through the receiver perfectly clear.

". . . terrific, Bill. My only problem is that I hate to clean them," he was saying. "You and Emily want some?"

"Sure. Bring them in tomorrow and leave them in the restaurant freezer for me." There was a pause, during which Randy pictured her father lighting his pipe. "Glad to see you had a good weekend for a change. Rita told Pat you were something less than a delight to work for after you got back from Cambridge."

*Cambridge?* Randy thought. So her father believed that Luke had been in Cambridge, not Maine. That sounded more like the Bill Dunne she'd always known. But why had Luke been moody when he got back? Because he'd taken the weekend far more seriously than he'd pretended to? Randy wanted desperately to think so.

"The secretarial grapevine strikes again," Luke answered wryly. "Sometimes I wonder just who runs this company."

"Then you'd better keep in mind that *I* do," Bill shot back. "So tell me, are you all set to tackle my *other* daughter?"

Randy almost lost Luke's answer—it was muttered in a low, disgruntled tone. "I only hope I do better with Miranda than with Linda."

"I thought you settled everything," Bill said. "You told me . . ."

"I did. And now I'm looking forward to meeting Miranda. Although after dealing with Linda it's a little hard to believe that two sisters could be as different as everyone says."

"Believe it," Bill replied. "And make sure you remember it."

"Oh, I will." The promise was drawled in a teasing way that Randy knew only too well. "I understand perfectly. Your younger daughter is as pure as the newfallen snow and I hope not as cold." There was a slight pause followed by Luke's laughing question, "Tell me, Bill, since you seem to think I'd make an acceptable son-in-law, do I have your permission to pretest the merchandise?"

"No." Bill sounded seriously irritated.

"Come on, Bill," Luke chided. "You wouldn't buy a new car without a road test, would you? Why should it be any different with a woman?"

After several seconds' worth of silence Luke gave another bark of laughter. "Okay, okay. Save the murderous looks for when the profits go down. I promise you that I'll behave myself. It means revising my game plan a little, though. I was planning to take her back to my office and seduce her on the couch."

At this point it seemed that Bill Dunne decided it was fruitless to overreact to Luke's gibes. He told Luke to go right ahead and do that and then changed the subject to plans for a new branch of C & D in Dallas.

If nothing else, Randy's eavesdropping had improved her mood. Judging from the conversation, she'd gotten under Luke's skin in Maine, just as he'd gotten under hers. A glance at her watch told her she'd only be five minutes early if she went inside now, so she replaced the receiver and switched the phone back to the first outside line again.

Bill Dunne let her in a few seconds after she knocked, affectionately pecking her on the cheek. "Hi, honey. I want you to meet your new boss. Luke Griffin, my daughter Randy."

Ghosts seldom frequent posh New York offices, but Luke paled so dramatically and stared so stupidly that one might have assumed that he thought he was seeing one. "Is something the matter, Mr. Griffin?" Randy asked, trying to keep calm.

"Uh—no. It's just that—I've met your sister."

Randy had never heard Luke stammer before, but he quickly recovered. "You look very much alike," he said, sounding a little annoyed.

She knew he'd jumped to exactly the right conclusion and felt a panicked temptation to confess. But there were too many excellent reasons for playing this role through to the end.

"People are always taking us for each other," she said. "But of course, Linda is older, Mr. Griffin, and much as I hate to admit it, thinner."

"'Mr. Griffin' is a little formal, honey," Bill remarked. "Why don't you make it 'Luke'?"

"I'd be more comfortable with Mr. Griffin," Randy

replied, giving Luke a cool look. "That way neither of us will be likely to forget our relationship is strictly business."

"I knew that phone call would get her back up," Bill told Luke with a sigh. "He was only teasing, Randy," he added to his daughter. "Why don't you forget it?"

When Randy didn't answer Luke plastered on one of those wretchedly charming smiles of his and announced, "I have no intention of being equally formal, Miranda. I hope you'll change your mind and follow suit."

Randy didn't budge an inch. "I don't think so, Mr. Griffin. Can we get to work now?"

"She's all yours." Bill shook his head in pretended dismay and motioned toward the door.

Randy followed Luke down to his private office, stopping for a moment to say hello to his secretary, Rita Washington. Rita had joined the company while Randy was in her last year of college, so the two women didn't know each other particularly well.

"You used to work for Oscar Levitan before he retired, didn't you?" Randy asked.

"That's right, but I'm happy about the change. Luke's not a bad man to work for—for a slavedriver, that is." Rita glanced at her boss. "Elroy thinks we're having an affair, I spend so many nights here."

Luke merely laughed. "Her husband is a former professional football player," he explained to Randy. "When Rita works late he usually walks over from the restaurant he owns a few blocks from here and picks her up. One look at Elroy and a man would have to be crazy to proposition Rita."

He took a few phone messages off Rita's desk and opened the door to his office, ushering Randy inside. The room was smaller than Bill Dunne's office and decorated with aggressively modern pieces of the type that C & D had long promoted and popularized.

The moment the door was shut Luke's lazy manner

132

disappeared. "What kind of game are you playing?" he demanded. But before Randy had a chance to answer his expression turned contrite. "I'm sorry, I shouldn't be shouting at you. What happened in Maine was entirely my fault."

Randy was heartily relieved. An apologetic Luke Griffin would be easier to cope with than an angry one. "I've never been to Maine, Mr. Griffin," she said with exactly the right mixture of bewilderment and stiffness in her voice. She suffered Luke's continued examination of her body and face, her discomfort very real.

"Don't tell me that," he said with a shake of his head, "because I just won't believe it. You tried to tell me who you were in Maine, but I wouldn't listen. If I hurt you—"

*If?* Randy thought. "Look, I don't know what you're talking about," she interrupted. "I just got back from Los Angeles. Before that, I was in New Hampshire with a friend. Now can we get to work?"

"No." Luke took a few steps closer to her, the fingers of his right hand closing over her upper arm, and bent his head to kiss her. "You may look a little different," he murmured, "but some things don't change."

Randy reacted with an anger that was only partially feigned. Did he really expect to pick up right where they'd left off, without even five minutes' worth of explanations? She jerked free and let fly with an open-palmed right hook, connecting squarely with Luke's left cheek. Then, as he stood there, staring at her in astonishment, she slammed out of his office.

He caught up with her when she was halfway to her father's office, grabbing her arm to turn her around. When he saw the tears in her eyes his expression became penitent to the point of self-mortification.

"Please forgive me, Miranda," he said a bit stiffly, removing his hand from Randy's arm when she showed no further signs of trying to get away. "I'm not usually this irrational. I realize I owe you an explanation."

"I'm not dimwitted, Mr. Griffin," Randy said coldly. "Obviously it has something to do with my sister. You can spare me the details. You can also spare me the cheap passes."

Luke's temper seemed to flare up out of nowhere. "Damn it, Miranda, I said I was sorry. I thought you were Linda. Or that Linda was you." He walked off in disgust, muttering to himself.

Randy watched his retreating back, pondering her next move. She certainly wasn't about to run to her father with some hysterical story about Maine when Bill Dunne had never gotten wind of that particular wrinkle in Luke's plan. On the contrary, her instinct told her to make her peace with Luke; if, in fact, they'd never met it was exactly what she would have done.

When she walked back into his office and closed the door he was standing by the window, staring down at the traffic on Lexington Avenue. He didn't turn around.

"Mr. Griffin," she said softly.

He glanced over his shoulder at the sound of her voice. "Did you decide not to run to Daddy?" he asked her.

Randy's tone was far warmer than Luke's, and conveyed her distress and uncertainty. "My father is extremely overprotective, Mr. Griffin. He thinks I don't know how to take care of myself. If I tell him what happened just now he's likely to come storming down here and chew you out. I realize that you can always get another job, but C & D can't get a vice president with your talents. I don't want to cause any trouble."

Luke relaxed and smiled, leaning against the window frame now. Obviously her answer had satisfied him. "Tell me," he drawled teasingly, "just what the logical conclusion of your philosophy would be. Suppose I walked over, picked you up and carried you to the couch. Would you tell your father? Or am I so valuable to the company that you'd let me make love to you?" To underscore his point he began to approach her slowly, a wicked glint in his eyes.

He was so irresistible that Randy longed to meet him halfway. She was suddenly grateful for her acting classes. She knew she couldn't freeze Luke off, but the Randy Dunne he'd heard about would have been too inexperienced to attempt it. The blush on her face probably made her look embarrassed, but the real cause of it was a sharp, hot memory of their night together in Maine.

She looked at the floor, as if she were totally outclassed and knew it. "Why—why do you get such a kick out of teasing me?" she asked.

He stopped. "I tease almost everyone, Miranda. Especially beautiful young women who put up cool facades to try to put me in my place." He came several steps closer.

"Look, Mr. Griffin," Randy said, backing away from him, "all my life I've been Daddy's little girl around C & D. Coming back from California wasn't an easy decision for me. I want the people here to take me seriously—including you."

To Randy's relief Luke ceased his forward march and strolled over to the couch. He sat down and lit a cigarette, took a few drags and then lazed back against the soft cushions. She continued to stand right where she was, apparently rooted to the floor by uncertainty.

"They take you seriously, Miranda—I assure you they do," he said. "I've been here less than a year, but I've already had my fill of hearing people talk about you. They do it on purpose, just to let me know that they resent the fact that I've usurped the position that so many of them seem to believe should be yours someday. I've heard about your almost being born in the back of a cab, and they pointedly add that you've been in a hurry ever since. I've heard about the time you took off all your clothes at one of the Memorial Day picnics—I think you were three. I've heard about the fashion shows you modeled in, and I've been told that even at sixteen you were one of the best salespeople that C & D had ever seen. I could go on and on. Your father's employees adore you. If you become president some day at least half of them will kneel at the coronation."

Conover-Dunne was like a large family and Randy had known many of the executives, salespeople and other employees since she was a little girl. Even so, she'd had no idea of their affection for her, and no knowledge of their hope that she would eventually take over the presidency of the store. She was very touched by what Luke had told her.

There was no need to put on an act with her answer; she could reply with the simple truth. "I didn't know all that, but I *am* aware that even though I worked at C & D for six straight summers I have a lot to learn about the executive end of the business. Maybe at some level I assumed that my father would hold on to the presidency until I was ready to succeed him, but rationally I understand that that wouldn't make sense—not if there's someone capable of replacing him. I know he has other responsibilities he'd like to concentrate on."

Luke nodded, looking so complacent in the wake of this answer that Randy couldn't resist taking him down a peg. "Besides, Mr. Griffin," she added, "you're so much older than I am. By the time I've worked my way up to a vice presidency you'll be . . . at a different stage of your life."

Her gibe failed to make the slightest impression on him. "Thanks a lot," he said with a grin. "I didn't know I'd be ready for Medicare in fifteen years."

"I didn't mean to insult you, Mr. Griffin," Randy persisted, "but you must be almost twice my age."

Luke burst out laughing. "Then C & D is taking its

toll. I'm thirty-four, Miranda, but I have the feeling you already knew that."

Randy permitted herself a smile. "Okay, you're right. I was only teasing you back. But I've had my fill of hearing about *you*, too. My father has you all picked out as my future husband, and it might have been nice if he'd consulted me about it. First, I'm not interested in marriage yet. Second, when I do get married, it will be to somebody closer to my own age. And third, assuming that I decide to make C & D my career, my ultimate goal will be the presidency itself, not just marriage to the president."

Knowing Luke as she did, Randy wasn't surprised when he took advantage of the opening she'd so generously provided and retorted, "I'm desolate. I don't know how I'll cope with the rejection."

He pointed to a spot on the couch about a foot away from where he was sitting. "Come sit down next to me, Miranda. I promise we'll keep it strictly business. My job is to give you some training and that's all I intend to do. Believe it or not, I agree with everything you said before."

Randy walked over and sat down. On the brass and glass coffee table in front of her there were recent issues of fashion magazines and copies of that day's New York newspapers.

Luke put out his cigarette and half turned toward her, his arm along the back of the couch. "I'll start by filling you in on how your father and I divide responsibilities." He was completely serious now, his tone and expression almost professorial. "Until Bill hired me, Oscar Levitan was responsible for the day-to-day details of running all the C & D branch stores. Your father retained direct supervision of the Manhattan store; it's his baby and he's not ready to let anyone oversee it. Along with your grandfather, he also made policy decisions for C & D as a whole."

Randy tucked one leg up under her and listened with

genuine interest as he went on, "Bill wasn't satisfied with the job Oscar was doing. In effect, Oscar was forced into an early retirement. When your father initially spoke to me in San Francisco about taking over Oscar's job I wasn't particularly interested. There was too little independence, not enough control. I told Bill how I felt and he made me a better offer. He threw in a seat on the board, an executive vice-president title and a major role in the making of company policy, particularly policy pertaining to the branch stores. Not everyone can accept the fact that I've been here less than a year and already have a stronger voice in the running of the corporation than vice presidents in areas like marketing, public relations and finance. Naturally I work very closely with your father. When we differ we usually manage to find a compromise. I never lose sight of the fact that he's the boss, Miranda, but there *is* a higher authority and on occasion we've resorted to him. Nobody argues with Jonathan Conover, least of all me."

Luke shifted his weight and propped his feet up on the coffee table. "Of course," he went on, "your grandfather has reached the stage in his life where he wants to enjoy himself. He loves to poke around the world on buying trips, so we only involve him where there are major disagreements or decisions. You probably know that for the past five years or so your father has been the de facto head of Conover-Dunne. You mentioned other responsibilities, and I assume you meant the chairmanship of Dunne Industries, the umbrella corporation of C & D and our other interests. You're quite right in thinking that Bill would like the time to concentrate on investments in areas like real estate and perhaps even manufacturing. I wouldn't have accepted his job offer if a shot at the top spot hadn't been part of the package. Within five or six years I expect to be president. Your father will run

Dunne Industries and your grandfather will retain the title of chairman of Conover-Dunne."

"I see," Randy said. Luke Griffin certainly didn't lack either ambition or self-confidence. Unable to resist needling him a little, she drawled, "I suppose I should polish up my rendition of 'Hail to the Chief.'"

She was surprised that Luke would take her seriously. "You sound unhappy about my role here," he said, "and I want you to know that I understand your feelings. But you also have a great deal to learn, and the sensible thing to do is to let me teach you."

Randy quickly corrected him. "I'm not unhappy about your role in the company, only a little in awe of your ego. As far as what I have to learn goes, I recall that on the phone you implied that the lessons would include more than business." Randy shot him the kind of provocative smile that had captivated more men than she knew. "Just what *do* you propose to teach me?"

She knew almost immediately that she'd gone too far. Luke was looking at her in the same intense way that he'd looked at her so often in Maine. But then his jaw clenched and his gaze swung to one of the magazines on the table.

"Your father wants you to start by getting an overview of the types of problems that come up," he said, taking out a cigarette and lighting it. "The reason he asked me to work with you is that my job involves solving problems in a wide range of areas—areas your work during the summers never exposed you to. Naturally I'm in the field a lot, and sometimes I'll take you along. I'll also have you do a lot of background reading. For example, we're in the process of reviewing feasibility studies for a store in Dallas, and we're in the middle of construction in Bal Harbour, Florida. We've got a serious problem in White Hills and in the next few weeks we've got to make some decisions about how to solve it. Once you've gotten an overall picture you'll be taking our executive training program. Then you can pick an area to work in, assuming there's an open slot for you."

"We?" Randy repeated with a seductive smile. "Is that the royal 'we' you're using?"

"We means Bill and myself," Luke replied coolly. "And Miranda—please stop what you're doing. I'm finding it damn hard to ignore."

Randy supposed she *had* been a little too flirtatious. In fact, if she'd behaved this way in Maine Luke would have pulled her into his arms and suitably punished her. In Maine, of course, she'd been a woman of the world. Here in New York she was only an innocent child who was presumably too naive to understand that she was playing with fire.

Holding out her hand, she said, "All right, Mr. Griffin. Let's shake hands on a successful professional relationship."

Luke took her hand for a couple of seconds but didn't release it afterward. Instead he turned it palm upward, the motion so subtle that had Randy not been aware that he was looking for the scar on her thumb she never would have guessed it. Fortunately she healed quickly and well and not a trace of the cut was visible. She caught Luke's fleeting frown out of the corner of her eye.

He got up from the couch and motioned for Randy to do the same. "There's a free office down the hall," he told her, walking to the door and holding it open for her.

The office was small, windowless and contained only the essentials: metal desk and chair, bookcase, lamp and phone. It wasn't very appealing, but then, Randy was only a trainee, even if her middle name happened to be Conover and her last name Dunne. Several thick, spiral-bound reports were sitting on top of the desk.

"I want you to look through these carefully," Luke said. "You'll find sales figures for the White Hills store for the last four years, broken down by department and analyzed in a number of different ways. When you're finished take a drive out to the store and look around. I want you to compare *our* location with our competitors' locations. You should also go down to the city government offices and check out things like planned construction, rezoning requests and so on. I want a recommendation from you as to whether we should close the store, renovate, look for a new location or make only minor changes."

"Will that be all, sir?" Randy said, trying not to be intimidated by this assignment.

"Isn't it enough?" Luke laughed, and walked out of the office.

During the rest of the week Randy threw herself into the task of becoming an instant expert on the White Hills branch of C & D. She saw nothing of Luke Griffin; he was out of the office more often than not, trouble-shooting on Long Island, checking the progress of renovations in suburban Washington or lending his considerable charm to a buyers' meeting in New York City.

Randy spent Tuesday afternoon and Wednesday morning poring over the detailed statistics contained in the reports Luke had left her. When inflation was taken into account the picture was depressing. Until three years ago the store had done moderately well. Sales per square foot, though not as high in most other branches, were acceptable. In subsequent years, however, although receipts in current dollars had risen, inflation and increased operating costs had meant an actual drop in earnings. Some departments, such as children's clothing, had resisted the trend and continued to do well; others, such as junior apparel, had experienced painful declines.

The store, C & D's first suburban branch, was located far from other major department stores in the city. There was a motor inn under construction in the area, which meant detours and traffic snarls, dirt and dust and general inconvenience to the shopper. With the streets ripped up as they were, Randy had trouble even finding her way into the parking lot.

She spent the rest of Wednesday in the store, remaining until it closed at nine o'clock. As she walked through department after department she tried to understand the reasons why some prospered while others were failing. It apparently had little to do with how well-displayed the merchandise was; the junior department, with its pop music and trendy appearance, was fun and appealing and yet it attracted fewer and fewer customers.

The signs of the building's age were everywhere. The architecture was boring, the space chopped up by pillars, the lighting old-fashioned. Basically it was a three-story stack of boxes. Yet the uninspired atmosphere didn't deter wealthy women from continuing to shop in the store's designer boutiques.

By the time Friday afternoon arrived Randy had waded through more planning documents, commission reports, committee meeting records and permits than she hoped to see for the next two years. The woman she'd talked to at City Hall, she thought wearily, had been too receptive for her liking. She'd learned that a major new county building was under consideration for a site near the store, and that the nearest highway interchange was scheduled for a complete reconstruction. A number of smaller projects were in various stages of planning and development, yet Randy estimated that it would be at least four years before all the proposed projects were completed. Unfortunately, there were no plans for any other retail outlets, which might have brought additional shoppers into the area.

On the other hand, should C & D decide on a new site, favorable locations were available. It seemed to Randy that no amount of renovation could turn a fundamentally mediocre store into the type of elegant building that housed the competition. Westchester County was a good market; many women preferred to avoid the transportation problems and crowds in Manhattan and shop locally. A new store in a good location would earn enough extra profit to justify the expense of site acquisition and construction.

Late Friday afternoon, as Randy sat in her office making notes on her conclusions, her phone rang. The ring, as opposed to an intercom buzz, meant that the call was coming from outside the building. She was puzzled when a male voice murmured something unintelligible in a foreign language.

"Uh . . . who were you trying to reach?" she asked with exaggerated distinctness, thinking that the man probably spoke very little English.

"Her Royal Highness Princess Elizabeth," was the response. "Randy? Is that you?"

Randy immediately placed the voice as that of Aaron Gregov, the professor she'd met in Cambridge. "Aaron! It's nice to hear from you," she said. "Where are you?"

"In New York. I came down last night to talk to some foundation people about funding one of my research projects. When can I see you?"

Randy had put in a long, tedious week and the prospect of going out was appealing. "I'd love to get out for dinner tonight," she said. "Why don't you stop by the apartment to meet my parents and have a drink and then we can go someplace to eat? And please come casual, Aaron. I think I'm too tired for anything fancy."

Aaron said it sounded perfect and told Randy he'd see her at six. At five-fifteen she went down to her father's office to walk home with him, only to find that he was tied up in a meeting and had left word that she should go ahead without him.

It was a warm, humid evening in New York. Randy,

perspiring from the eight-block walk, headed for the shower as soon as she walked into the apartment. Then she dressed in snug-fitting jeans, a red tube top and a short-sleeved print blouse which she left unbuttoned and tied at the waist.

She was brushing her hair when her mother peeked into the room. "Umm—very sexy," she teased. "Is that in Luke's honor?"

Randy was baffled by the question. "Luke? What does he have to do with it?"

"He's coming over for dinner. We're having the fish he caught last weekend. I assumed you knew, Randy."

"I haven't seen him since last Tuesday, Mom. I have a date with a guy I met in Cambridge."

"He came all the way from Cambridge to see you?" Emily asked, sounding as baffled as Randy had been only moments before.

"He's here on business. His name is Aaron Gregov and he teaches history at Harvard. Respectable enough for you?" Randy's mouth quirked at her mother's befuddled expression.

"Well, of course, darling. But Luke . . ."

"What about him?"

Emily regarded her daughter for several long seconds, then lifted an expressive shoulder in a half-shrug. "I told your father to let you live your own life. Serves him right!" She flashed a slow wink at Randy and left her to finish dressing.

Randy, both annoyed and amused by her father's presumption, quickly finished brushing her hair and applying her makeup. She walked into the living room to find Luke and her parents talking, a bottle of sherry on the table in front of them.

"Hi, Dad. Sorry I missed you at the office," she said. She turned to Luke, who had made himself completely at home in her parents' living room. "And I'm sorry I'll miss your fish tonight."

144

"Somehow I doubt that," he said, apparently uncon-
cerned by that fact. "But you should be. It's not every
night you get a chance to eat dinner with me."

"Really?" Randy glanced at her father and couldn't
pass up the opportunity to pay him back for his
matchmaking. She knew that Luke wouldn't take her
comments seriously, but Bill Dunne certainly would. "I
was under the impression from Dad that all I had to do
was snap my fingers and you'd come sniffing after the
family fortune like a bloodhound hunts rabbits, Mr.
Griffin."

Bill Dunne almost choked on his sherry while Emily
calmly sipped hers and attempted to suppress a smile.
Bill was revving up for a stern lecture when Luke
laughed and remarked, "You seem a bit jumpy tonight,
Miranda. Am I working you too hard?"

Randy smiled back at him. "Definitely, Mr. Griffin.
That's why I'm going out."

"You should have said something. It seems to me
that if I'm the cause, I should get first shot at providing
the remedy."

"What did you have in mind?"

"I couldn't possibly tell you in front of your parents."

This verbal sparring, a substitute for a far different
sort of love play, was setting Randy's body on fire. She
wondered how she could possibly spend hour after
hour in Luke's company without giving up and throwing herself into his no-doubt astonished arms. Fortunately for all concerned, at that moment the intercom
buzzed and the doorman announced that Dr. Gregov
was downstairs. Randy opened the front door and
waited for him, but when he walked up and looked her
over his confusion was apparent. "Do I have the right
apartment?" he asked. "The Dunnes?"

"You've found them, Dr. Gregov," Randy said.

"Randy?" He studied her face. "But—your
hair . . ."

"Was a wig." She took Aaron's arm and led him into the living room. "Don't you like me as a blonde, Aaron?"

His response, in full view of her parents and Luke, was to tip her chin up and kiss her lightly on the mouth. "I like you any way at all, princess," he said.

Randy introduced him to her parents and Luke and then poured him a glass of sherry. Once he was seated he started to explain how he and Randy had met.

"You have a charming daughter, but the only time I've seen her she was wearing a dark wig. She and your older daughter cooked up some scheme to pass her off as a Yugoslavian princess, and it worked beautifully. Everyone was falling over himself to meet her." He smiled at Randy. "Not that they wouldn't anyway. I teach European history, so I knew she was a ringer. I lured her into the garden and made a pass at her, just to see what she would do. She never stepped out of character till I told her I knew she was a phony. I'm afraid I exacted payment for my silence—a kiss in the garden and this dinner date."

"I'm surprised you didn't insist on a quicker payback," Luke said casually. "In Cambridge, that is." Only Randy understood the reason for his comment, and it was all she could do not to laugh.

"I would have," Aaron answered, "but she was leaving town for New Hampshire."

"Then we'll have to let you go," Luke drawled. "We can't allow Miranda to welsh on her obligations."

"I'd hardly call it an obligation, Mr. Griffin." Randy looked up into Aaron's eyes, her smile entrancing. "I only wish all my royal duties were as pleasing as this one, Dr. Gregov," she murmured, using her Princess Elizabeth accent.

"You can see that the world lost a promising actress when C & D gained a future executive," Bill told Aaron.

Randy rose to leave, taking Aaron's hand to pull him

up along with her. "Don't you mean *president?*" she said with a wink.

A friend of Aaron's, a professor of Asian history, had recommended an unpretentious little restaurant in Chinatown. Although the place had a plain linoleum floor and paper placemats on its formica-topped tables, the aromas wafting out of the kitchen promised a superb meal.

"Jim told me that they serve Americans different food from Asians," Aaron explained. "I thought we'd try something authentic." When the waiter approached, he proceeded to order in a combination of some Chinese dialect and English, asking for items that weren't on the menu and communicating well enough, since the waiter kept smiling and nodding and writing.

The food, when it came, was unlike any Randy had tasted. The flavors were stronger, the soup fishier, some of the ingredients unidentifiable. When Aaron asked if she'd feel reassured to know what she was eating she quickly shook her head. "I'll enjoy it more if I *don't* know where it came from," she admitted.

They took their time over dinner, talking about Randy's experiences in Hollywood and Aaron's travels in Eastern Europe. On the way back uptown they stopped for American dessert and coffee, returning to the Dunnes' apartment about ten. Randy's parents and Luke had finished dinner and were back in the living room, discussing business.

"Don't you three ever stop?" Randy asked.

"I'm getting a private report tonight, darling," Emily told her. "After all, I'm a major stockholder. Since Mother and Dad are off poking around Europe, the least these two handsome men can do is to keep me informed about what they're doing with my money."

Randy led Aaron into the kitchen and poured him another cup of coffee. They talked for half an hour until Randy, yawning, apologetically explained that it had been a hard week and she was tired. At the kitchen door Aaron turned her into his arms and tipped her chin up for his kiss. The touch of his mouth against her own wasn't unpleasant, but her body failed to ignite the way it always did when she was near Luke Griffin.

Sensing her minimal response, Aaron lifted his head. "What's the matter, princess? Too tired?"

"I suppose," she murmured.

"Come on, Randy. What's wrong? Something's changed between Cambridge and New York."

It was only fair to be honest with him. "I'm sorry, Aaron," she said. "I met someone else, and . . ."

"Griffin? Your boss?"

"How could you tell?"

He shrugged. "There's an electricity between the two of you that's pretty hard to miss." He took her hand and led her to the center of the kitchen, well away from the door. "Look, Randy, I'm not going to stand here and pretend I had only friendship in mind when I called. But if you're not interested, you're not interested. Why don't I call you next time I'm in town? If your feelings have changed, fine. If not, I'd enjoy getting together for lunch, or maybe a play. Okay?"

"You're very understanding," Randy said.

"Understanding has nothing to do with it. I enjoy your company. Besides, I figure I can sponge a free meal from your parents, or better yet, a place to stay."

"Any time," Randy answered. She and Aaron returned to the living room, where Aaron shook hands with the two men and kissed Emily's hand with practiced smoothness. Randy walked him to the elevator afterwards, raising her face for a good-night peck as the door opened and waving goodbye as it closed.

She was yawning when she let herself back into the apartment. Her mother got the first good-night kiss and her father the second. Then she came to Luke.

"Don't stop now," he grinned.

She was just tired enough to call his bluff. When her lips provocatively lingered against his mouth she felt

148

him stiffen slightly and draw away. The fact that he so obviously wanted more than a kiss did wonders for her frame of mind. From time to time over the past few days she'd had her doubts about what she was doing, but now she pushed them aside. Things were going to work out perfectly.

# Chapter Seven

 $\mathcal{I}$ t only took till Saturday morning for Randy to realize that if she didn't put some distance between herself and Luke Griffin she'd wind up securely in his arms. Given her behavior he probably had every right to assume it was what she wanted, and on some level he seemed to want it, too.

Her sister Linda clearly thought she was hopeless. She called Sunday night for her first progress report, listening to Randy's account of events with growing dismay.

"For heaven's sake, Randy, there's a limit to how good an actress you are," she said when Randy was finished. "You can't let him get that close to you. You were supposed to be businesslike and unimpressed, remember? And let me tell you, Luke was suspicious going in. He called Roger last week and asked some very telling questions. Roger gave him some story about meeting you when you came back from New

Hampshire and being startled by how alike we are, but still—Luke's not *stupid!*"

"I can't help it," Randy answered weakly. "I want him to be attracted to me, Lin. He teases me, so I tease him right back. After all, if I freeze him off—"

"But you don't have to issue invitations to the man," Lin interrupted. "Find a middle ground, Randy. You want some time to sort out your feelings, don't you?"

"Of course I do. I just seem to forget that whenever I'm in the same room with him."

Linda gave an exasperated sigh. "And you have to ask yourself if you're in love with him? What on earth do you *think* you feel?"

"I don't know. We hardly know each other. After all, I thought I was in love with Sean. . . ."

"We've been through that before. I think you know that Sean Raley isn't fit to shine Luke Griffin's boots."

"I suppose." Randy also supposed that having the same conversation all over again wouldn't accomplish anything. "I'll try to keep a grip on my common sense, Lin. So how are you and Roger doing?"

"Wonderfully. I'm going to Paris with him in a few days. He's trying to lure some obscure director whom he claims is a genius into doing a movie for him."

Randy immediately suggested to Linda that as long as she was going to be in Paris anyway she might take a look around the shops for merchandise suitable for C & D's boutiques. "You're one of the world's champion shoppers," she teased. "If you could discover some unusual items that no one else has come across I know Dad would be impressed."

After talking over the idea Linda asked Randy to put their father on the line. He seemed pleased by his older daughter's interest, but wary of taking her too seriously. At least Linda understood that the ball was squarely in her court, which Randy considered a positive sign.

* * *

When Randy walked into the office on Monday morning she found a note on her desk from Rita Washington, Luke's secretary, saying that Luke wanted to see her at ten o'clock to discuss her recommendations for the White Hills store. She just had time to review her notes and the data Luke had given her before going down the hall to his office. On the way she passed a grim-looking Rita Washington. Although Randy smiled and murmured, "Good morning," Rita kept right on going, as if she'd scarcely noticed.

The door to Luke's private office was slightly ajar, so Randy poked her head inside to see if he was ready to meet with her. He was standing in the center of the room, facing her; in front of him, with her back to Randy, was a willowy blonde almost as tall as Luke was, her arms carelessly twined around his neck. Luke's hands were resting lightly on the woman's waist.

Their eyes met over his companion's shoulder, but he made no attempt to disengage himself from her grip. "Come on in, Miranda," he said.

The woman glanced around, decided that Randy was no one important and kissed Luke softly on the mouth. As her hands dropped from around his neck they paused to straighten his tie. Randy decided that it had been perfectly placed until the woman touched it.

She managed a friendly smile, a major tribute to her ability as an actress. "You're Katrina Sorensen, aren't you?" she said. "I recognize you from your work in commercials, but you're even more beautiful in person than your photographs." The statement was true, even if Randy hated to admit it. Katrina was stunning, her hair a thick and sensual lion's mane, her eyes cat-like and glowingly green, her facial structure feline and exotic. Even her figure was sensuously rounded, not bony and angular like so many models' bodies were. Despite Roger Bennett's comments on the woman's shortcomings it was impossible not to be jealous.

A perfectly shaped eyebrow was cocked in Randy's direction. "Thank you. And you're . . . ?" Katrina let the question dangle, as if to indicate that whoever Randy was, she was of absolutely no consequence.

Luke casually removed his hands from Katrina's waist and made the introduction. "This is Miranda Dunne, Katie. She's Jonathan Conover's granddaughter and Bill Dunne's daughter. Needless to say, she's also a future V.I.P. around this company."

"Why didn't you tell me that before?" Katrina scolded huskily. Randy thought irritably that even her *voice* was marvelous. "I'm very glad to meet you, Miranda. Your grandfather and your father are charming gentlemen, and I certainly hope I'll have the opportunity to work for them."

"Randy and I have some business to take care of, Katie. Run along now. I'll talk to your agent about a contract some time in the next couple of days." Katrina didn't take offense at being talked down to in such a manner, but merely smiled and thanked Luke very prettily for his time. Then she strode out the door, her body swinging from side to side with lithe, tawny grace.

Her soft, little-girl manner reminded Randy of some of the starlets she'd come across in Hollywood. They seemed so feminine and helpless that men lined up to take care of them, but in reality they were as tough as stevedores, with ambition clogging every pore.

Irritated by Katrina's performance, she reacted before her better judgment could stop her. "Your tie is crooked," she said, approaching Luke as she lisped out the words. "Let me fix it for you."

His failure to comment as she reached up and pulled the knot over a fraction should have warned her about his mood, but she never even noticed. "That's much better," she cooed. "But you know, Mr. Griffin, you *really* should have shut your door. I *do* hope I didn't interrupt anything."

When he frowned Randy realized that he hadn't

cared for her advice. "If I'd wanted to do something that was worth keeping private," he said a little curtly, "I would have done it at home." He walked over to his desk and sat down, motioning toward a chair on the other side. "Have a seat. Let's talk about what you've learned."

His clipped tone of voice made Randy uncomfortable, as did his choice of seating arrangement. She'd assumed that they'd sit on the couch and talk informally, as they had on Tuesday, but instead Luke was turning the session into a kind of interview. Less than confident about her conclusions, yet eager to earn his respect, she was hesitant to even begin lest she choose the wrong opening. Luke, who was watching her almost coolly now, offered absolutely no help.

"Do you want me to tell you what I think about the White Hills store?" she finally asked.

"That's what you're here for." He pulled out a cigarette but didn't light it. "And not, as you seem to think, to indicate your opinions about either Katrina or myself."

I should have kept my mouth shut, she thought, but said aloud, "I was only kidding. You didn't—"

Luke cut her off. "Something you're very good at. But I'm spending time I really don't have to work with you today, so you might try to be serious about it."

Randy bit back the urge to retort that she was *very* serious, and that furthermore, if he were really so all-fired busy she'd come back another time. She had to remind herself that she'd learned all about his temper in Maine, and that he'd undoubtedly get over what was bothering him soon enough.

"Okay." She shifted her position slightly, as if greater physical comfort would somehow help matters. "I think we should close the present store as soon as we can open a new one in a better location. It will be years before all the construction in that area is finished, and in the meantime, it's dirty and confusing. We're not losing money yet, but we will be within two years if the current trend continues. Besides, we'd still be the only major retail outlet in the area, and the store is old and unattractive."

Luke didn't seem particularly impressed by her analysis. "Why are we losing money?" he asked.

Randy thought she'd already told him, but elaborated. "The area's full of dirt and noise, the streets are all ripped up and there are so many detours you have trouble finding your way into the parking lot. When you add the fact that the store is old and unexciting to shop in, it's not surprising we have a problem. I realize that some of the departments are doing well, but they're the exceptions."

"Why have they done well?"

By now Randy was beginning to resent not only Luke's failure to respond to anything she was saying but also his rapid-fire style of questioning her. Nonetheless she went on evenly, "C & D's children's clothing departments are known for having an excellent selection of good-quality merchandise at competitive prices. The designer boutiques have apparently attracted a faithful clientele that will come to the store in spite of the hassle. For major purchases like carpeting or draperies people will comparison shop to find the best buy. But those are all special cases. In general we've lost a lot of customers, and if we don't do something soon I'm afraid we'll lose them permanently."

"What's under construction there?" Luke lit up his cigarette and leaned back in his chair.

"A major new hotel, a medical office building and a highway interchange. There might be a new county building also, but no decision's been made yet."

"How do you know that?" Luke asked.

Randy was more than a little exasperated by the question. "How do you *think* I know?" she demanded. "I asked about it, of course!"

"Then you asked the wrong person," Luke told her curtly. "The project will be approved."

Randy quickly voiced a protest. "If that's inside information I don't see how I was supposed to find it out."

"Simple. All you had to do was ask me if *I* knew, which I did. The projects you've mentioned—will they be good for business?"

"Probably they will—eventually," Randy said. "But it will be years before everything is finished, and we'd still be stuck with an old-fashioned, deteriorating building that's unpleasant to shop in and—"

"Can the building be renovated?"

Randy's temper was fast approaching the breaking point. "I suppose so. But it would still look like a stack of cigar boxes, and all the other stores have modern—"

"Is there anything we can do about that?" Luke interrupted yet again.

"How should I know?" Randy flung back. "I'm not an architect, just a persecuted trainee!"

Luke paid no attention to her outburst, but reached into the side drawer of his desk and took out a file folder. He tossed it on the desk facing Randy, who silently opened it, her body stiff with reproach. Inside were architect's blueprints and sketches showing how the present building could be enlarged and renovated. The shape would be changed from a box-like structure into a graceful arc and the interior would be redesigned to remove or disguise columns and break up the space in interesting, innovative ways.

"If you're not an architect," he said blandly, "then hire one. Howell and Morita specialize in this type of job."

Randy didn't answer. She simply closed the folder and stared angrily at Luke, feeling that he had deliberately withheld the sketches in order to set a trap for her.

"The city officials we've talked to feel that that area of town could become a vital part of the central business district again, given enough help from private business," he stated. "C & D has always been a community-oriented company. Don't you think we should be a part of that effort?"

"I suppose it would be good public relations," Randy answered. "Even profitable over the long term."

"What's on the land adjacent to the store?"

Here we go again, she thought with a sigh. She tried to picture the surrounding area. "An abandoned service station and a vacant lot—and some partially occupied buildings, and, uh, parking spaces."

"Who owns the land?"

"I don't know."

"Why didn't you look it up?"

"It didn't occur to me to look it up, Mr. Griffin." Randy glared at him. "Should it have?"

"Obviously, yes. But since it didn't, I'll tell you. Dunne Industries does. So what do you propose that we do with it?"

"You could have told me that before I went up there, just like you could have shown me the blueprints! Do you enjoy setting people up? Is that it?"

Luke frowned and repeated the question in the tone of voice he might have used with an annoying adolescent. "I asked you what you propose that we do with it."

The only thoughts in Randy's head concerned where Luke Griffin and his bloody land could darn well go. "I don't know," she muttered.

"Don't tell me you don't know. Think about it until you can give me an answer."

Randy looked down into her lap. She found it impossible to think about anything except her own anger and hurt. There was no question in her mind that Luke had deliberately set out to give her a hard time, but why? Because of a mild little joke? Because he'd had a lousy morning? Or because he actively disliked her? After the intimate ways he'd touched her in Maine the possibility was insupportable. It didn't matter that he believed she was someone else. She wasn't thinking too rationally just then.

He leaned forward, picked up a pencil and began to tap it on his desk. "I'm waiting, Miranda."

"I—I don't know," Randy stuttered, suddenly close to tears. "I can't think when you . . . sit there and glare at me that way."

"I wasn't glaring." Luke threw down the pencil in disgust. "Is that what you plan to do when you're a vice president of this corporation and the board puts you on the hot seat with an hour's worth of tough questions? Sit there and cry?"

As an actress Randy had often been forced to listen to painful criticism and try to learn from it. She was no crybaby; on the contrary, in two years of acting classes and repertory she'd broken down exactly once, around the time that Sean had left her.

"You weren't only questioning me," she said in a low, intense voice, "you were attacking me. It was personal, so that's the way I took it."

Luke stared at her a moment longer and then ran a hand through his hair. "The land," he said. "What should we do with it?"

Obviously he didn't intend to deal with her accusation, but Randy read regret in his eyes and it was all she really needed to see. She tried to concentrate on the question, more or less thinking out loud. "I suppose we could sell everything if we change locations—a bigger lot would be worth much more to a developer," she said. "Or we could stay where we are and sell off the portion that we don't need for the store. Or we could develop it ourselves."

Luke leaned back in his chair again. "And which are you recommending, Miranda?"

There was a warmth to his tone that hadn't been

there all day. Startled, Randy asked him, "What happened to your rotten mood?"

"I think you shamed me out of it," he admitted with a half-smile. "Go over to the couch and think about how we should use the land, and I'll get us a couple of cups of coffee."

"Cream, no sugar," Randy said, getting up. "And . . . thanks." She'd seldom felt such relief.

When Luke returned a minute later Randy was already settled on the couch. She held out her hand for the mug of coffee he carried, smiling at him. "Why did you do that?" she asked.

He sat down a healthy distance away from her, saying, "Why did I do what?"

"You know perfectly well what. It made me feel as though you hated me. Did the stuff about Katrina really make you that angry with me?"

"Only because I was three-quarters of the way there." Luke took a few sips of coffee and put the mug down on the glass table. "Should I tell you about my weekend, Miranda? I worked, all day Saturday and most of Sunday. Then last night I went out to dinner with a woman I'd just met who turned out to be a royal pain in the neck. The restaurant was supposed to be first-rate, but I wound up with a case of food poisoning, probably from the fish I ate. When I got into the office this morning Rita told me she has to have four half-days' worth of dental work done in the next few weeks. My office goes to pieces when Rita is away."

When he paused for another sip of coffee Randy risked a teasing suggestion. "You could tell her to have all of them pulled and get herself dentures. That would only take *one* day."

Luke laughed and shook his head. "As a matter of fact, that's exactly what I did say, but not in quite that tone. I can't believe I actually yelled at Rita over her teeth. I hope she doesn't send Elroy after me. But there's more."

"More?" Randy repeated.

"Katrina. She's one of the most beautiful women I've ever met, but she makes the lady I went out with last night seem like a sweetheart. I spent twenty-five minutes convincing her to do the Dallas promotion for us, soothing her supposed fears that it was more complicated than anything she'd done before. And then she puts on that little-girl act of hers and starts negotiating. I don't know why she bothers with an agent. Do you know what it's like to try to talk to a woman who keeps putting her hands all over your body? When at the same time she's holding you up for every dime you have?"

"I can't say that I do." Randy smiled to herself, very happy to know that Katrina Sorensen drove Luke right up the wall.

"Then you're lucky. If she weren't perfect for the job I wouldn't put up with her. And then *you* come in, Miss Dunne, and start handing out your usual quota of snide comments at a time when I wasn't about to put up with them."

"But I was only . . ."

"Joking, I know. But like I said, you picked the wrong time. I started to wonder whether you're more interested in cracking jokes than you are in learning something about this company."

The accusation stung. "Of course I'm not," Randy said a little stiffly. "I'm sorry I gave you that impression." The temptation to tell him how hard she'd worked was strong, but she knew that words wouldn't impress him at all. He was looking for the right analysis of the problem and she had to give it to him. The land, she repeated to herself. Hadn't Dunne Industries recently sold off a health-food store chain?

"We—Dunne Industries that is—we have quite a bit of cash to invest, don't we?" she asked.

"I see you're finally thinking in the right direction," Luke drawled.

"So we could take the cash and develop the area ourselves. We could put in a shopping mall connected to C & D on one side, with a tiered parking structure to hold the cars."

"We could do that," Luke agreed, smiling. "In fact, it's a very good idea. So good that your father first thought of it five years ago."

"Five years ago?" Randy repeated. "You mean to tell me that all of this was decided five years ago and you made me read through all those reports and traipse around White Hills—"

"Did you learn anything?" Luke interrupted.

"Well, yes. Of course I did," Randy admitted. "But still . . ."

"But nothing. I could have sat you down and explained our plans and you wouldn't have picked up one-tenth as much as you did this way. The store manager in White Hills is active in the community. Five years ago he started to pick up rumors about the new county building. He told Bill and your grandfather and the result was that Dunne Industries quietly began to acquire the land surrounding the store. It's taken us this long to buy everything we wanted. Yes, the profits have gone down in the short term, but when we reviewed the situation last month to make a final decision our calculations indicated that we should be able to make an acceptable profit out of that location over the next several decades, both on the store itself and as the developer of an adjacent shopping area. So tell me, did I waste your time?"

Randy knew exactly what he wanted to hear. "No, Mr. Griffin. You didn't waste my time. You're a wonderful teacher."

"Do I detect a sarcastic note in your voice?"

"From *me?*" Randy looked astonished. "Of course not."

Luke gave her a skeptical look and started to explain the proposed development, saying that preliminary discussions had already been held with city officials and with a number of prospective tenants. Her next assignment, he promised, would be far less taxing than the first had been. Handing her financial information on the corporation and marketing and site location studies for the Dallas store, he told her to familiarize herself with the project by Thursday morning. That afternoon she'd be attending the quarterly store managers' meeting with him.

Even if Luke Griffin never set another trap for her, Randy was determined to know those reports backward and forward. They accompanied her everywhere, even to bed at night. She even astonished her father by declining his invitation to accompany him to a play. He'd stopped by her office late Wednesday afternoon, saying that Emily was tied up with a client and couldn't use her ticket.

He immediately assumed that his daughter must be suffering from some life-threatening ailment to refuse a chance to attend the theater and announced that he would take her home in a taxi and take care of her.

"I'm perfectly healthy," Randy assured him. "It's just that I need to work tonight. I didn't do as well as I would have liked with the White Hills project and I want to be well-prepared."

"Anxious to impress Luke, hmm?" Bill teased.

"Anxious not to be trapped again," Randy corrected. "Luke can be terrifying when he puts his mind to it."

"In that case, put down the reports. Luke doesn't expect you to eat, breathe and sleep them, honey." Bill took the papers out of her hands and walked around to Randy's side of the desk. "Dinner first, then the play," he said, pulling her up.

Later she thanked him for being so insistent. The play dealt with the familiar subject of family conflict, yet the characters were so sensitively drawn and the dialogue so true-to-life that she found herself deeply involved in what was happening. Most of all she envied the young actress who played the daughter of the family, but when she said as much to her father he merely laughed and told her that next time he took her to a play he'd check to make sure that all the female roles called for actresses over forty.

The next morning Randy reviewed her notes on the Dallas project until she was sure that nothing Luke could ask her would faze her in the slightest. Then she marched down the hall to his office. His door was closed and Rita was on the phone; when she noticed Randy she mouthed, "He's busy."

A few seconds later, just as Rita hung up, a small, portly man came scurrying out of the office, a large black briefcase clutched in his hand. *"He* was sure in a hurry," Randy observed as he rushed out the door. "Who is he?"

"Katrina's agent. She's signing a contract to do the promotional work for the Dallas store. I guess you can go in now, Randy. Your dad sat in on the meeting, by the way."

Randy gave a knock and opened the door to find Luke and her father sitting together on the couch, laughing at something.

"What's so funny?" she asked.

"It's unrepeatable," her father answered, getting up to leave. "I assume you're here to speak to Luke." He glanced at Luke, adding, "She's memorized all that stuff on the Dallas store. I don't want to be the one to tell her that we've decided against the project." He chortled to himself and walked out the door.

Randy was totally bewildered. "But Katrina's agent . . . ? Rita said . . ."

"He was kidding, Miranda. Pat spent a good part of Monday tracking down your grandfather in Italy. He's solidly in favor—your father and I have been the cautious ones. Our capital isn't unlimited and we don't want to overexpend it, especially given the current economy. But you must know our financial situation from the reports I gave you."

"Yes, and last year's annual report showed that—"

"You must need something else to do," Luke interrupted.

"But aren't you going to ask . . . ?"

"No."

"Not *anything?*" *After all the work I put in?* she added silently.

"Not right now. I'm sure you've done your homework, and I've got some material to review for the meeting this afternoon." A number of papers were scattered on his desk and he gathered them together and shoved them into a file folder. "Skim as much of this as you can before lunch. I'll stop by your office at about twelve-thirty and take you out to eat. It will give us some time to talk. We can come back to the meeting together afterward."

Randy took the folder and walked halfway to the door before she stopped and turned around. "Just as a point of information," she drawled, "was that an invitation or an order, Mr. Griffin?"

"It's an invitation if your answer is yes and an order if it's no," Luke shot back.

Randy put a hand on her hip and smiled. "One of these days I'm going to have the last word, you know. I hope you realize that."

"Naturally. I have to let you win a round or two just to keep up your spirits," Luke agreed.

But obviously not *this* round, Randy thought as she walked back to her office. The folder Luke had given her contained the minutes of previous quarterly meetings and numerous reports explaining how various problems had been handled. There were also examples of materials from successful promotional campaigns and summaries of recent market research. Randy quickly saw that the meetings conducted under Oscar Levitan, Luke's predecessor, had been less than productive and poorly attended. Luke had taken over as vice president in September, and while the October meeting had been primarily a forum for listening to the managers' problems and complaints, the minutes for January and April reflected solid accomplishments in a number of important areas.

Luke poked his head into Randy's office a few minutes early, before she'd had time to finish her reading. "I still have a couple of things left to do," she said. "I'd better skip lunch."

"All you have to do this afternoon is meet our managers and listen to what they have to say. No one's going to cross-examine you—not this time."

Thus reassured, Randy allowed Luke to take her to a German restaurant down the street, where she ordered half of what she would have loved to eat and declined a glass of wine, explaining that alcohol was fattening and that dieting was a way of life for her.

"I've seen your diaper commercial," Luke teased. "You must be at least twenty pounds lighter now."

"Only ten pounds," Randy corrected with a smile. "The camera really does add weight."

"Your father mentioned that you'd been starving yourself for a movie role. Were you disappointed not to get it?"

Randy decided to take a calculated risk. Linda's advice to the contrary, she and Luke were never going to get any closer to each other if she didn't permit him a glimpse of her personal thoughts and feelings at times.

"Actually," she said, toying with her napkin, "it wasn't a movie role at all. It was a man. But there was no point in telling my father that. It only would have upset him."

"But it happens to everyone sometimes," Luke answered.

After what Randy had told Luke in Maine he surely must have understood, but she explained the situation anyway. "The point is, even though Dad's had his

165

troubles with my sister he's never had to spend a day worrying about me. I was always the sensible one, the good one, the *backward* one—until I met a guy in Los Angeles who wound up ditching me to marry someone else. I took it harder than I probably should have. It's funny—I saw him at a party when I was back in L.A., but the woman he was with wasn't his wife."

"So you figure you were lucky."

"I suppose."

Randy was no mindreader, but Luke's searching look virtually announced that he was thinking about who'd been up in Maine with him. Perhaps he assumed it would be a waste of his time to ask her, because he merely remarked, "I hear that your sister is dating Roger Bennett these days."

Randy told him he'd heard right, adding that Linda and Roger were in Paris at the moment and that Linda hoped to do some buying for the store. "Lin seems to have straightened out a lot since her last divorce," she said. "She's a little less frenetic and more sensitive to people's feelings. I hope things work out with Roger, because I liked him when I met him and I thought he was the right kind of man for her. He's strong enough not to give in to her and he expects the best from people."

"And what's the right kind of man for you?" Luke promptly asked her.

Even if Randy had known the answer she wouldn't have touched the question with a ten-foot pole. She'd told Luke enough for one day. "Anyone but Sean Raley," she said with a smile.

After that they stuck mostly to business, talking about the Dallas project and what would be covered in the meeting later that afternoon. Randy listened far more than she talked, asking an occasional question and discovering just how little she really knew. Her liberal arts education, with its single course in economics and lack of exposure to statistical methodology and computer science, had evidently left her ill-prepared for a career as a modern corporate executive.

The branch managers' meeting was being held in the company conference room on the top floor of the C & D building. Luke and Randy walked in fifteen minutes early and joined Rita Washington and a group of executives by a sidetable laden with drinks, pastry and fruit. Promptly at two-fifteen Luke invited the thirty-five-plus people present to be seated and started the meeting. Randy was on his left near the end of the table, while Rita had positioned herself halfway down from the end in order to take notes.

Luke began by introducing Randy and welcoming the new assistant manager of the Boston store. Then he asked everyone present to give his or her name and title. The preliminaries attended to, he gave a mock sigh. "Okay, let's take the complaints first. You don't like the fall merchandise we pushed at you. It's all wrong for your customers and the stuff you found on your own is ten times better."

There was a ripple of laughter. In fact, the managers were pleased with the fall lines. Most of the merchandise was selected from suggestions made by buyers operating out of headquarters, but an important percentage came from buyers employed by the individual stores and tended to reflect local taste. For several minutes the managers shared names and addresses of their "finds," most of whom were local manufacturers or even independent artisans.

The first item on the formal agenda was the financial statement for the second quarter of the fiscal year. Balance sheets and sales figures for the fifteen branch stores and the Manhattan store were passed out and studied. With a few exceptions it had been a good spring. One problem area was in White Hills, and another was in Philadelphia. Luke questioned the manager of the latter store in a low-key, unthreatening manner, but Randy caught a hint of steel in his voice as it became apparent that his suggestions had been largely ignored. The assistant manager of the same store sat there trying to conceal her delight. Obviously she assumed that she was in line for a promotion.

The discussion of quarterly earnings led to protests about a new corporate accounting practice that Luke had put into effect. The managers clearly felt that due to the change, store expenses appeared to rise while corporate expenses dropped, whereas Luke argued that his only concern was an accurate accounting of actual expenditures by the central corporation. He promised to have the comptroller's office send out a memo further explaining the matter, saying that if there were still questions about it people could ask them at the next meeting. It was obvious that he had no intention of backing down.

C & D had always stressed the value of training its personnel, so Luke took half an hour or so to ask his managers' opinions on what types of training their employees needed. The group worked out tentative dates and locations for training seminars, and Rita jotted down suggestions about content. The most frequent request seemed to be for Luke's personal presence as a speaker, something that impressed Randy as much as anything she would hear that day.

The next block of time was reserved for sharing successful ideas in areas such as promotion, display, public relations and management. Randy had expected a free-wheeling session full of generalizations, but quickly realized that Luke Griffin would never tolerate such a waste of everyone's time. His managers came fully prepared with copies of advertising material, photos of displays, lists of steps taken to implement their ideas and written summaries of their presentations to pass out. Although the atmosphere was informal enough to permit quiet trips for coffee and cake, there were no undercurrents of conversation and no signs of restlessness.

As the meeting continued more and more senior company executives wandered in to listen. Randy had known many of these men and women since she was a girl and time and again she received a smile or a peck on the cheek before they sat down in one of the extra chairs along the wall. Eventually there were nearly two dozen observers in the room.

The final hour of the meeting was devoted to problem-solving. The managers were specific and concise in describing their difficulties, with Luke acting as a sort of catalyst to help them pinpoint the real causes. Bill Dunne arrived just as this section of the meeting got underway, so Randy gave him her seat and found another by the wall. Just as Luke was wrapping up the meeting with a brief summary of what had been covered and accomplished, Emily Dunne came into the room to remind everyone that they were invited back to the house for a buffet supper. It was typical of her mother, Randy thought, that she would take the time to reextend the invitation in person.

Luke walked back to the apartment with Randy and her parents, the two men slightly ahead of the women, discussing how the meeting had gone.

A few blocks from the store Bill stopped and turned around. "So what did you think, honey?" he asked.

"It was fantastic. I can't believe what they accomplished in just three and a half hours. The meeting was disciplined, nobody wasted time, everyone was prepared. . . ." Randy's voice trailed off when her eyes met Luke's. He was smiling the smuggest smile she'd ever noticed on his face.

"So I finally managed to impress you," he drawled.

"I've *always* been impressed, Mr. Griffin," Randy drawled back. "The problem is, nobody could possibly be as impressed with you as you are with *yourself.*"

Her gibe failed to find its target. "That's only because no one knows me as well as I know myself," he laughed. "Would you care for the opportunity to try?"

Randy rolled her eyes. "Suppose I said yes. What would you say?"

"I'd say, 'Name the time and date.'"

Determined not to let him have the last word, Randy suggested archly, "How about now?"

He nodded, walked back to her and put an arm around her shoulders. "Excuse us, Bill, Emily," he said. "Miranda and I will be staying at my house tonight."

Randy's sheer blouse provided very little armor against his touch. Aware that her parents were watching with amused interest, Randy started to blush. When Luke pulled her away with him and whistled for a cab, her eyes slid to the sidewalk in defeat.

"Luke, do leave her alone," Emily scolded. "She's no match for you and you know it."

He complied with a knowing wink at Randy, leaving her ready to sink through the concrete. At a minimum he knew that she wasn't as innocent as her parents believed, and at a maximum he might be aware that he himself had sampled her favors on more than one occasion. Mercifully he didn't actually say anything, but merely walked back to Bill and started to talk business again.

"I'm going to have to fire Heywood," he said as they continued toward the apartment. "The Philadelphia store should be doing five percent more business. I've given him as much help as I can, but it's been a waste of our time and money."

"Eight to ten percent more business," Bill corrected, "and I told you that a month after you came on board. I understand why you wanted to wait, but I think you underestimate just how much respect you've earned in this company. Have you decided who to replace him with?"

Luke glanced back over his shoulder at Randy. "What do you think, Miranda? How about the assistant manager, Sheila Kane?"

Randy hadn't cared for Sheila Kane and she told Luke why. "She can't wait to get rid of him. Instead of working as a team for the good of the company, I get the feeling that she's been standing around with a sharpened knife waiting for opportunities to plunge it into his back."

Luke nodded. "I agree with you. You get an A for picking it up so fast." He turned his attention back to Bill. "I was thinking of Don Jacoby, the assistant manager in Garden City. He's got three kids, so if I'm going to make a switch it should be soon, before the school year begins. I'll deal with Heywood and Kane tomorrow, then talk to Jacoby afterward. I thought I'd take Miranda down to Philadelphia with me for a couple of days next week to get a better picture of what's going on."

They'd reached the Dunnes' building now and were waiting for the doorman to let them in. "Would you like that?" Luke asked Randy.

"Very much." She realized that they'd be staying overnight and wondered what the sleeping arrangements would be. Very proper, no doubt—but would they stay that way?

As usual, Emily Dunne had mounted a major production, with twin buffet tables piled high with cold cuts, salads, breads and desserts. The first group of guests walked in some fifteen minutes later to be followed by a dozen successive waves. Apparently word of the dinner had filtered through the corridors of C & D's executive offices, because eventually nearly seventy people found their way to the apartment.

Randy mixed with the crowd, greeting those she knew well with a hug or a kiss and introducing herself to the others. But eventually the smoke and noise took their toll in the form of a nagging headache, so she slipped into the kitchen for a glass of ice water and some aspirin and carried them down the hall to her bedroom.

She was lying on her bed with her eyes closed when two quick knocks captured her attention. They were followed by the appearance of a wavy, blond-streaked head of hair and concerned brown eyes. Luke didn't wait to be invited inside; he simply closed the door behind him and sat down on the bed.

"You looked a little pale," he said. "We were worried about you, Miranda."

The situation was much too familiar for Randy's peace of mind. The last time she'd had a headache was in Maine, and she remembered all too well exactly how Luke had taken care of her—not just during the afternoon, but all night long.

"I'm okay," she said. "I just have a slight headache, that's all." She reached for the ice water and took a few sips, more to have something to do than because she was particularly thirsty. It was a serious mistake; her hand was trembling from nervousness, almost causing the water to slosh out of the glass. Luke could hardly fail to notice.

He removed the glass from her hand and set it back down on the night table. "The first day we met you made it clear that you weren't interested in me as anything but a teacher, but within ten or fifteen minutes you started to broadcast the opposite message. You can't have it both ways, Miranda. Just how do you feel?"

Putting him off was sheer self-preservation. "Does it matter?" she asked. "You agreed with me, remember?"

He was searching her face in a way that both unnerved and aroused her. Every part of her body seemed to be throbbing, her head with pain and the rest of her with a mixture of tension and desire. Staring into her lap, she was hardly aware of raising a hand to absently rub the back of her neck.

If she hadn't been so wrapped up in her own emotions she would have anticipated Luke's reaction. With a husky, "Here, let me," he brushed away her hand and started to massage the knotted muscles of her neck, smoothing away the pain. Always the doctor, Randy thought to herself, turning onto her side to allow him freer access.

Just like before, his fingers were firm and gentle as they worked their way from her neck to her temples to her scalp. Randy's eyes fluttered shut within moments, but she could feel Luke's muscular thigh lodged against her back and hear the regular sounds of his breathing. Her own breaths were coming a little too quickly now as pain gave way to relief and then arousal. In time his hands dropped to her back, lightly kneading it through the sheer material of her blouse and then pulling the blouse out of the waistband of her skirt to slip underneath and stroke the bare skin. She had no bra on, only a camisole top, and his fingers occasionally approached the side of a vulnerable breast as they worked their magic, heightening her anticipation.

The intimate feel of Luke's hands on her body was quickly rekindling the smoldering embers of the Maine firestorm, tempting Randy to twist around and offer her lips. But suddenly his hands stilled and then dropped away.

"Miranda," he murmured.

Randy opened her eyes and turned onto her back to look at him. His features were taut, as though he were under considerable strain. She automatically stretched up a hand to soothe away the tension, but he captured it at the wrist and pressed a hard kiss into the palm before releasing it. "I'd better go," he said.

Randy didn't want him to, but she didn't waste words objecting. Instead she arched up, her hands reaching for his neck to pull him down to her. He didn't resist her invitation for very long; within moments his mouth was nuzzling her lips, then urgently parting them. His tongue hungrily probed and conquered, as if he were starved for the sweetness and softness of her mouth. But the kiss, as hot and searching as it was, came to an abrupt end when Luke all but yanked his head away.

Randy wouldn't have physically detained him a second time, but apparently the look on her face accomplished the same result. Her eyes were languid with desire, her lips moist and wantonly parted, her hair sensuously tousled. With a helpless groan Luke buried his face against the curve of her neck, seeking the sensitive little spot below her ear. Randy wasn't so carried away that she failed to remember that responding to his gentle nips with the passion she'd shown in Maine would be a clear confession of who she really was. It was too soon, she thought hazily, worrying that in another few seconds she wouldn't be able to help herself. But Luke soon turned his attention elsewhere, tracing the outline of her collarbone with his lips.

At the same time his fingers started to deal with the buttons of her blouse. She eased herself down and stretched out, her hands reaching out to hold him around the waist. Her blouse unbuttoned, the camisole impatiently shoved up, Luke quickly trapped a hardened nipple with his teeth and gave a sharp little nip that sent sensual shock waves through her body. What little control Randy had left abruptly snapped.

She groaned as he continued to tease her breasts, and when his hand stroked her stomach and then moved lower her flaming body restlessly responded. Somehow she managed to unfasten his belt so that her fingers could reach down and caress him in turn.

He stiffened, choking out her name. The next moment he'd swung his legs onto the bed so that he lay fully atop her body. She returned his demanding, rhythmic movements almost wildly, her lips opening submissively to receive his kiss. Between the thrusts of his tongue and the urgency of his body Randy knew only that she wanted him more than she ever had. When he ran his hand up her leg and started to unfasten the side closing of her skirt, she helplessly moaned out her wishes—a breathless, "Luke—oh, Luke—please . . ."

The knock on the door sent Randy on the quickest trip back to reality that she'd ever taken. She had time for only one frantic thought—*Please let it be Mom*—before the door opened and William Dunne came striding into the room.

Luke rolled off her and started to fumble with his belt while Randy bolted up and pulled down her camisole, then clutched at the sides of her blouse. She knew her face must be scarlet.

Although her father looked absolutely stunned there was no explosion—at least, not right away. "I came to see how you felt," he said a little distantly.

Luke was standing up by now, his face drained of color. Some loose change and a comb had fallen out of his pocket and Randy automatically gathered them up with her free hand. The only thing she could think to say was, "I'm sorry."

Bill Dunne's jaw clenched. *Now* he was getting angry, it was obvious. But he totally ignored Randy's apology and instead shot a tight-lipped look at Luke. "When you're finished getting your clothes back on," he said, "I'd appreciate a few words with you. In the den."

Luke glanced at Randy, then nodded. "Just a minute," Randy said as her father turned to leave. "You're acting as though I had nothing to do with this, like it's somehow Luke's fault. That's ridiculous. And you had no right to walk into *my* bedroom without an invitation—"

"In *my* house, young lady," Bill interrupted. A vein in his neck was throbbing with anger. "And as long as you live in my house you'll obey my rules."

*Young lady?* Randy thought furiously. At *twenty-four?* She'd never yelled at her father in her life, but his attitude made her livid. "So I'll move," she spat at him. "Maybe clear back to California."

Bill's reaction was to glare at Luke and then mutter, "You don't know what you're saying, Randy."

On the contrary, she knew exactly what she'd said. She also knew that it was easier for her father to blame Luke than to admit that she'd had an equal part in what he'd witnessed. She was about to point that out when Luke laid a quelling hand onto her shoulder to stop her.

"Let me handle it," he murmured. "If you're ready?" he said to Bill.

The two men walked out, Bill Dunne in front, Luke Griffin following.

# Chapter Eight

As Luke followed Bill Dunne down the hall to the den he wondered how it was possible to hold a woman in his arms, to kiss her passionately and intimately caress her flesh, yet still not be sure of who she was. Half of the evidence seemed to point in one direction and half in the other. He now knew that "chubby vestal virgin" was a preposterously inaccurate characterization of Miranda Dunne; in fact, Sean Raley had apparently cost her not only her innocence, but a good twenty to thirty pounds as well.

Raley's name was familiar from a TV movie Luke had once seen and brought to mind dark macho looks and a strapping physique. Raley was about as handsome as they come, and had obviously hurt Miranda very badly. Although she seemed to have recovered quite nicely by now, Luke realized that he was angered by the idea that Raley had treated her so carelessly. He didn't even like the idea that Raley had touched her.

Of course, in order for him to believe that the

"Linda" of Maine and the "Miranda" of New York were one and the same person, Luke would have had to disregard a whole host of very logical evidence. He would have had to believe that Miranda had never breathed a word of what had happened to anyone, with the obvious exception of her sister and Roger Bennett. He would have had to believe that Roger had purposely misled him on the phone. And he would have had to believe that Miranda had skillfully altered her appearance, and was a good enough actress to have altered her behavior as well. After all, "Linda" had gone half-crazy when he'd nipped at that little spot below her ear, but Miranda had scarcely noticed. "Linda" had been the image of self-possession in Maine; whereas Miranda had come almost unglued on Monday morning when he'd given her a rough time about the White Hills project. And he just couldn't picture the "Linda" of Maine rushing to his defense with the hotheaded impetuousness exhibited by Miranda only a few minutes ago.

Despite all this evidence to the contrary, however, he would have laid odds that he was dealing with the same woman. The reason was very simple. If he strained his memory to the utmost, he might have been able to come up with a handful of women over the years who'd attracted him so powerfully that his usually perfect self-control had slipped. It stretched his credulity to believe that it could happen twice in less than a month with a pair of sisters who were purportedly very different.

The only problem was that no matter what his body told him, his brain persisted in demanding proof. He'd checked around the Dunnes' apartment, but there wasn't a single picture of Linda as an adult. If she hadn't been in Paris he might have flown up to Cambridge for a firsthand look. And now, as if the whole situation weren't driving him crazy enough to begin with, he had to pacify his boss. After the way Bill had reacted inside Luke could well understand why Randy hadn't told him about Sean Raley. He'd treated her like a child, and she'd responded exactly the same way.

Bill opened the door to his den and motioned Luke inside. At least, Luke thought as they sat down in a pair of oversized club chairs, Bill wasn't going to sit behind his desk and interview him as though he were an errant employee.

While Luke sat there feeling uncomfortable Bill took his time about lighting his pipe, puffing it a few times before he spoke. "She's in love with you, Luke," he finally stated flatly.

Luke had no idea what to say. He'd half expected Bill to chew him out like a top sergeant and wouldn't have been all that surprised by a request for his resignation. But this deadpan announcement about Miranda's feelings for him left him speechless.

When he sat there with his mouth shut Bill continued a little angrily, "The way she acts with you—I've never seen her like this before. If she isn't trading quips to get your attention then she's working her tail off to impress you. I'm not proud of losing my temper in there—I've never had to yell at Randy in my life. Obviously I should have taken into account who she was *with*." He shook his head. "Damn it, Luke, you were in there seducing my *daughter!* What in hell did you think you were doing?"

"I don't know what to say, Bill, other than that I'm sorry," Luke finally managed. "And that it's entirely my fault, of course." A lie, but an honorable one. "I, uh, I was massaging her neck—she had a headache—and things somehow got out of hand." He paused before attacking what Bill seemed to consider the heart of the matter. "And . . . as far as Miranda's feelings are concerned, I think you're forgetting that we've spent a total of maybe four hours alone together." Or was it four hours and a three-day weekend? "People don't fall in love that fast," he finished a little lamely.

179

"You have a lot to learn about life," Bill retorted. He tapped his pipe on the table, an expression of leashed aggression. "I would have proposed to Emily the first night I met her, but she was only eighteen and I was afraid she would think I was after her money. But all that's beside the point. All you need to understand is that I don't want to see Randy hurt. Especially not by you. I don't believe I'm capable of separating my feelings as a father from my judgment about what's best for my company. Do I make myself clear?"

How do I manage to get myself into these things? Luke thought, suppressing a groan. "Perfectly," he said aloud.

Bill nodded his satisfaction. "That leaves us with only one problem," he said. "Randy expects to go to Philadelphia with you next week. Under the circumstances, I think she should stay home."

Bill Dunne, thought Luke, didn't know his daughter even half as well as he thought he did. "Miranda will tear a strip off both our hides if either one of us allows a personal situation to get in the way of what she wants to learn about the business. There's no way I can tell her she can't come. But I promise you that I'll keep things under control, Bill."

"Meaning?"

The word was flung down as coldly as a challenge to duel. Luke immediately adopted his most reasonable tone. "That I'm attracted to your daughter—very attracted to her—but that I'm not in love with her. At this point I would certainly like to get to know her better, but . . ." He hesitated, trying to find a tactful way of stating the obvious. "At a certain point . . . What I'm trying to say is, this isn't the eighteen-hundreds, Bill. I'd like your permission to take Miranda out, but I can't promise not to lay a finger on her."

Bill started puffing his pipe again, looking much too calm for Luke's peace of mind. "Lay a finger on her. Delightful euphemism, but both of us know what you mean. And it seems to me that you've already reached that 'point' you alluded to." He paused, then added a little curtly, "I'd suggest that you don't take her out at all unless you're damn well serious about her—very serious."

There was nothing Luke could say beyond an irritated, "I won't." The only saving grace to this whole blasted situation was that it no longer mattered *who* he'd been with in Maine. He'd been warned away, and he wasn't crazy enough to argue or disobey. No matter how much Miranda attracted him, she wasn't as important to him as his career.

Randy had very little success in calming her simmering emotions, so she did the next best thing. She changed out of her wrinkled skirt and blouse into a fresh dress and sat down on the bed to wait for either Luke or her father to come in and tell her just what those two men of the world had decided. When fifteen minutes went by with no sign of either one she started toward the living room, intent on demanding a few answers. She didn't see either Luke or her father, but she did notice that a cluster of bodies, mostly male bodies, was surrounding one of the upholstered chairs on the far side of the room. Curious, she went over to find out what the attraction was.

The minute she found out she started to wish she'd stayed in her room. Katrina Sorensen was holding court in the chair, her long legs crossed sensuously and revealingly, the slit of her emerald-green silk dress exposing a provocative length of suntanned thigh. Luke was half sitting and half leaning on the arm of the chair, casually fondling the back of Katrina's neck with one of his hands. Randy didn't know whether to cry or try to strangle the man.

Emily approached her just as she was about to turn away, her sympathetic look virtually announcing that she'd heard about what had happened in the bedroom.

"Come meet Katrina, darling," she urged Randy. The sea of bodies obediently parted as, taking Randy by the hand, Emily led her into the model's presence.

Randy's murmured, "But we've already met, Mom," was met by a whispered, "Straighten up and smile, darling."

"Katie, dear," Emily said to Katrina, "I'd like you to meet my daughter, Randy. I'm sure that she joins all of us in telling you how delighted we are that you'll be working for C & D."

"How sweet, Emily, but I had the pleasure of meeting Randy last week, in Luke's office." Katrina smiled warmly at Randy, then gave Luke a look which mingled possessiveness with seduction.

He stood up and extended his arm to her, totally ignoring Randy, who somehow managed to keep on smiling, even though she dearly wanted to kick him. "Up you go, Katie," he said. "If you're sitting in a chair, you aren't earning the outrageous amount we pay you."

Katrina giggled and tucked her arm around Luke's waist. As he led her off to mingle with those in the room Emily said to Randy, "Come into the bedroom with me. You're doing fine."

Randy, who felt anything but fine, obediently followed. Only when the two women were sitting together on the bed behind a locked door did Emily continue to talk. "Your father told me what happened," she said. "He also told me that he informed Luke that you're in love with him, which probably terrified the poor man, and that he'd made it clear to Luke that if he hurt you he could think about finding himself another job, which would account for his very bizarre behavior with Katrina."

Randy was now as furious with her father as she'd been with Luke only a minute ago. "Bizarre?" she raged. "How dare Dad talk to Luke like that! And how *could* he touch that—that woman after the way he touched me?" She brushed away an angry tear. "I could kill him."

Emily gave a soothing cluck and made a gracefully dismissive gesture with her hand. "He used to date her, but everyone knows that he got tired of her within a month, darling. I suppose that paying attention to Katrina is his way of telling you that he's not interested in you, but of course, if he weren't interested in you, he wouldn't bother to pay attention to Katrina. True?"

"I suppose." It did make a convoluted kind of sense. "But, Mom . . . Dad has to stop interfering in my life. My relationship with Luke is nobody's business but mine, and I won't have Dad treating me like a child."

Emily stroked her hair, murmuring, "But darling, you've only known Luke a short time. Don't you think you were rushing things—just a little?"

Randy's response was a burst of mildly hysterical laughter. This whole situation was ridiculous. At first she wasn't sure just how much she was going to tell her mother, but somehow after twenty minutes of nonstop talking she'd given Emily a shorthand version of everything from Sean Raley onwards.

Emily Dunne's clients weren't always the easiest people in the world to deal with, and in the course of her career she'd developed a talent for remaining absolutely tranquil in the midst of total chaos. When Randy finished her story her only reaction was a thoughtful, "It *is* a complicated situation, isn't it?"

Calmer now, Randy realized that she'd just handed her mother a very big pill to swallow in the space of less than half an hour. "Are you very disappointed in me?" she asked meekly.

"Disappointed?" Emily moved her hand up and down Randy's back, gently massaging the tense muscles. "For making a mistake with that actor? Of course not. I never really believed that anyone who loves to eat as much as you do could bear to diet away all that weight for a movie role. And as far as Luke is concerned"—she smiled knowingly—"he's a *very* attractive man. If I were fifteen years younger and single I'd go after him myself. But if you're serious about him, darling, you really should stop playing games and get to know him. Luke won't be easy to pin down—he's been single for a long time and there must be a reason for it. And don't worry about your father. If things don't work out for you and Luke I'll make sure he understands that C & D's two biggest stockholders would look very unfavorably on Luke's departure."

Randy couldn't quite believe what she was hearing. Her mother seldom involved herself in the business and never challenged her father's decisions. "You're talking about yourself and Grandpa—but would you really do something like that? Dad would be furious with you."

"If it's necessary I will," Emily answered firmly. "Your father is being very unfair, not only to Luke and you, but to the company also. But I doubt it will come to that. After over thirty years of marriage to a man you know him very well. You've always been your father's favorite and it isn't easy for him to accept the fact that you're a woman now and that your love for another man could lead you to disregard what he considers to be his proper authority. But don't you think he deserves a little time to get used to the situation? Do make your peace with him, Randy."

Randy absently agreed, her mind fixed on the phrase, "your love for another man." Why was everyone in her family so convinced that she loved Luke Griffin when she herself wasn't? And even more important, how long would it take before she was finally sure that he wouldn't turn out to be just another wild, ultimately painful infatuation?

When Emily and Randy returned to the living room a minute later Katrina and Luke were still standing side by side, making their way from group to group and apparently charming everyone in sight. With only a little prodding from her mother Randy walked up to her father and slipped a hand through his arm.

"She's really something," she said, nodding toward Katrina. "Exactly what is she going to do for us?"

Bill seemed startled by his daughter's friendly attitude. "It was Luke's idea," he began, then mumbled under his breath, "One of his *good* ideas, as opposed to his bad ones. Are you all right, honey?"

Randy blushed slightly and said that she was fine. "And . . . I'm sorry that I lost my temper before," she added.

"Me too." Bill looked greatly relieved. "About Katie—we figured that she attracts media attention wherever she goes, and that's the basic reason we're using her. We'll start by running a series of ads in the Dallas papers—you know the type of thing I mean. The first one will be a picture of the construction site with Katie surrounded by a group of hardhats, and copy reading something like 'C & D says "Howdy!" to the Big D.' We'll do several more as construction proceeds, and from now until we're ready to open Katie will make personal appearances for us. Her basic job is to act as a spokeswoman and keep our name in front of the public—to help us generate excitement about the store. I admit I'm nervous, Dallas is our first major market outside the East, and you know how rough the competition there is."

As her father talked Randy watched Katrina work the crowd. She was such an expert that if she'd wanted to she could have charmed a Bengal tiger into purring like a kitten. Luke continued to stick to her side like glue, his arm draped over her shoulders. If he hadn't been so careful to avoid even glancing in Randy's direction his behavior might have provoked her into some foolhardy sort of retaliation.

\* \* \*

Randy spent the next two days working as a saleswoman in the children's department of the Manhattan store. An army of flu germs was marching through the city, and Conover-Dunne had been one of the prime casualties. Perhaps because children were especially susceptible to the strain of the disease that was going around, the staff of that department had been continually exposed and thus hardest hit. Randy had had very little experience with children, but she'd always enjoyed the imagination and sense of wonder which can turn any little girl or boy into a superhero or T.V. star. When she wasn't ringing up orders or helping customers she was playing games with the children, keeping them occupied while their harried mothers shopped for late summer bargains or the first clothes of fall. By the time the store closed at five o'clock on Saturday, however, all she wanted to do was soak in a hot tub with a good book. All those hours of entertaining had left her drained.

The last she'd seen of Luke was his departing back as he walked out the door of her parents' apartment Thursday night with Katrina Sorensen on his arm. He'd spent Friday morning closeted in his office, first with the manager and then the assistant manager of the Philadelphia store. In the afternoon he'd driven out to Garden City. She knew his schedule because Rita Washington had stopped off in the children's department Friday evening with a note for her and had mentioned what a tough morning Luke had had with Marvin Heywood and then Sheila Kane.

Randy didn't envy him that part of his job. After only a few weeks at C & D she now understood just how hard he worked and why he was successful. She realized that people like Luke and her father had a great many qualities she admired: they were organized, openminded and knowledgeable, yet capable of putting up a tough, unemotional facade when it was really necessary. Most important, they inspired and held the loyalty of those who worked under them despite the inevitable clashes and disagreements. Randy was beginning to suspect that she wasn't cut out for clashes and disagreements. She didn't want to be responsible for thousands of people's jobs. Areas like public relations or training appealed to her very much, but she could no longer picture herself as president—at least not for many years.

The note was from Luke, and took the form of a brief memo quite obviously dictated into a machine and transcribed by Rita.

"We'll be leaving at eight A.M. Monday and staying overnight," it read. "I'll pick you up in front of your building. Please wear jeans and a tee shirt. I would like you to look as much like an average college girl as you possibly can. We'll spend a few hours shopping in the store, then meet for lunch to discuss our reactions. On Tuesday I plan to hold a series of meetings with the staff, which you can skip or attend as you wish." There was no signature.

The tone of the memo was so completely impersonal that Randy read it twice, searching for some hint that Luke really cared about her. She couldn't find what wasn't there, and his behavior in the car after he picked her up on Monday only underscored his attitude. After an unsmiling hello he clicked on the radio and completely ignored her existence.

Randy might have attributed his distant behavior to her father's heavyhanded warning but for one fact: since she was dressed in faded jeans and a tee shirt, with almost no makeup and her hair in a ponytail, there was no way Luke couldn't recognize her as the "Linda" from Maine. What they'd already done together rendered Bill Dunne's lecture a little absurd.

Randy decided that the logical explanation was that

Luke was angry with her, so she gave him a full hour to calm down before she turned off the radio and asked submissively, "Luke, don't you think we need to talk?"

He gave her a cool look. "There's nothing to talk about. I've been told to stay away from you and I will. As far as your father is concerned the past never happened, even though both of us know that it's a little late in the game for his threats. Don't we?"

It was a rhetorical question; Randy didn't bother to answer it. It was hard to believe that Luke wouldn't take into account who she really was. In fact, she'd assumed that he'd be eager to pick up where they'd left off. Then again, she remembered, he was obviously still angry. There was no point in trying to reason with him until he'd cooled down. But still, she argued back, was his job so much more important to him than she was that he wasn't willing to take even the slightest risk to see her? The thought hurt dreadfully.

When he turned the radio back on she bit her lip and kept her mouth shut. Her eyes misted over and a few tears slipped out, but if Luke noticed her brush them away he didn't say anything.

They reached the store shortly after it opened and walked silently inside. "Just look around, pretend to shop and see how you're treated," Luke instructed. He was treating her as though they'd met only that morning. "I'll meet you in the restaurant at twelve-thirty."

At least, Randy thought resignedly, his impersonal tone was an improvement over his earlier sarcasm. She offered a meek, "Okay, Luke," and walked off to look for the junior department.

It was where she seemed to belong. Her blue jeans had come from a discount store in Los Angeles and her tee shirt had the logo of a friend's band on it. In short, nothing about her appearance indicated that she was anything other than a typical middle-class girl. After two hours of shopping in the junior department and several others, she'd decided that the attitude of the salespeople in the store ranged from pleasant to bored and unhelpful. No one was actually nasty to her, but the friendly warmth that C & D was known for was largely absent. Given the reception she'd probably receive it was sheer perversity to check on the designer boutiques, but Randy couldn't resist.

She was carefully looking through some formal gowns when a saleswoman walked up to her. Although the traditional "May I help you, miss?" sounded polite enough, the woman's manner clearly indicated that Randy was in the wrong department.

"I was just looking," Randy answered pleasantly, continuing to look through the dresses.

The woman's smile turned wintry. "These dresses are very expensive, dear," she informed Randy in a patronizing tone. "Perhaps you should try the junior department."

"I was looking for something special," Randy explained. "I do have a C & D credit card, ma'am."

"I'm sure you do, dear. And it probably has a limit of several hundred dollars. Most of the gowns in this department cost over a thousand dollars."

"Gee," Randy said, as though overwhelmed by the price. "How would I know what my credit limit is?"

"We punch your number into the computer," the woman said impatiently, indicating a small terminal on the counter nearby. "Give me the card; I'll check it for you."

Suppressing a smile, Randy took out her wallet and removed the gold card, turning around to hand it to the saleswoman. She noticed Luke standing several feet away, watching her. She was sure he'd been forcing back a smile until their eyes met, but he quickly frowned and gave her a disapproving stare.

The saleswoman examined the card, which read "Miranda Conover Dunne," and above that, the number "000 00 006." There was no need to consult with a computer to determine if her credit was good. The VIP number and a name identical with that of the store she was shopping in made such a formality unnecessary.

The woman's eyes jerked up to Randy's, her face fire-engine red as she stumbled over her apology. "I'm terribly sorry, Mira—I mean, Miss Dunne. The teenagers—these clothes are so delicate—we have to be careful. . . ."

"Of course you do," Luke put in smoothly, glancing at the woman's nametag, "Mrs., uh, Healy. I'm sure Miranda is sorry she trapped you that way, aren't you, Miranda?" Luke's tone brooked no disagreement.

"Yes, I am, Mrs. Healy," Randy obediently parroted.

"Who are *you?*" the woman blurted out, staring at Luke.

"My name is Luke Griffin, and I'm—"

"Dear God, the vice president," Mrs. Healy babbled, now thoroughly rattled.

"That's right," Luke agreed with a smile. "I know you're having a few problems in the store, and Miranda and I are here to have a look around. You don't seem to be too busy at the moment, so why don't we take a few minutes off and talk about what you think is wrong here?"

At first Mrs. Healy was intimidated and defensive, but inside of ninety seconds Luke had charmed her into confiding in him like he was a long-lost friend. After she completed her monologue with a tale of being blamed for a gown which had been ripped by a careless debutante, Luke thanked her and asked her not to disclose their presence. Then he clasped his fingers around Randy's upper arm and hauled her off to the privacy of the stairwell.

"That was a damn stupid thing to do," he barked. "If I hadn't shown up everyone in the store would have known we were here."

"You thought it was funny," Randy said. "I saw the

look on your face before you noticed me watching you. Besides, we were done shopping."

Luke's lips twitched helplessly before he finally gave up and laughed. "I don't believe you," he complained. "'How would I know what my credit is?'" he mimicked, following up the imitation with an exasperated look. "What you need is a good spanking."

Since Randy had already sampled Luke's notion of a spanking she found the threat more delicious than intimidating. "A spanking, huh?" she repeated, her eyes dancing mischievously. "You mean like in Maine, Mr. Griffin?"

"No, Miss Dunne, I *don't* mean like in Maine," he retorted. But his eyes admitted the opposite.

Randy adored him in this kind of devilish mood. "Would you strip off all my clothes first?" she asked, contriving to sound terrified.

He nodded and growled, "Absolutely. The punishment is more effective that way."

"Sounds okay to me," Randy said airily, and laughed. But when Luke scooped her up, tossed her over his shoulder in a fireman's hoist and started climbing the stairs with her, Randy began to squirm vigorously. "You wouldn't dare!" she hissed.

"On the contrary," he said, "there are plenty of places in the furniture department that would be perfect for it."

He paused to catch his breath when he reached the landing between the two half-flights, then continued his ascent. Reaching the top, he kicked the door open and strode into the empty corridor, prompting a horrified, "Luke, please—put me down!" from Randy.

Her plea accomplished nothing but a firm little slap on the rear. Randy began to believe that he would actually carry out his threat when he marched through the corridor into the display area. They were in a deserted section of the store now, in a model room decorated for a teenaged girl. Luke lowered Randy to the floor next to a canopy bed, holding her wrist in a firm grip.

When he reached for the snap on her jeans she tried to twist away, whispering, "You're crazy!"

"Obviously," he drawled, pulling her into his arms. "Otherwise I wouldn't have started this."

Her arms were around his neck in seconds, her lips parted to invite his kiss. Their embrace, with its aura of flaunting propriety, was as erotic as anything Randy had ever experienced. Their mouths and bodies clung in a sensuous dance that continued for second after dangerous second until Randy was so aflame with need that when Luke broke the kiss she moaned in protest and sought his lips again.

"Miranda—no," he said hoarsely, putting her away from him. "It isn't going to work."

After the passion they'd just shared his statement simultaneously chilled her blood and made her sick to her stomach. It was all she could do to manage a husky, "What do you mean?"

"Don't look at me like that." Luke ran a hand through his hair, his expression grim. "I mean—I can't make any commitment to you."

"But nobody asked you for one," Randy said.

"Your father did. And I told him . . ."

"I know about all that. But my father doesn't run my life, Luke. And there's no reason for him to know *anything* about what I do."

Randy stopped arguing when Luke shook his head and insisted that they would have to talk about it later. She understood that the furniture department of a public store was hardly the appropriate place for a private conversation. As they started over to the restaurant she forced her mind back to business, aware that Luke would respect her more if she managed to keep it there for the next several hours.

He asked her to tell him about her morning and then

relayed a number of experiences similar to her own. "What I don't understand," she said, "is how the manager can make such a difference. Why do so many of the people here seem so unhappy?"

They'd ordered their meals by now and were waiting for the food. "First of all," Luke began, "it's reasonable to assume that we would have gotten better service if we'd been dressed more expensively. But to answer your question—suppose you'd made suggestions and been ignored? Or wanted to change workdays or alter your vacation schedule and been mired down in red tape? Or had difficult customers and received no help from your superiors? You can list a dozen situations where the manager decides policy that affects the salespeople. Heywood was inflexible. He seemed to think that he was commanding a regiment, not supervising a department store. When you drown people in regulations and treat them like buck privates you wind up with a mess on your hands. Your employees become resentful; they come to work because they're afraid of not finding another job, and they can't wait to leave at the end of the day."

"How did he get the job as manager?" Randy asked.

"Oscar put him in six months before I started. For the first few months after I came I was so busy learning the ropes that I had no time for individual stores unless a major crisis was erupting. And this situation didn't explode, it developed very gradually. Your father told me Heywood would have to go, but I was afraid that moving too fast would scare people off or build up resentment. I was also conceited enough to think I could change the guy's style of doing things. I was wrong. He sees any disagreement as a personal affront and becomes even more rigid. He does have certain strengths—intelligence and an incredible intuition about what's going to sell. That's why he was promoted in the first place, and the merchandise he'd personally brought into this store has been so attractive to customers that they'll shop here despite the changed atmosphere. But he's deadly with people. Basically he's got the wrong job. I offered him a position as a buyer on the West Coast. He'll do a lot of scouting for new suppliers. He'll be able to work on his own and I think everyone will be much happier."

"And the assistant manager, Sheila Kane?"

Luke shook his head. "Her record up to now was clean, but if she had been having problems with Heywood and saw what was happening in the store she should have come to me or your father. Instead she sat back and waited for Heywood to hang himself. We don't need employees like that."

"You fired her outright," Randy stated. She hated the thought of having to do that to someone.

Luke nodded. "I told her I'd be happy to write her a recommendation I considered fair. I'm not out to destroy her career, but I don't want her working for C & D."

By the time lunch arrived they were discussing plans for the afternoon. Luke intended to talk informally with the store's employees, both the salespeople and those in the office, in order to let them air their grievances to someone from headquarters and to provide some reassurance. He already knew what he would hear, he admitted.

By the end of the afternoon it was apparent to Randy that Luke's assessment of the situation had been accurate. One salesman, a veteran of men's suits, was blunt to the point of brusqueness. "It's about time you people did something about this," he said. "There are salesmen here who could write their own ticket at other stores, but they stick it out out of loyalty to C & D, and"—he nodded at Randy—"your father and grandfather. Of course, we knew you were trying to work with Heywood, but we could have told you you were wasting your time."

"Next time, Mr. Corelli, I hope you'll sit down and

write me a letter. Although I trust there won't be a next time." Luke shook the salesman's hand and started wearily toward the next department.

Later, as he and Randy walked out of the store, he said with a grimace, "I really got raked over the coals today. I'll bet you enjoyed every minute of it."

"Raked over the coals?" Randy repeated, puzzled. "They were complaining about Heywood, not you."

"He was my responsibility. I should have come out here months ago, but I knew he was a smart guy and I was convinced I could make him see the light. It's probably the toughest lesson I've ever learned—that my judgment is so far from infallible."

It was nice to know that Luke admitted it. Since he was obviously a little depressed it was the wrong time to bring up their personal situation, but Randy assumed that over an intimate dinner for two that evening they would talk honestly about the past and make a decision about the future. Everything was suddenly so clear in her mind that she couldn't understand her confusion of only a few weeks before. Naturally she and Luke would continue to see each other—it was obvious that neither of them could stay away from the other. It would be wonderful if they eventually decided to marry, but if not, she'd manage to survive the pain. She was no longer so afraid of being hurt or of making a mistake that she needed to play it safe. She realized that she couldn't live her life that way.

The only thing wrong with Randy's scenario was that Luke had entirely different plans. Once they'd checked into separate rooms a few doors away from each other he informed her that he was sorry that he couldn't have dinner with her because Don Jacoby was flying in from New York to meet with him that evening, and that he was already late for the airport.

"But this afternoon you said we'd talk later," Randy reminded him. "It's later, but you're still putting me off. Why?"

They were standing in the middle of the corridor outside their rooms; Luke waited while a young couple and their two children passed by. "I told you it wasn't going to work," he said. "Why can't you just accept that?"

Randy told him exactly why. "Because five hours ago you grabbed me and kissed me like you were dying to throw me down on that canopy bed and make love to me. Doesn't that count for anything?"

"It only proves that I have trouble keeping my hands off you. I've *always* had trouble keeping my hands off you—in Maine, in New York, even in the damn furniture department here in Philadelphia. But I don't have any choice, Miranda. If we start seeing each other and things don't work out, I can kiss the presidency of C & D goodbye. And I'm not about to put myself in that situation, even for you."

Seeing that Randy was about to argue with him, he went on firmly, "And don't tell me that your father won't find out. The last time some guy broke your heart you lost thirty pounds." Before she could say a word he was striding away from her.

She started to go after him, then stopped and turned back to her room, wiping away a tear. There was a limit to how far she'd chase a man and she'd just reached it. For the next thirty minutes she sat in her room and stared out the window, thinking about Maine and trying not to cry. Then she remembered that it was dinnertime and realized that she had absolutely no appetite.

Suddenly she was furious with herself. She wasn't going to put herself through six more months of hell over a man; not eating, not dating, driving herself crazy with feelings of remorse and rejection. One gradual decline was more than enough.

The hotel had dining and dancing nightly, and she decided that she'd be a masochist not to take advantage of them. Within an hour she was dressed in the brightly colored sundress she'd brought along for dinner with Luke, waiting for the elevator to come. A couple of middle-aged businessmen walked up a moment after she did, talking about whether the hotel restaurant was any good.

"Have you tried it?" one of them asked her.

Randy shook her head. "I'm here on business myself, but I just got in today. I didn't feel like sitting alone in my room, so I thought I'd go downstairs to eat."

In the end one of the men went over to talk to the desk clerk, who steered them to an Italian restaurant about twenty minutes away by car. Randy didn't hesitate to accept an invitation to join them for dinner—she recognized the name of their company, and both of them looked completely respectable.

Given her troubles with Luke she didn't expect that the evening would turn out to be particularly pleasant —especially not with a pair of computer salesmen as companions—but she wound up eating more than she should have and laughing at impossibly corny stories. After dinner the three of them went for a ride around the city, so that it was close to eleven by the time Randy thanked them and said goodnight.

She was in the middle of undressing when the phone rang. Luke? she wondered. Or perhaps her father, checking to make sure that she was sleeping in her own room.

Her uncertain, "Hello?" was met by a peremptory, "I've been calling you every ten minutes for the last hour. Where in hell have you been?"

Never had a fit of temper been so welcome. "At dinner," Randy said matter-of-factly. Her lips curved into a triumphant little smile.

"I checked downstairs. You weren't there."

She couldn't resist handing Luke back some of the grief he'd given *her* lately. "I went out," she said.

"Where to?" he demanded.

"An Italian restaurant. It's about twenty minutes away by car."

"By car," he repeated. "You took a cab?"

"A rental car. It belonged to the man I was with."

"Oh." It was the curtest "Oh" that Randy had ever encountered; it was obviously time to explain.

"Actually there were two men, Luke. I met them by the elevator on my way downstairs to eat. I happened to mention that I was alone and they invited me to join them. Both of them were my father's age. Now what have you been calling me about?"

"I wanted to make sure you were okay." He sounded nettled that he'd cared. "I thought that maybe you'd be upset."

How perceptive, Randy thought. "And if I was?" she asked aloud. "What did you plan to do about it?"

"I—I don't know. Apologize, I guess."

Suddenly Luke's reaction was no longer either amusing or exasperating. His tone was filled with such uncharacteristic defensiveness and uncertainty that Randy's heart softened, then completely melted. The least she could do would be to offer him some help. "I could phone room service for some brandy for two," she said softly. "It's a little cold and lonely in here."

There was a strained silence lasting a good ten seconds before Luke finally answered. "I can't," he muttered. "You know I want to, but I can't." He hung up the phone.

Randy could cheerfully have ripped her own phone out of the wall, carried it down the hall to Luke's room and thrown it at him. What was a woman supposed to do with a man who checked up on her like a jealous lover and then refused to even touch her? Did he really believe that they could continue to work together without the sparks of mutual attraction flaring into passion? Perhaps they could, Randy admitted, but only if she were willing to play the game Luke's way. And she wasn't.

She'd brought along the only really sensual night-gown she owned, a graduation gift from Linda two years before. It was white—"For purity," Linda had teased—with a lace bodice and ankle-length silk skirt. Randy's pulses were beating a little too quickly as she slipped it on and covered it with the matching robe. She grabbed her key on the way out of her room and pulled the door firmly shut behind her.

What happened when she knocked on Luke's door wasn't entirely a surprise to her. Luke wouldn't open it up until he knew who was there, but when Randy identified herself he brusquely told her to go back to bed. Since his hoarse tone of voice all but announced that it was the last thing in the world he really wanted, Randy had no intention of listening to him.

"Luke, please," she murmured, willing herself to sound miserably sick. "That Italian food—I must have eaten too much of it."

"So take an antacid tablet," he said.

"I don't have—oohhh." Randy cut herself off with a heartbreaking moan, dropping to her knees and clutching her stomach in pretended agony. That was the way Luke found her when he hastily opened the door, wearing only the robe she remembered from Maine.

"Okay, just take it easy, honey," he said as he helped her up. They started toward the bed, Randy leaning on Luke for support.

"Tell me what you ate," he ordered.

"Uh, antipasto, minestrone, a pasta dish and prawns with a tomato and garlic sauce. . . ." Randy doubled over again, as if pain precluded a further inventory.

"No wonder you're sick," Luke muttered as he eased her down on her side. "I'll see what I can find."

He walked off into the bathroom, returning a few moments later with a couple of chewable tablets and a glass of water. Randy, figuring they certainly couldn't harm her, gingerly sat up and accepted them, a look of adoring gratitude on her face. Fortunately the tablets tasted almost like candy, and the water washed away the chalky aftertaste.

Luke, who was sitting beside Randy on the bed now, remarked a little irritably, "Obviously I don't affect your appetite the way Raley did."

Randy decided to ignore that. "I feel a little better already," she said, "but it's so hot in here, Luke. Do you think I could have a fever?"

As Luke felt her forehead she untied the sash of her robe and slipped it off. His eyes dropped to the cross nestled between her breasts and then lower, to what the lace of her gown so cleverly emphasized. "Your temperature is normal," he said in a slightly strangled voice, "but too much more of this and *mine* won't be."

Randy fluffed up a pillow and lay back against it. "Would you rub my stomach for me, Luke? It hurts."

He did as she requested, but not without a certain inner struggle. His gentle fingers, though initially quite impersonal, turned caressing as he continued to stroke her skin. The warmth of his hand seemed to suffuse the surrounding area, especially when his fingers wandered just a little too low.

He abruptly pulled away his hand, and then, as if unable to help himself, started to finger the gold cross Randy wore, branding her in the process. "I used to think how inappropriate this was in Maine," he murmured, "but it isn't, not really. It's a beautiful piece of jewelry. Who gave it to you?" He traced the path of the chain with his index finger, then dropped his hand.

"Lin did. It was a present for helping her with her apartment in Cambridge. I'd decided to stay instead of going to New Hampshire, and it was easier not to tell my father that I'd changed my plans because I was leaving soon anyway. Linda went on a trip with Roger the next morning, but I stayed in the apartment to wait for the last delivery—and you, of course."

All the time Randy was talking she was wondering how Luke could manage to sit less than a foot away from her, looking at her with desire burning in his eyes, yet do nothing more than fondle her necklace. She was aching to be in his arms.

"How do you feel?" he finally asked.

"Okay."

"Then you'd better put your robe back on and go."

But you don't want me to, Randy thought. I know you don't. Totally unpracticed in the role of temptress, she swallowed nervously and shook her head. "My head just started to hurt," she said.

"No it didn't." Luke stood up, reaching for his lighter and cigarettes, which were sitting on the night table by the bed. Randy noticed that his hand was trembling as he lit up a cigarette. "It doesn't hurt any more than your stomach did. Am I right?"

"You're always right, aren't you?" Despite the husky statement Randy could barely think straight by now. She wanted Luke so much she was shaking from it, and if he really wanted her to leave he was going to have to throw her out.

With a convulsive little shudder she slowly pulled down first one slender strap of her nightgown, and then the second. Luke stood and watched impassively, staring into her eyes, his only movement a jerky drag on his cigarette. When she slid down the bodice to reveal firm, high breasts and dusky, erect nipples his gaze dropped to the floor and he cursed very softly.

He seemed to be in severe pain. "Do you make a habit of this sort of thing?" he groaned.

Randy wanted to fling herself into his arms, but even more than that, she wanted to entice him into making the first move. "What kind of thing do you mean?" she asked.

"Seduction." He looked up at her, the hint of a twinkle in his eyes. "Torturing helpless men." His lips twitched just a fraction. "Driving them so crazy that their common sense atrophies and every inch of their bodies starts to ache."

When his smile broadened Randy knew he'd given up. "Actually," she said ingenuously, "it's the first time I've tried it. How did I do?"

"Let's just say that you're one hell of a beginner," Luke drawled, stubbing out his cigarette.

Randy expected him to sit down next to her and pull her into his arms, but instead he walked around to the other side of the bed, lazily removed his robe, and lay down on top of the covers. "It seems to me," he said, "that the least I can do for you is to give you the opportunity to practice a little more."

Incredulous at his self-control, Randy blurted out, "How can you stand it? I'm ready to explode, Luke."

"It's called delayed gratification," he answered with a grin. "I know I can make love to you as many times as I want to tonight, so waiting becomes a very pleasant kind of agony." He took her wrist to coax her closer. "I'm all yours," he drawled. "Experiment all you want."

Randy knew every hard sinew of his body by touch, but she'd never really studied him with her eyes. He was magnificent, she thought, running her fingers over his muscled arms. And he was also right about waiting. Knowing what was to come, she could manage to live through another few minutes of frustration.

She continued to teasingly explore, massaging each calf and thigh in turn, running her fingers over his shoulders and chest, and tracing the planes of his face. Luke lay there and watched, so unnaturally still that if it hadn't been for the film of perspiration on his body and the fact that his heart was thumping like he'd just run the hundred-yard dash, Randy might have wondered whether her closeness was having the effect he'd earlier alluded to. Except, of course, that it obviously was.

Touching him so freely had excited her as much as it had excited him. She forgot her inhibitions in her eagerness to goad him into losing his self-control and allowed her mouth to continue what her hands had begun. Luke moaned as she captured a nipple with her lips, his hand reaching out to find her breast and gently knead the flesh. As his fingers became more and more demanding the world seemed to recede, leaving only Luke's body to give pleasure to. Randy was nuzzling his stomach now, the feel of his hands on her inner thighs driving her wild, all but ordering her to continue. The more intimate his touch became, the greater the liberties that she herself began to take. And then Luke pulled her around and replied in kind, until the need to give and the need to take mingled and intensified, reaching a mindless fever pitch before both were finally fulfilled.

It was the last time that night that Luke would bother very much with delayed gratification. Time and again he reached out for her, making love to her with all the fiery passion he had shown in Maine but also with a tenderness and caring that hadn't been there before. Randy woke up again early in the morning and stole back to her own room, wanting to avoid the risk of running around in her nightgown once people were up and about. As she snuggled back into bed she wondered how she could possibly have failed to realize how much she loved Luke. Her feelings were so much deeper for Luke than they had ever been for Sean. In addition to physical attraction she felt respect and admiration, and also a selfless concern that was entirely new to her. It seemed impossible for any human being to be as happy as she felt at that moment.

At first it didn't occur to Randy that Luke's "Good morning," when he phoned the room a few hours later, sounded a little off, but when he invited her to join him for breakfast in his room the strained discomfort in his voice finally penetrated. She refused to panic while she showered and dressed, yet when she walked into his room and saw only regret and guilt in his eyes, anxiety almost got the better of her. It was an effort to smile good morning, to sit down at the table and pretend to calmly sip her juice when she felt like choking on it.

"I'm crazy about you," he began. "You *do* realize that."

A statement like that had to have a "but." Randy resignedly waited for it, and it wasn't long in coming. "But I've been up since you left this morning, trying to figure out what to do, and I'm just not getting anywhere. I wish I could ask you to marry me, Miranda, but I just can't. Not yet."

"Not yet" were two of the sweetest words in the English language, Randy decided. Things weren't nearly as bad as she'd feared. "I'm not asking for a proposal," she told him. "I realize we don't know each other very well, except, well, physically." She blushed slightly.

"Exactly. The fact is, I don't know you at all. There was 'Linda' in Maine, 'Miranda' in New York and somebody else here in Philadelphia. Sometimes I wonder if there *is* a real Miranda Dunne, or only the roles she plays."

Randy had known that sooner or later they'd have to talk about what she'd done, and was relieved that it was finally out in the open. "Are you very angry that I pretended we'd never met?" she asked.

Luke shook his head. He wasn't paying any attention to his food, Randy noticed, but then, neither was she. "At first I was, but not anymore. I *would* like to understand, though."

Randy studied her plate a moment, then pushed it away. She wasn't going to eat a thing until this was over. "It was just—I'd made such a bad mistake with Sean, and I was so guilty about it. I was afraid of doing it again, of getting involved again. After the way you'd treated me in Maine—sweet half the time, cruel or arrogant the other half—I was confused about what I felt for you. And I thought, if only I had more time I could figure it out. Pretending that we'd never met was actually Lin's idea."

Randy looked him straight in the eye, her heart racing. "But I'm not confused anymore, Luke. My father was right. I love you very much. I'm willing to wait until you know what you want. And as far as my father goes—"

"If your father finds out what happened last night he'll lynch me, Miranda," Luke interrupted. He looked downright distraught. "I gave him my word I'd leave you alone. I don't want to hurt you any more than Bill wants me to hurt you, but I can't be sure I won't. And I've told you, the presidency of C & D means a hell of a lot to me."

Randy urgently explained that her father's common sense would eventually surface, and that her mother had promised to prevent any attempt by her husband to let his personal feelings interfere with business. But her arguments failed to sway him.

"It would be impossible for me to function effectively without your father's support," he pointed out. "I have this scene that plays through my head all the time. You and I are seeing each other, or even married, and we have a fight. Your father spends the next week scowling at me. I just can't—"

"That's ridiculous," Randy broke in. "I'm not going to run to my father every time we—"

"No, wait. Just hear me out, Miranda. I'm thirty-four years old and I'm still single. I've never come close to asking a woman to marry me and it isn't because I haven't met anyone suitable, because I have. Maybe part of the reason has something to do with my father walking out on my mother, or with the man my mother eventually remarried. I think it's scared me off. But it's also true that I've never wanted to take the time out from my career for personal relationships, except of course for my sister. I never starved as a kid, but there were things I never had—lots of things—and I want them now. Let me tell you something that I've learned about myself. If I'd become a doctor the way I'd originally planned to, I wouldn't have practiced selfless family medicine in some small town somewhere. I would have become a New York surgeon and made myself a fortune."

His explanation, far from clearing anything up, only confused Randy more. Was he saying that he didn't want to get involved with her because that might jeopardize his career? Or that he didn't want to marry at all? "I just don't understand what you want," she said.

"Neither do I," he admitted. "At first I thought that all I wanted was to sleep with you. Both of us know that if you started to take off your clothes I'd be helping you do it inside of ten seconds. But that isn't getting us anywhere, Miranda."

Randy stifled an exasperated sigh. Obviously Luke was even more confused than she was. "So what *would* get us somewhere?" she asked.

"I don't know, but maybe we should let things ride. Okay?"

Randy took a drink of water, thinking, Mom, you were so right. Luke isn't going to be easy. Then she stood up to leave. "Knock on my door when you're ready to go, Luke. I *would* like to attend the meetings today." Without another word she briskly crossed the room and let herself out.

It wasn't easy to sort out the tangle of emotions she felt, but by the time Luke stopped by half an hour later she'd largely succeeded. She realized that there was no point in being angry. Luke wasn't deliberately being difficult. All the things he'd touched on—how little they really knew each other, the problems with her father, the feelings left over from his childhood—were valid concerns of his. In a way, there was no point even being hurt, except that Randy was human and simply couldn't help it.

She knew that, given Luke's feelings, continuing to force the issue as she had last night wouldn't accomplish anything. She had no choice but to get on with her life and give him the time he needed. She'd "let things ride."

But if you don't do the same, Luke Griffin, she thought as she grabbed her suitcase, I'm going to give you the tongue-lashing of your life. If he alternately chased her and put her off she'd go crazy.

Luke seemed surprised when she opened the door with a friendly smile and asked him to give her thirty seconds. "I'm always leaving things behind. Just one last check."

She walked back with a pair of pantyhose and saw his fleeting smile. As they drove back to the store she asked him what he hoped to accomplish that day, and learned that his primary goal was for everyone to meet Don Jacoby and start to feel comfortable with him. He hoped to leave the store's employees with renewed confidence in the company and an eagerness to repair C & D's slightly tarnished local image.

Watching Luke in action that morning, Randy decided that the man could have run for public office. Both he and Don were well-prepared, encouraging honest and creative answers to their questions and stimulating an enthusiasm and excitement that Randy wouldn't have believed possible. She'd planned simply to observe, but became so involved in the discussions that she made a few well-received suggestions and comments on her own.

Most of all, however, she was fascinated by how Luke skillfully manipulated each of the meetings. Initially everyone in the room would look to him for leadership and guidance. He was the blazing star of Conover-Dunne and no one could fail to feel it. Yet in meeting after meeting he somehow managed to shift the spotlight onto Don Jacoby, so that by mid-afternoon, when everyone gathered together for a final session, the new manager had taken control of the proceedings and Luke was able to laze back and watch, more of an observer than even Randy was.

Since Don drove back to the city with them there was no opportunity for personal conversation. The two men talked business almost the whole way, scarcely coming up for air even when Luke stopped in front of Randy's building. It seemed impossible for her that the man who opened up the trunk and handed her her suitcase with such a formal smile could have held her and caressed her all night long—and not once, but twice—but he had. And no matter what he wanted to pretend, both of them knew it.

# Chapter Nine

$\mathcal{R}$ andy spent the next week and a half filling in for flu-stricken salespeople in C & D's Manhattan store. For the first three days she worked a summer white sale that was sheer madness, but at least it kept her too busy to think about Luke during the day and left her so tired that she had no energy to lie awake nights.

When the doorbell rang on Friday night she was sitting at dinner with her parents, eating as much as she could manage to swallow and trying to act cheerful lest Bill Dunne decide that Luke Griffin had broken her heart. Her mother knew a little of what had happened in Philadelphia, but Randy really hadn't felt like talking about it.

"I'll get it." She was relieved to have an excuse to leave the table. Their visitor had to be someone familiar to the doorman, or else he would have buzzed the apartment by now.

She opened the door to find her sister and Roger Bennett standing outside, Linda with a large suitcase and Roger laden down with three bulging shopping bags. Somehow everything wound up on the hall floor as Randy embraced first one, then the other.

"Paris was fabulous," Linda said, picking up the suitcase and striding inside. By now the Dunnes had come into the foyer. "Just wait till you see the stuff I brought back," Linda told her parents as she hugged them hello. Then she seemed to remember Roger, who was still standing near the door with the shopping bags.

"Darling, you remember my parents from the fashion show," she said. "Mom, Dad, Roger Bennett."

Roger put down the bags and shook hands with the Dunnes, saying that it was a pleasure to see them again and adding, "You have a captivating daughter."

"Two of them," Bill said with a smile.

The older captivating daughter promptly announced that she was hungry, but fortunately for her stomach her mother could always be counted on to rustle up a meal to ward off starvation. As for Randy, between her pleasure in seeing Roger and her sister and her interest in the details of their trip she forgot that she wasn't hungry and finished her veal. After dinner everyone went into the living room for coffee and Linda dumped out the contents of her suitcase and shopping bags.

Even Bill Dunne was impressed by the treasures she displayed. There were exquisitely beaded handbags at half the New York price, handmade lingerie, bulky, hand-knit sweaters, and a group of clever kitchen gadgets in bright plastic colors that Randy fell in love with. Linda explained that while Roger was tied up in negotiations with his temperamental French director, she'd gotten a little restless and decided to do some traveling. Her notion of "some traveling" encompassed nearly half a dozen European cities, and each of her "finds" seemed to come from some posh but out-of-the-way shop that only the local "in" crowd knew about.

"Just in case you're interested, I did a little preliminary negotiating on prices," she told her father, taking a piece of paper out of her purse and handing it to him "You know how rotten I am with figures, so I had Roger translate the local currency into dollars using last week's exchange rates. What do you think?"

Bill glanced down the list of numbers, then handed it to Emily. "I think that if I don't get you onto my payroll I'm crazy." He paused, frowning at his own enthusiasm. "You understand," he added sternly, "that I expect you to take this seriously, Linda."

"Of course I will," Linda answered. "I've finally found my true calling in life—becoming a professional shopper."

But as the evening wore on the woman that Randy had seen glimpses of in Cambridge emerged more fully. Not only did Linda seem serious about a career, she wanted a career in the family business. Randy knew that when Linda put her mind to something she had an ambitiousness and an aggressiveness that she herself couldn't match, but heretofore those qualities had been utilized almost exclusively in the pursuit of either pleasure or men. Should Linda decide to go to business school and pursue an executive position at C & D she would probably give Luke Griffin a real run for his money some day.

When Randy mentioned that C & D was shorthanded due to a flu epidemic Linda immediately offered to stay in New York and help out. Working in various departments would give her a chance to refamiliarize herself with the merchandise, and remaining in New York for a week or two would give her and her father the opportunity to discuss the details of her future job. Besides, she admitted with a wink at Randy, she'd been looking for an excuse to spend more time with Roger.

Toward the end of the evening Emily reminded everyone, including her husband, that Thursday was their anniversary, saying that nothing could please her more than to have the family together at dinner. The fact that the invitation included Roger Bennett left Randy jealous of her sister and guilty over the fact. And when Roger and Linda walked out of the apartment arm-in-arm a little later and Bill Dunne said exactly nothing about it, Randy couldn't help but resent his double standard. She didn't bother to hide her feelings when she said goodnight to him. Several times over the next few days she was sorely tempted to argue with him over Luke Griffin, but every time she complained to her mother Emily merely told her to be patient. In the end Randy held her tongue.

At least having Linda in New York provided partial compensation for not seeing Luke. She and Roger came over for dinner most nights and the two sisters met for lunch on workdays. On Monday they went shopping together for an anniversary present for their parents, finding a small Persian rug in a store specializing in oriental imports and chipping in for it. Randy took Linda's word that even though the rug cost the moon and the stars, it was well worth the price.

Most other days the weather was so hot and muggy that they stayed in the building and ate at the store restaurant, talking about everything from Linda's trip to Paris to the latest difficult customer. Not surprisingly, however, their primary topic of conversation was their respective men. Although Linda was now completely serious about Roger, she was also very cautious. She pointed out to Randy that she hadn't even met his children yet—they wouldn't be returning to New York until school began in the fall. She wasn't about to rush into another marriage where there might be hostile stepchildren to contend with.

When it came to Luke Griffin Linda had no advice for Randy beyond the resigned observation that if Bill Dunne would only come to his senses, things would surely proceed in a satisfactory fashion.

"But it's been over a week," Randy said. "How long

am I supposed to humor him for? Another week? A month? A *year*, for heaven's sake?"

"Why don't you give it till the end of the week?" Linda suggested. "And then the three of us can gang up on him and make him see reason. He has to have noticed that the women in his family all disagree with him." Linda smiled a little wistfully and laughed softly. "Do you remember the fit Dad had the first time I stayed out all night? I suppose I wasn't the easiest daughter to raise, but at least I paved the way for you."

"Paved the way?" Randy repeated, laughing herself now. "You wore him down where you were concerned, but what good does that do *me?*"

They finished their lunch in increasingly good spirits, laughing and reminiscing over the foibles of fathers.

Luke knew he'd been acting like an infatuated high school kid ever since returning from Philadelphia, but he couldn't seem to help himself. With the exception of a three-day weekend spent in Dallas he'd been in the store constantly for the last week, and perhaps that was part of the problem. As long as he kept his mind on his job he was fine, but all too often during the day he'd find himself wondering what department Miranda was working in and how she was doing. It wasn't so bad to lie in bed at night and remember how sweetly passionate she was in his arms, because at least no one was around to notice the effect it had on him. But one of these days he was going to allow his attention to wander during a meeting and wind up totally embarrassed.

Yesterday he'd reached either the high point or the low point of his folly. He'd actually called around to find out where she was and then gone down to housewares to look at her. Not to speak to her, just to look at her. That in itself was bad enough, but then, when she wasn't around, he'd approached one of the other saleswomen in the department and asked where she was. Upon learning that she was eating lunch in the store restaurant he'd taken the elevator back upstairs again.

He shook his head in disbelief, thinking that some mysterious virus must have afflicted him, to send him up to the restaurant after her. But virus or not, he had felt like killing her when he finally found her. She was sitting with another woman and laughing about something. What right did she have to laugh, he asked himself, when he was going quietly out of his mind? In his more honest moments he admitted to himself that sooner or later he was going to cave in and confront Bill Dunne about her, but he hadn't quite reached that level of desperation.

At first he didn't pay any attention to Miranda's companion, but then the resemblance between the two of them hit him with almost physical force, and he realized that he was looking at Linda Franck. The two were very much alike, so much so that if Miranda hadn't just changed her hairstyle, a casual acquaintance who met one of them in the street might have wondered which sister he was seeing. Luke began to feel a little less stupid about the mistake he'd made.

He grimaced as he watched them talking and laughing, wondering if the two of them were cooking up another diabolical scheme to drive him crazy with. Probably not, he supposed. Miranda could easily have manufactured some excuse to come to his office if she'd wanted to see him, but she hadn't. Up till now she'd done most of the chasing, but things had obviously changed. Or maybe it was her feelings that had changed. He couldn't help but notice that she'd finished almost an entire chef's salad.

Totally disgusted with how much that frightened him, Luke had gone back to his office and thrown himself into his work. And the next day, as Bill Dunne wrapped up a meeting with Luke and a group of senior executives, he firmly dismissed the temptation to ask for an extra five minutes alone with the boss. He was a rational man, after all, and as such, he understood that he'd have to be a fool to jeopardize his career for a woman he'd met less than six weeks ago and thus couldn't possibly love. Not only did they barely know each other, but he wasn't about to get trapped into any commitments just yet. It made no difference that he couldn't get her off his mind, and had absolutely no desire to see anyone else.

Logic, however, failed to explain why his heart started pounding double-time when Bill said casually, "Luke, stick around for a while, will you?"

Everyone else filed out of the room, leaving the two of them alone, facing each other across Bill's desk. "Today is my thirty-first anniversary," he said.

Luke realized that Bill looked almost as uneasy as he himself felt. When Bill didn't come to the point, he made the obvious comment. "Congratulations. I envy you and your wife—she's a very special lady."

Bill picked up his pipe, stared at it and then put it back in the ashtray. "Damn it, Luke, at the rate I'm going there won't be a thirty-second. Emily never yells, but she's made it clear that she thinks I was wrong about you and Randy. Okay, I *know* I was wrong about you and Randy. Your relationship with my daughter has nothing to do with your performance as an executive, and I never should have tied the two together. I'm sorry."

"Apology accepted." Luke was far too cautious to say anything more. Obviously Bill wasn't through with him yet, and he wanted to judge the lay of the land before he responded.

"But that doesn't mean that my feelings as a father are any different from what they were two weeks ago," Bill went on. "It's just that if I keep interfering the women in my family are going to openly revolt. It was bad enough when it was just Emily and Randy I had to contend with, but now that Linda's in town. . . ." He ran a hand through his hair in a defeated gesture and then winced at his own words. "Uh . . . does that present any problem for you? The fact that Linda's around?"

"No," Luke said. He might have explained that his opinion of Linda Franck had undergone substantial revisions, but he didn't bother. "As a matter of fact, I saw Miranda and Linda in the restaurant yesterday."

"Did you?" Bill shook his head. "I only hope Randy was eating for a change. I know she's unhappy—Linda and Roger are the only people who seem to be able to get a smile out of her lately. That's Roger Bennett, by the way. He and my older daughter are what I think you'd call a 'hot item.'"

She doesn't eat? Luke thought. She doesn't smile? He felt as euphoric as a kid who'd just stolen home. Naturally he didn't admit that, but calmly remarked that Miranda had once mentioned that her sister was dating Roger Bennett, and that he hoped that whatever was troubling Randy would work itself out.

In the past Bill Dunne and Luke had laughed over the latter's talent for playing it close to the vest, but on this occasion it seemed to seriously annoy Bill. "You know bloody well what's troubling her!" he said. "Do I have to spell it out for you, Luke?"

"It would be nice," Luke answered evenly.

But instead of spelling out anything, Bill smiled sheepishly and admitted that part of the reason he'd hired Luke was for his ability to outflank the competition. "But I don't much care to have you use that poker-faced routine on me," he told him. "I'll make it easy for both of us. Emily and I are going out for our anniversary tonight, to Windows on the World. The two girls and Roger are coming along also. Why don't you join us? Our reservation is at seven-thirty."

Luke wasn't taking any chances—not when victory

was so close. "Does that constitute an official bless-
ing?" he asked.

"More or less. I'll trust that your intentions are what
we used to call honorable, Luke. Why don't you go
downstairs and talk to Randy? She's selling shoes
today."

Luke got up and started to leave, then turned around
and held out his hand. The handshake was more than
an empty formality. It signified that they'd reached an
understanding, and Luke didn't know which of them
was more relieved.

"Why is it," Randy complained to her co-worker in
the shoe department as she headed toward the stockroom, "that I always get the ones with the weird feet?
Do we even *have* anything in 11AAA?"

"If you'd read our ads you wouldn't have to ask," the
woman informed her with a laugh. "We're the ones
who like to boast that we're the best department store
in the city for narrow sizes, remember? But you'd
better grab the ladder, Randy. We keep the narrowest
widths together, all the way in the back on the top few
shelves."

At least I'm not afraid of heights, Randy thought as
she climbed to the top of the ladder. A bulb was
missing from one of the overhead fixtures, making it a
little hard to read the writing on the boxes. She reached
up for one, only to nearly drop it when a male voice
called out, "Miranda?"

Luke, of course. Everyone else called her Randy.
"All the way in the back," she called to him. The only
reason she *hadn't* dropped the box was that his appearance wasn't a total surprise. One of the saleswomen in
housewares had mentioned that he'd stopped by yesterday when she was at lunch, and the news had made her
day. She knew it had to be personal—if it had been
business he would have sent her another one of his
blasted memos.

He walked over and looked up at her, commenting that he didn't understand how she could see what she was doing.

"I manage," she told him. "You've come at a very good time." She threw down the box of shoes, saying, "Here, catch!"

Two more boxes containing the only pumps in the store even vaguely resembling the customer's request quickly followed. "I have an 11AAA out there," she explained as she started to back down the ladder.

She was pleased with herself for appearing so calm when actually she was fast becoming a nervous wreck, wondering what Luke wanted to say to her. Her pulse rate jumped when he set the shoes on the floor and placed a hand on either side of her waist, gently lifting her the rest of the way down.

He didn't release her once her feet touched the ground, however, but took a few steps forward until the front of his lean body was pressed against her back. "The 11AAA can wait," he murmured into her ear. Randy stiffened when his mouth moved lower, nipping at the spot he'd first discovered in Maine, and then made a helpless, guttural little noise.

After a week of not seeing or touching him his lips were even more effective than usual, arousing her to pliant cooperation even more quickly than before. "Unfair," she moaned. "Illegal offense."

Luke turned her around in his arms, twining a hand through her hair to firmly tilt her head back. His lips brushed across her mouth, then lifted a fraction. "I always play dirty when I'm desperate," he said.

The next instant their lips were clinging, their tongues hungrily tasting and exploring. As Randy arched against him her hands slipped around his waist to hold him close. It feels so right, she thought to herself. Like being home again.

She pulled away to break the kiss, but their foreheads were still touching, their lips playfully meeting every few seconds for a gentle kiss. "The 11AAA," she murmured.

"Such dedication." Luke traced the line of her jaw with his lips, then turned his attention to her earlobe. "There's one thing you don't know about me, Miranda. I go wild over shoes. Any other department and all I would have done is kiss you a few times and then tell you that I'm coming to dinner with you tonight. But shoes . . ."

"Are you?" Randy twisted away to free her earlobe from his teeth, acutely interested in the conversation all of a sudden. "You mean you talked to Dad?"

"Umm. I think I have his seal of approval as long as I behave with reasonable propriety. But you should have stayed out of the stockroom, Miranda." Without warning Luke picked her up and started toward the darkest corner of the room.

"Luke, where *are* you going?" Randy asked with a giggle.

He nodded straight ahead. "Over there. I'm going to throw you down on the floor. I told you, shoes drive me wild, especially size 11AAA pumps. I can't control myself around them."

When he put her down, pulled her roughly into his arms and sweetly ravaged her mouth, a bemused Randy began to wonder if he were serious. She was clinging to him with a kind of confused abandon when he finally decided to release her.

"The 11AAA," he groaned.

"She's probably gone by now," Randy murmured, her lips exploring the curve of his neck.

He put his hands on her upper arms to hold her a safe distance away from him, then took a few steps backward for insurance. "Don't you know you could get into trouble for messing around in the stockroom during working hours?" he demanded.

"With the boss?" Randy asked.

"I'm not the boss in Manhattan." Luke put an arm around her shoulders and nudged her toward the waiting trio of shoe boxes. "I'll see you tonight, okay? I have some work to finish up, so I'll meet you at the restaurant."

"Windows on the World at seven-thirty?"

"Right, angel." Luke pecked her on the lips and picked up the three boxes of shoes.

Randy's first problem was to placate her irate customer, but Luke solemnly apologized, explaining that he was a vice president taking a special inventory of the shoe department that had required Miss Dunne's cooperation for a few minutes, and the customer nodded in bewilderment and allowed Randy to show her the shoes.

Randy was so happy with the thought of having Luke at dinner that night that it was hours before she realized that Linda would be there also. She wondered if Luke knew.

Her conversation with her father as they walked home that evening reassured her that Luke not only knew but didn't mind, and that Bill Dunne had indeed decided to remove himself from her personal life. She wasn't naive enough to believe that he could really accept a love affair between herself and Luke, but realized that he simply preferred to look the other way and pretend it wasn't happening. Randy had no intention of doing anything that would remind him.

Like Luke, Linda and Roger were meeting Randy and her parents at the restaurant, which was located on the 107th story of the North Tower of New York's World Trade Center. Randy had never been there, so the first thing she did when she walked out of the elevator and into the lounge was to look out the window. She could make out the Statue of Liberty guarding New York Harbor. She was so wrapped up in the view that when she felt a man's lips on her bare shoulder she started violently and whirled around. The gown she wore, a one-shouldered dress of silk chiffon in shades ranging from royal blue to deep violet, almost invited such liberties.

Luke smiled and kissed her cheek, telling her that she looked beautiful. "You look beautiful, too," she answered, running a hand down the lapel of his dark suit. "But I like you better naked," she whispered mischievously.

"Patience, woman." He smiled and led her back to her family. Roger and Linda had just arrived, and Randy felt as though her own smile were plastered to her face as she made the introductions. To her great relief both Luke and Linda smiled and shook hands as though delighted to know each other.

It was left to Emily Dunne to finally bring up what was on everybody's mind. Dinner had gone perfectly, from the champagne and sushi to the special anniversary cake that Bill had ordered delivered to the restaurant. Perhaps they'd had a trifle too much wine, but it certainly hadn't hurt any of them. And then Emily smiled at Luke and blithely asked him how his sister and her husband were getting along.

To his credit, the stunned look on his face passed almost at once, and he answered that they were doing much better. "They're seeing a very good woman therapist," he added. "Tom was having problems with his job and Annie was frazzled from being at home all day with two small children. Neither was very sympathetic to the other's problems, but I think that they now understand each other better. They'll work things out."

Emily said she was pleased to hear it and announced that it was time to open the presents. The celebration picked up without missing a beat. Emily adored the Persian carpet, saying that even though a client was looking for one exactly like it she intended to hang it in the bedroom. Roger handed them an IOU for house seats to a couple of plays set to open in the fall, and Luke had brought along two bottles of a very expensive French wine that was almost impossible to find outside of someone's private cellar. Eventually all six people wedged themselves into the Dunnes' limousine and drove uptown to finish off the evening in the apartment.

Randy fixed the coffee while everyone else made themselves comfortable in the living room. After an evening filled with passionate little looks and subtle caresses she was glowing with happiness. But the smile on her face abruptly disappeared when she walked into the living room to hear Linda giggle and say, "Who would have thought that things would turn out so well?"

Randy almost dropped her mother's sterling silver tray. "Have some coffee, Linda," she said, setting it down on the cocktail table.

But Linda didn't seem to hear her. "I mean, after all that business with you and Luke in Maine. . . ." She winked at Randy and giggled again.

"Roger, did you happen to notice how much wine she had tonight?" Randy asked with a sigh.

"Obviously too much," he answered. "Come on, darling, have a cup of coffee."

"Maine?" Bill Dunne repeated, looking totally bewildered. "What is everyone talking about? What business in Maine?"

"Oh, nothing," Linda said. When she picked up the silver coffeepot and a delicate china cup Randy held her breath until she'd safely finished pouring.

Bill Dunne's gaze slowly traveled around the room. Randy was watching Linda sip her coffee, her face rather pale. Roger looked as though he were dying to laugh but understood that such an act would be an unpardonable breach of good taste. Luke seemed tense and angry and Emily was smiling beatifically, as though

Linda hadn't just dropped a potential bombshell into the conversation.

"Emily," Bill said at last, "do you know what Linda was talking about?"

Emily nodded.

"And?" he demanded.

Emily gave an apologetic little shrug at Randy, then repeated the process with Luke. "Actually, it's rather a complicated story, darling, but to give you just the basics, when Luke went up to Cambridge to talk to Linda about Tom—that's his brother-in-law, you remember—he decided that perhaps it would be more —effective—to take her some place out of the way for a while. I'm afraid his motives are rather a mystery to Randy, and since she's the one who told me the story in the first place I suppose you'll have to ask Luke to enlighten you. Because with men, who knows? Isn't that true, Linda? Do you remember your friend Buffy Cabot, the one who got involved with that ghastly dentist who seduced her when she—"

"Emily," Bill interrupted with a heavy sigh, "don't pull that number on me. Not after thirty-one years. I'm not going to forget what I asked you in the first place, so just get on with it."

"I can't understand it," Emily observed blandly. "It works perfectly with most of my clients."

"Emily . . ."

"Yes, darling." Emily settled back in her chair, looking a little chastened. "It's just that Luke got Randy instead of Linda, and somehow he never realized it, so when she came back to New York she pretended they'd never met, and—"

"What?" The question was bellowed out with all the ferocity of a wounded rhinoceros. "What in *hell* were you doing in Cambridge?" he said to Randy. "You were supposed to be in New Hampshire!"

The whole conversation had taken on the inevitable air of a Greek tragedy—or perhaps a Roman farce.

Randy knew that sooner or later the whole story would have had to come out, but later—much later—would have been better than sooner. Preferably, she thought to herself, after she and Luke had been married for ten years and had produced a pair of adorable children. Ugly ones wouldn't have served half as well.

Having told this tale first to Linda and Roger and then to her mother, it was understandable that she'd lost a little of her enthusiasm for it. Nonetheless, she obediently repeated to her father just why Luke had mistaken her for Linda and what had happened afterwards. It wasn't so much that she purposely left anything out as that she simply forgot to mention that Luke had touched her a time or two when they were in Maine.

She didn't really suppose that Bill Dunne would be gullible enough to swallow her version of events without asking a few pointed questions—and she was right.

"First of all," he said to Luke, "you can explain just what made you think I would approve of your drugging one of my daughters, flying her up to some remote part of Maine and keeping her there against her will for three solid days. Second, you can tell me how someone to whom I pay a six-figure salary, who's widely acknowledged to be one of the smartest men in our business, can possibly have been *stupid* enough to have mistaken my younger daughter for my elder one. And third"—his voice rose by a good twenty decibels—"you can tell me what the hell you were trying to accomplish!"

Luke reached for his cigarettes. Randy had already noticed that he tended to light up a cigarette whenever he was angry or upset, but in this instance there was already a cigarette burning in the ashtray. He stared at the pack, as if suddenly aware of that fact, and threw it onto the table.

"I knew you wouldn't approve," he said. Randy was

amazed by how calm he could sound when she knew he was thoroughly rattled. "That's why I didn't ask you. I believe that Miranda has already explained why I thought she was Linda. And I certainly didn't intend to harm her—I just wanted to, uh, take her mind off Tom."

"Well, from what I've heard about it," Linda drawled, "you certainly would have succeeded!" She giggled again, then clapped a hand over her mouth. At this point it seemed that Roger Bennett couldn't contain himself a moment longer. He grinned from ear to ear and then burst out laughing.

Both Bill and Luke ignored the pair of them. In retrospect, Randy decided, the story was kind of funny, even if Luke didn't think so. But then, she wasn't the one her father had just called stupid, or the person who Linda and Roger were laughing at.

"Obviously," Bill said to Luke, "you didn't succeed in taking my daughter's mind off anyone by telling her to carry wood. I will therefore assume that you took a typical male approach and took her to bed."

Suddenly even Linda sobered up. Randy's hands clenched into fists, the nails of one digging into the palm of the other. She didn't want to see her father hurt, but even more than that, she couldn't allow Luke to be put on the spot this way. "Daddy . . ." she began.

Luke cut her off with a short, hard stare. "Obviously *not*," he said. "If I had, I would have known it wasn't Linda."

Randy went limp with relief, so sure that the worst was over that even when her father bit out the curt question, "And Philadelphia?" she paid very little attention to him. She'd intended to tell him about Sean Raley, but if Luke wanted to substitute a harmless little lie or two, that was all right with her.

"I don't think it's going to do our future relationship any good for me to lie to you," Luke said. Randy bolted up like a puppet whose strings have been yanked taut. He couldn't possibly intend to admit what had happened, she thought. But she was wrong.

"If you're asking me whether I've made love to Miranda, the answer is yes," he added.

"Then I trust that you have a solitaire diamond in your pocket," Bill snapped back.

Oh, no, Randy thought, here comes the shotgun. She rolled her eyes toward the ceiling and then looked over at her mother, who shrugged helplessly. Emily's expression said that *both* men were crazy.

Luke glanced at Randy, saw that she was more exasperated than upset, and told Bill, "Not at the moment. Perhaps eventually."

Randy could see that her father was absolutely furious. He'd given his word not to interfere and had certainly intended to honor it, but Luke's clear admission of what had happened in Philadelphia was too much for him to swallow. "I strongly suggest," he said, "that tomorrow morning you take Miranda to Tiffany's, Luke."

"I'm busy tomorrow morning," was the measured response. "Maybe some other time."

Suddenly Randy had had enough of both of them. "Would you just stop it?" she yelled. "In the first place, Daddy, I have no intention of marrying a man who has to be backed into a corner before he'll agree, and in the second place—in the second place, this entire conversation is absurd. If you insist on getting out your shotgun, why don't you point it at—"

"That's quite enough, Miranda." The rather overbearing interruption came from Luke, who promptly turned his attention back to Bill. "Obviously we're upsetting her," he stated. "I suggest that we finish this conversation in the den."

But Bill had paid very little attention either to Randy's outburst or to Luke's quashing of it. He seemed to be deep in thought, lost in some world of his own. "I learned in California that you can be a tough negotiator," he finally remarked. "Do you happen to recall what Dunne Industries closed at this afternoon?"

"Thirty-two and a half," Luke answered.

"Exactly. I hold options to buy ten thousand shares at twenty-six even. I think that one thousand of those options would be a reasonable sum. And then there's the matter of the presidency. I've told you six years, but I could be persuaded to reconsider."

Luke settled back on the couch, apparently at ease now. "I'm listening," he said.

If Randy had been close enough to hit him she probably would have. How dare he negotiate with her father as though dowries were still in style? She heard another giggle from Linda, turned to glare at her and noticed the expression on her face. Over the years she'd learned that if Linda thought something was *that* funny, it probably was.

"Do you believe the two of them?" Linda asked Randy, still laughing. "They sound like two characters out of a Regency romance!"

Randy smiled in spite of herself. "Really, Luke," she teased, "those options are only worth, let me see, sixty-five hundred dollars. Don't you think you're worth a little more? I mean, it isn't every day a woman gets to marry—"

"Nobody asked you." Luke obviously saw nothing funny in the situation. "You were saying?" he asked Bill.

"I could be persuaded to give up the presidency in, let's say, five years."

Now Emily chimed in. "Luke, dear," she said solemnly, "I think you should hold out for stock. The problem is, my father and I hold most of the stock, so you really should be talking to *me*, not Bill."

"Mom, you're outrageous," Randy said, laughing

along with Linda and Roger now. In fact, the only two people in the room who didn't find the situation amusing were Luke and Bill Dunne.

"I think," Emily went on, "that five hundred shares would be a very nice wedding present. And don't you dare try to bargain me up, Luke Griffin, because I won't have it. That's worth over sixteen thousand dollars, and even if you are the handsomest, most charming, most *desirable* man in Manhattan there's a limit to what you can extort from me."

"I wouldn't think of it," Luke retorted. "Thank you, Emily. It's a very generous gift." He looked back at Bill. "Four years. No longer."

"You've got yourself a deal." The two men stood up almost simultaneously and shook hands.

"I'll pick you up at ten o'clock tomorrow, darling," Luke said to Randy.

*Darling?* she thought. "What for?" she said aloud.

"Tiffany's," he stated.

"You're out of your mind." Suddenly Randy's sense of humor had fled. "I'm not going to be part of some—some financial package that you've negotiated with my father."

"Why not? In Philadelphia you told me—"

"Never mind what I said in Philadelphia! I'm not going to marry a man who has to be *bought* for me!" Without another word Randy turned on her heel and stormed into her bedroom, slamming the door viciously shut behind her.

Luke joined her within moments. The minute he walked into the room Randy rubbed the tears out of her eyes and glared at him. "What do *you* want?" she demanded.

"I have a proposition to make," he said, sounding utterly sane and reasonable. "I can understand that you wouldn't want to marry me under the circumstances we discussed in the living room, but *you* have to understand that only a fool would give up what I was offered. At the same time, though, I refuse to put myself into a situation where your father constantly interferes in our relationship. So if you don't want to marry me, you're going to have to live with me."

It took Randy less than five seconds to spot the flaw in his logic. "I'll get my own apartment," she said.

Luke shook his head, walking to the bed and sitting down next to her. "I'd be lonely," he murmured, trailing a finger down her arm. "My house is in Westchester and you'd be in Manhattan."

Randy edged away from him, unwilling to be talked into anything. But he put a hand around her waist to prevent further escape and went on seductively, "Do you realize that all night long I've been dying to do *this?*" Before Randy could stop him he'd slipped her gown off her shoulder and down to her waist. She wasn't wearing anything underneath, a fact that seemed to please him immensely.

Even though she arched away from him his mouth managed to imprison a nipple, nipping it until it was hard and then sweetly punishing its twin with equal effectiveness. The old familiar fire started to burn its way through her body, but still she resisted, trying to twist away.

Luke was having none of it. He rolled onto the bed and pinned her body beneath his own, ignoring the hands that pushed against his shoulders. "You're beautiful," he growled. "And I'm tired of lying in bed at night and thinking about you. I want you with me."

When his lips brushed her mouth she shuddered with desire. Her hands dropped to her sides, then crept around his waist. After a smoldering kiss that said he wanted much, much more from her, he raised his head and murmured, "Okay?"

Randy looked into his eyes, too aroused and confused to think straight. "Okay what?"

"It would be easier to get married than to live together, Miranda."

Randy didn't answer, but as Luke captured her lips again she knew that she'd marry him if that was what he wanted. She wanted it too, so what difference did his reasons make?

# *Chapter Ten*

*R*andy was looking at herself in the full-length mirror in her mother's dressing room, her hand shaking slightly as she smoothed the ankle-length skirt of her white silk dress. Although her wedding gown, with its mandarin collar, fitted lace top and long sleeves, looked enchanting on her, her face was almost as pale as the fabric was. She fingered the chain of her gold cross, which was hidden beneath the neckline of her dress, and wished for the tenth time that day that the ceremony was already over with.

Luke was more than half an hour late, and Randy became more and more agitated as the minutes ticked by. Ever since Friday, when she and Luke had picked out simple gold wedding bands and a ruby and diamond engagement ring, everything had seemed to go wrong.

After taking out a marriage license and lunching together in the city, they took the train up to Luke's house in suburban Westchester County. Luke had already warned Randy that he had a very busy schedule for the next few weeks; he was ostensibly showing her the house so that she could shop for mundane items like decent pots and new linen. Emily had promised to help him decorate, he said, but he'd never found the time to sit down with her. There was very little furniture as yet.

She loved the place on sight. It was a large, colonial-style home surrounded by shrubs and trees, sitting on almost an acre of land. They walked inside arm-in-arm, but Randy barely had time to glance into the nearly empty living room before Luke was lifting her into his arms and carrying her up the stairs. He made love to her with a burning passion, whispering how much he wanted her and how beautiful she was. And afterward, as she lay replete in his arms, he murmured a tender "I love you" and everything seemed perfect.

Unfortunately, Randy had seen Luke exactly once since that afternoon. When he wasn't working in the office he was traveling—first to Florida, then to Texas. They managed to have lunch together on Wednesday, but Randy's grandparents joined them so the meal was anything but intimate. The Conovers had interrupted their European trip to fly back to New York for the wedding, but were delighted to be thus inconvenienced. Randy smiled and thanked them when they announced their intention to give her and Luke a thousand shares of Dunne Industries stock as a wedding present, but she couldn't help adding in the gift to all the other assets Luke would derive from their marriage.

But the most stressful part of the whole thing was the way the wedding had snowballed from a quiet ceremony for the immediate family into a major affair complete with white gown, catered dinner and over a hundred guests. The whole reason for marrying so quickly was that Luke wanted something small and private, but the minute Jonathan Conover heard about the wedding he insisted that his family and close friends would never forgive him if they weren't invited. He knew perfectly well that his daughter was one of the few women in New York who could arrange dinner for one hundred in less than a week.

Randy didn't have to see Luke to know that he was displeased. They talked on the phone every day and he'd made his attitude crystal clear. Right now he was probably stuck in traffic on his way back from picking up his mother and stepfather at the airport. It was bad enough, Randy thought, that Linda and Luke's sister Annie were standing in the same room at this very moment, without adding in the presence of a mother and stepfather from whom Luke was quite obviously estranged.

She was looking at a chair, dying to sit down but afraid of wrinkling her gown, when Linda came into the room. "Luke just got here," she said. She took in Randy's frayed appearance, then added, "He looks even more wiped-out than you do. A huge truck jackknifed on the parkway and tied up traffic for miles. I think he's been sweating bullets, afraid you'd think he wasn't going to show up. Anyway, Dad sent him to your bedroom to change. He's not too pleased with the black tie routine."

"I know that." Randy brushed away a tear. "Lin, this is supposed to be the happiest day of my life and it's been totally awful. Luke is furious about the big wedding and upset about having his family here. I feel like I'm making a terrible mistake rushing into this, and, and . . ."

The next moment she was in Linda's arms, sniffing, "Lin, the dresses . . ."

"The world can survive a few wrinkles," Linda said, rhythmically stroking her neck. "Just take it easy; things will be fine. Luke loves you, he told you that."

Randy straightened and grabbed a tissue, dabbing at

her eyes. "Me, my money, who knows what he loves? I wish he'd refuse it all."

Linda smoothed a few stray wisps of her french knot back into place. "That's what I told Roger," she said, "but he thinks Luke would have to be crazy. He says that if he were Luke he'd take you and the money and live happily ever after. Men think differently than we do. They're pragmatic instead of romantic."

When Linda saw how little her explanation helped, she went on, "At least I have *one* piece of news that should help you relax. I've just been talking to Annie Havemeyer. She's quite a lady. She came up, introduced herself and actually thanked me for trying to straighten out her husband. I stood there stammering like a ninny until Roger came along and rescued me."

The thought of Linda at a loss for words coaxed a slight smile onto Randy's lips. She turned to the mirror to repair her makeup and Linda left the dressing room, saying she would check on Luke's progress.

A minute later Randy heard someone open the bedroom door and walked out of the dressing room to find out what was happening. She froze in her tracks at the sight of Luke, thinking that if she excused his slightly skewed bow tie and wan complexion, he looked terribly handsome.

"It's supposed to be bad luck," she mumbled.

"Lin told me how upset you are." Luke walked up to her and kissed her gently on the lips. "Don't be. Everything will be okay." He caressed her face, then took her in his arms and parted her lips for yet another kiss, this one passionate rather than tender. "Come on," he murmured against her mouth. "Let's get this over with."

Despite Randy's fears, the ceremony and reception went very well. She'd noticed that Luke's mother looked uncomfortable in the glittering world where her son was so at home, but Emily made sure that she and her husband had plenty to eat and introduced them to some old friends who could be counted on to keep them entertained.

The first person Randy spoke to after the ceremony was Annie Havemeyer, who admitted rather hesitantly that she almost hadn't come to the wedding, but couldn't bear the thought of not seeing her brother married.

"I just want you to know—I met your sister Linda and I thought she was very nice. What I'm beginning to realize is that I used to run to Luke for every little thing, especially after he moved back to New York. It made Tom feel as though Luke were more important than *he* is, and between the problems with his job and my troubles with the kids, everything started to go wrong. Someday I'll tell you about it, but I guess you have a lot of people to say hello to right now."

Randy answered that the next people she wanted to say hello to were her two new nieces, who were standing with their grandmother on the other side of the room. When Annie introduced her mother and stepfather there was no hint of discomfort or dislike in her voice; she seemed to have put the past behind her, even if Luke had not. The couple seemed perfectly nice to Randy, and she was relieved when she noticed Luke talking easily with them about an hour later.

Although everything went better than Randy had dared hope, she was more than happy to toss her bouquet to Linda, change out of her dress and leave the apartment with Luke. She fell asleep during the drive home, only waking up when Luke pulled the car into his garage. Carrying her in the back way wasn't exactly romantic, but Luke admitted that he was just too tired to walk around the house with her.

The next few days were as hectic as Luke had warned her they would be. He was out of the house by seven and returned late each night. He was tense and distracted, even when they made love, and couldn't or wouldn't respond to Randy's efforts to talk to him. She kept herself busy shopping and looking at furniture, but with every passing day was more unhappy and unsure of herself.

When Luke finally managed to make it home for dinner on Thursday she kissed him hello, served him his meal and kept the conversation light. But her feminine instinct to placate him was at war with her need for reassurance, and the latter finally won.

They were lying in bed together, watching a TV movie, when she asked softly, "Are you sorry you married me?"

Luke stared at the screen for several seconds, then looked at her like she was crazy. "What are you talking about?" he demanded.

His anger unnerved her. "You seem . . . unhappy," she stammered.

He sighed and reached for his cigarettes. "Miranda, I'm busy as hell; we've been having problems with the Dallas project contracts, and last week some teenager set off a bomb near the Florida store and knocked out half the windows. If I'm unhappy it doesn't have anything to do with you."

Randy wanted to believe him, but couldn't. "I feel as though you don't love me," she said. "Or at least that you have mixed feelings about the marriage. The fact is, if Lin hadn't said anything about Maine and if my father hadn't bribed you with things you wanted very much, we wouldn't be married at all."

When Luke didn't answer, she repeated, "We wouldn't, would we."

"No." Luke took a drag on his cigarette. "But I'm the one who pushed it, not you. You just have to understand that after so many years of avoiding marriage I needed . . . an incentive. Something to talk me into it. But that doesn't mean I regret it, or that I don't love you."

"Will you give everything back then?" Randy asked. "Wait the six years to take over?"

Luke frowned at her. "You can't be serious, Miranda."

Randy was about to answer that she was *very* serious when the phone rang. It was Aaron Gregov, who'd just seen the announcement of her marriage in the paper and wanted to congratulate her. Randy got him off the phone as soon as she decently could, but Luke wasn't too pleased by the call.

It was ridiculous to feel defensive—Aaron hardly qualified as an old boyfriend—but Randy couldn't help it. Luke went back to watching the movie and Randy lay beside him pretending to do the same. Eventually, though, he smiled at her and started to toy with the cross around her neck. She snuggled into the crook of his arm and began to unbutton his shirt.

He turned his head to kiss her, his hand reaching under her nightshirt to caress her breast. Even though the TV was on, Randy finally felt that Luke's full attention was on *her*, not on his work or on the need for physical release. She murmured a tender "I love you" and melted into his arms.

And then the phone rang again. Luke reached for it with a muttered curse, barking a curt "Hello!" into the receiver. Judging from the conversation, Randy concluded, the caller wasn't one of his favorite people.

"Yes, she is," he said. "No, you can't." A pause. "No." Another pause. "Yes." A third pause. "I'll do that. And please don't call her or try to see her ever again." He slammed down the phone.

"That was Sean Raley," he informed her, looking at her as though she were somehow responsible for the unwanted call. "He sends his best wishes."

Randy was surprised and rather pleased by Luke's jealousy. "I don't feel anything for Sean anymore," she said, "but you might have been a little more polite to him. It was considerate of him to call."

"Considerate?" Luke shook his head incredulously. "Are you really that naive? He's in New York, Miranda. Now that you're safely married he obviously wants to start sleeping with you again." He added a terse epithet that described his opinion of Sean Raley most effectively.

"I'd rather sleep with *you,*" Randy whispered.

Luke reached out for her, but the tender mood of only minutes ago had been lost. Randy couldn't respond to what she considered pure animal lust, and Luke quickly sensed it. The interrupted lovemaking left both of them hurt and touchy. Angry words were exchanged, and they wound up in a blazing argument when Randy demanded that Luke cancel his trip to Dallas the next day and he flatly refused. His goodbye kiss the next morning was perfunctory at best.

Randy was so dejected that she spent most of the day at the movies, but in the evening Linda and Roger appeared at the house with Chinese food for three, and a little of her depression lifted. Linda explained that Bill had mentioned Luke's trip to Dallas, so they'd decided to keep her company for a while.

It didn't take Randy very long to admit that things were less than perfect between her and Luke, or to become as angry as she'd been the night before. After ten minutes of pouring her heart out, she fumed, "So he's down in Dallas now, with Katrina Sorensen. And I'm not supposed to mind, even though he threw a tantrum when Sean Raley called me!"

"Randy, he's only doing his job," Roger pointed out. "And as far as Katrina goes, you should feel sorry for him, not angry. He's going to have his hands full shooting that advertisement."

"Well, poor little Luke. I don't see why he had to chase down there to sign those contracts and watch them take a few pictures. Dad could have done it."

"Because he knows how to handle Katrina better than anyone else, and because it's his responsibility to sit down with your attorneys and check over the contracts. He negotiated them," Roger reminded her, "not your father."

Randy wasn't interested in Luke's devotion to duty. "So where do I come into it?" she demanded. "In a couple of weeks I'll be starting the company's executive training program. Every time I bring up a honeymoon Luke claims he's trying to clean up his work so we can go away, but he just seems to get busier and busier."

"You won't get any sympathy from Roger," Linda said with a sigh. "He's as bad as Luke at times."

"If it were only the work I suppose I could cope with it," Randy replied. "But I can see that it's not. Something's eating at him, but he won't admit it, much less talk about it. Maybe we'd have a chance to work things out if I could only get him away from his damn job, but you can see how much success I've had with *that*. Tomorrow is Saturday, and he won't even be home till two o'clock."

Linda smiled, giving Roger a sidelong, calculating little glance.

"Okay, Lin," he laughed, "I know that look. What do you want from me?"

"Roger darling," she purred, "have you ever staged a kidnapping?"

Randy was standing in the hall looking out the window, nervously watching the street in front of the house. It was almost two-thirty now. Linda and Roger, meanwhile, were sitting in the kitchen, talking and drinking coffee. Also in evidence were two hulking young men whom Roger had introduced as Pete and Clint. Pete was the largest male nurse that Randy had ever seen, while Clint, an out-of-work actor, looked more like an out-of-work wrestler.

When Luke's car turned into the driveway Randy's heart began to slam against her ribcage. "Roger," she yelped, "he's back." Luke didn't bother to pull into the garage, but parked the car in front of the house. He got out, immaculately tailored as usual, whistling to himself. When he caught sight of Randy at the window he smiled at her and waved.

A moment later he let himself in. Roger had positioned himself about two yards back from the door, with Pete on one side and Clint on the other. Randy and Linda were standing on the first step of the stairs. Luke looked around at everyone, his expression puzzled. His eyes met Randy's. "What are you doing back there, honey?" he asked.

"Okay, fellas," Roger drawled. Pete and Clint, moving incredibly quickly for such large men, rushed over and grabbed Luke from behind, one of them holding his arms, the other his legs.

"What in hell is going on here?" he demanded. "Miranda? Who *are* these people?"

No one paid any attention to the angry outburst, least of all Roger, who removed a plastic bag from a leather satchel on the floor by his feet and started toward Luke. Luke spotted the handkerchief inside and started to struggle impotently. "Damn it, Roger, I have plane tickets for—"

He never had the opportunity to finish the sentence.

Pete eased him gently to the floor. Roger, kneeling down to finger the lapel of his jacket, remarked, "Nice suit. Come on, fellas, let's get him into something more rustic." The switch to blue jeans was accomplished with speedy efficiency.

When Roger withdrew a small bottle of medicine from the leather satchel Randy began to feel mildly queasy. "Is that really necessary?" she asked.

"Take it easy, Randy." He handed the bottle to Pete. "This will keep him asleep for a couple of hours, that's all. I don't want the guy cursing me all the way to Lake George." Randy turned away as Luke moaned, protesting the taste of the medicine Pete was dropping onto his tongue.

Afterward Roger pulled some rope out of his satchel and tied Luke's arms and legs. Then he cocked an eyebrow at Clint. "He's all yours, friend."

Pete had gone outside to retrieve a yellow station wagon from in front of the neighbor's house. Clint carried Luke in a fireman's hoist to a mattress lying in back of the wagon, laid him down and covered him with a blanket. Several suitcases were tossed in after him. Randy, Roger and Linda climbed into the front seat, and were headed for upstate New York ten seconds later.

Randy had gotten very little sleep the previous night. Kidnappings were not her usual *modus operandi*. But somehow, from the moment Linda had mentioned the idea the evening before, events had rushed on of their own volition, entirely out of her hands. Roger was enjoying himself enormously; he said with a wink that arranging a kidnapping was even more fun than producing a movie, because everything was real.

Within forty-five minutes he'd made half a dozen phone calls, arranging to borrow the wagon, a friend's cabin on an island in the middle of Lake George in upstate New York, and Pete and Clint. Roger Bennett, Randy decided, was the first man she'd met who could keep up with her sister.

She repeatedly reminded herself that if she didn't get Luke away from the office he would continue to work sixteen-hour days while their relationship went to pieces. She reminded herself that since he had kidnapped her, this was only poetic justice. But she didn't want to think about how angry he would be when he woke up, or what he would do to her once they were alone. Of course, as long as his hands and legs were tied, he was really quite helpless.

Eventually the motion of the car and simple exhaustion put her to sleep. The smell of hamburgers and fries woke her up, the change in scenery telling her that they'd traveled quite a distance in the meantime. Roger was just pulling back onto the highway after stopping for dinner at a local diner.

"Are we nearly there?" Randy took the hamburger that Linda held out to her and unwrapped it.

"Almost," Linda answered. "Luke's been tossing and muttering to himself back there. I think he's about to wake up."

As if on cue, Randy heard a hoarse curse from the back of the wagon and turned around to see Luke struggle into a sitting position. "Miranda," he said irritably, "don't you think this has gone far enough?"

Randy's blank expression gave no clue to the frightened turmoil she felt. "Are you hungry?" she asked. "Roger got some hamburgers."

"How am I supposed to eat one?" Luke demanded. "Damn it, Miranda, when I get these ropes off—"

"You'll get them off when Randy cuts them off," Roger interrupted with a laugh. "I was an Eagle Scout, Luke. I tie the best knots in New York."

This boast was met with a pithy suggestion from Luke as to just what Roger Bennett could do with his knots. Randy, ignoring Luke's ungentlemanly language, offered sweetly, "I'd be glad to feed you, Luke." When he gave a curt nod she unwrapped a burger and held it up for him to bite. He looked at her as though he would cheerfully take off her finger as well.

Half an hour later they pulled up to a pier where a medium-sized cabin cruiser lay gently bobbing in the water. After disposing of a hamburger and a packet of fries Luke had turned his attention to removing the ropes that were binding his wrists. He hadn't been successful.

Roger parked the car and opened the back of the wagon. "Time for a spin across the lake, Luke. Come on, get out."

"Like hell I will," Luke said.

"You want me to knock you out again?" Roger pointed to the boat. "I'm strong enough to carry you in there if I have to."

Luke glared first at Randy, then at Roger. "You might explain how I'm supposed to walk," he snapped.

Roger only laughed. "Say please, Luke, and I'll cut the ropes."

There was such a thing as going too far. "Roger," Randy began, "don't you think . . ."

But Roger merely grinned and said to Luke, "I figure I've owed you one ever since you swiped Katrina."

"You should have thanked me for that, not taken her back," Luke retorted. "Your stupidity isn't my problem!"

Roger thought it over for a moment, then conceded the point. "I suppose you're right. Okay, I'll cut the ropes."

With a rather extravagant curse for Roger, Luke edged his way out of the wagon, letting his legs dangle over the tailgate. Roger took out a pocket knife and quickly cut through the ropes on Luke's ankles.

"Okay, Luke, move it," he ordered lazily.

Luke, his face a study in cold fury, eased out of the car and stood up. Roger promptly gave him a forceful shove in the direction of the boat, prompting a sigh of dismay from Randy.

Livid over such treatment, Luke stopped dead. "You're enjoying every minute of this, aren't you?" he accused.

Roger only smiled again, putting his arm around Luke's shoulders and leading him a few feet away. He whispered something in Luke's ear and checked that the ropes were secure. Then both men began to laugh and walked to the boat together.

Randy and Linda exchanged a puzzled shrug, but said nothing. Luke was no longer angry with Roger, but it soon became obvious that he was eagerly anticipating the revenge he would take on Randy. He stared at her during the entire trip to the little island where Roger's friend had built his cabin, refusing to speak.

As they approached a small wharf Randy glimpsed a rough, wooden cabin about ten yards beyond, surrounded by trees. Roger helped Luke out of the boat, winked at Randy and announced, "We'll be back tomorrow night."

"Do have fun, you two," Linda added.

Randy and Luke stood watching as the boat slowly disappeared. Neither one spoke or moved. After several minutes Randy finally murmured, "Are you very angry with me?"

"You could say that," Luke answered coldly. "Are you going to untie me? Or do you plan to keep me this way until tomorrow night?"

"As long as it takes," Randy answered, her eyes fixed on his chest. She began to undo the buttons of his shirt, her fingers unusually clumsy as she bared his chest. Luke didn't tell her to stop or try to walk away. When she was finished she pulled off her own tee shirt, wound her arms around his neck and looked into his eyes.

"Am I supposed to be impressed?" he asked. "After all, it's hardly the first time."

Though disappointed by his failure to respond, Randy rubbed her half-naked body sensuously against his, standing on tiptoe to gently nip at his lower lip.

Luke stood there like a statue. "Untie me, and then we'll talk," he said.

"No." Randy dropped her arms to her sides. "I haven't had your complete attention for the entire week we've been married, but I aim to have it now. I'm going inside. You come in, lie down on the bed and let me do what I want, and when I'm satisfied that your mind is on *me,* then we can talk." She picked up the two suitcases she'd brought along and started toward the cabin.

It had only one room and contained a variety of furniture including a sofabed and a small dinette table. There were a stove and a sink, but the cabin had no indoor plumbing or electricity. Several gasoline lanterns sat on the table and the pump was located out the back door.

One of the suitcases Randy had taken up with her contained food, which she unpacked and put in one of the cabinets. Then she opened up a bottle of what she had gathered to be Luke's favorite wine and methodically drank down a six-ounce glass of it. Finally she opened up the sofabed, made it up with sheets and blankets she found in a dresser, and sat down to wait.

It seemed like hours before Luke finally came inside, and by then Randy had gone through a second glass of wine. He silently sat down on the bed, swung his legs up and lay back against the cushions that served as a headboard. When Randy didn't immediately join him he drawled, "I thought this was another one of your famous seductions, Miranda. What are you waiting for?"

He finally sounded like the man she'd fallen in love with. Greatly encouraged, Randy began to remove his shoes and then his socks, and was unable to resist running a teasing finger along the bottom of his foot.

He quickly jerked away, threatening, "Miranda, if you start tickling me. . . ."

"What will you do?" The wine had gone to her head by now. She turned her attention to his belt, unfastening the buckle and unsnapping the jeans. "I need a little cooperation," she scolded.

Luke merely smiled and lifted his body to permit her to remove his clothing. Randy sat down beside him and ran her hands up and down the full length of his body. "Something tells me you aren't angry anymore," she teased.

"At a certain point one's hormones take over," Luke

admitted. "But isn't this doing things backward? I thought that the idea was to get my attention. Believe me, Miranda, you've got it."

Randy gave his objections due consideration and then dismissed them. She didn't feel like talking, she felt like touching him and kissing him until he begged for mercy. "We'll get to that," she said, pouring him a glass of wine and holding it up to his lips. "Come on, drink up."

He sipped the wine, then shook his head and laughed. "Isn't this setting a little rustic for Château Lafite?" he asked.

"But it's your favorite." Randy pouted. "Isn't it?"

"True," Luke agreed, "but a little expensive to get me drunk with. Unfortunately, I think it's too late for you. Come on, honey, untie me before you pass out."

Randy ignored him in favor of pouring and drinking another half-glass of wine. She held Luke's glass up to his mouth for him to drink, and with a shrug he complied. Then she slowly stripped off the rest of her clothing, well aware that he couldn't take his eyes off her.

She felt pleasantly dizzy as she lay down next to him, one leg draped over his thighs, her sensitive breasts pressed against his chest. Her kisses were featherlight, meant only to tantalize and arouse, but Luke didn't seem to understand that. He repeatedly tried to capture her lips, only to have her tease him with the soft inside of her mouth and then repeatedly pull away. By now, of course, she knew exactly how to touch him and didn't hesitate to take advantage of the knowledge. She stroked and caressed him until he restlessly responded, moaning with a mixture of pleasure and frustration.

Her own pulses were also racing by now, so that continuing to tease him turned into a self-inflicted torture. When he murmured hoarsely, "Miranda, please let me kiss you," she couldn't refuse. She eased fully on top of him and offered her parted lips, which were taken in a devouring, bruising kiss. Though he clearly ached to possess her body as well Randy made him wait. As she moved above him she could feel his wild urgency and delighted in it. Finally satisfied, she raised her head and smiled. Luke stiffened and looked up at her, breathing raggedly.

"If I thought you knew what you were doing to me I'd tan your backside," he said. "Cut the ropes off, Miranda."

Randy rolled off him, pretending to consider the matter, while Luke rolled onto his side. "Miranda," he growled, "now!"

"I have to find a knife," she said, running her hand over his chest and tracing the dark arrow of hair to its point.

What came next happened so quickly that Randy never even saw it coming. One moment she was playfully caressing him, and the next she was pinned flat on her back, Luke on top of her, his knee aggressively parting her legs and his hand roughly claiming her breast. He lowered his mouth to hers in a fiery kiss that ended long before Randy wanted it to.

"How did you . . . ?"

He looked down at her with the most devilish glint she'd ever seen in his eyes. "Never mind that. Now you're going to pay the price for the last few hours," he announced. "You have two choices, Mrs. Griffin. One, I take you right now, and I do mean *now,* or two, I tease you the way you've just teased me. In either case I promise to leave you *very* frustrated."

Randy studied his crooked grin for a moment, then protested, "Luke, those are *terrible* choices. Give me a third."

He shook his head. "One or two, Miranda."

Of course he didn't mean it. "The first, I suppose," Randy told him.

Luke grunted and lowered his head. Randy could feel him trembling as he kissed her, his mouth gentle, thorough, tender. His hands were feverish on her body, yet he made no move to press his physical advantage. Instead he caressed her until she was arching toward him, hungry for his possession. For such a large man he could use his body with exquisite sensitivity, and as he moved against her her need increased until she was burning up with it. And then he stopped.

Randy stared at him, unable to believe that his threat had been serious.

"Do you have my attention?" he asked hoarsely.

She nodded, unable to get a word out.

"Good. Then listen carefully. I love you, Miranda. Do you hear that?"

"Yes," she whispered.

"You're sure?"

"Yes."

"Positive?"

"Yes," she said urgently.

"No doubts?"

"Luke," she moaned, *"please . . ."*

He cut her off with a kiss, suddenly out of control. Randy didn't mind at all. She was so recklessly excited herself that she stayed with him every step of the way, right through to the tempestuous finale.

And afterward, as they lay in each other's arms, everything felt so right to her that she wondered if her imagination had been running away with her all week.

"Miranda?" Luke murmured.

"You're the only one who ever calls me that," she told him sleepily.

"Because I like the name. Always have, ever since the first time I read *The Tempest.*" He kissed her nose. "You were right, you know."

"About what?" she asked.

"My feelings. Things happened too fast. It wasn't only work this past week."

Randy straightened up and pulled away from him, tense all over again. But Luke quickly stroked her hair and pulled her back. "It's okay now," he said. "I did a lot of thinking in Dallas, especially about the way I reacted to Raley's call. When I realized that the thought of being without you made me physically sick I figured it was time to stop analyzing all the reasons why we should have waited and trust my emotions."

He reached for the wine, smiling at her. "Any woman who thinks to bring along a bottle of my favorite wine is too good to lose."

After he'd refilled their glasses and settled back on the bed Randy said, "But you were the one who insisted. You admitted that. You knew as well as I did that my father would calm down by Friday morning. So why, if not for the money?"

"I admit that it seemed like too good a deal to pass up. And I was also a little angry at the way the four of you were laughing at me. But basically I wanted you with me. I told you that."

Randy sipped her wine, hating every single stock option and certificate.

"So we'll give it all back," Luke sighed.

She started in surprise, almost spilling her wine. "How did you know . . . ?"

"It's obvious, if you understand women. What *you* don't understand is that cutting a deal with your father gave me a rational excuse to justify what I wanted to do in the first place. It would have taken me some time to give in to my emotions, but the end result would have been the same. And if you want to return the stock. . . ."

"The truth is, it's much less than what I already own," Randy told him. "I guess we can keep it."

Luke's complacent smile said that he'd known all along that Randy would eventually see things his way, and when he promised that in the future he'd talk about what was bothering him she decided that the stock was really very unimportant. But as she silently sipped her wine it occurred to her that if he'd already sorted out his feelings in Dallas, there was no reason for him to have been angry about being hauled to Lake George.

"Luke," she said, "earlier today—all that cursing and all those dirty looks—did you mean them?"

He shook his head, grinning at her. "Of course not. I enjoyed every minute of it, especially once you started taking off your clothes. Although you *did* go a little too far, Miranda. My self-control isn't quite as great as you seem to believe."

"Oh." Randy started to play with a lock of his hair. "Were you planning to work tomorrow? Did I foul up your schedule?"

"If you could look in the pocket of my suit jacket you'd find a pair of airplane tickets to London. I told you that I was trying to clean things up so we could get away, didn't I? Unfortunately, the flight leaves tomorrow morning."

Randy moaned, "Oh, no!" and then, thinking that perhaps he was teasing, asked him, "That's true? You're not just saying it?" When Luke assured her that he was serious she exclaimed, "But why didn't you explain! We could have driven straight back!"

"Because I was having too much fun. You're the first woman who's ever kidnapped me, and I was finding it very erotic. Didn't you wonder what Roger whispered to me, or why we were laughing?"

Randy admitted that she had, but that she was so nervous that within moments she'd forgotten the whole incident.

"He said, 'You'll never play Hamlet at this rate, Luke. You're overacting.' Then he slipped me a metal file to cut the ropes with. Unfortunately, it took longer than I thought it would. You damn near drove me crazy, Miranda, especially since I'd been thinking about making love to you ever since I stepped on the plane in Dallas."

Randy meekly apologized. "I guess I had too much wine. But to think I could be packing for London right now . . . !" She sighed. "I suppose all's well that ends well, but still. . . ."

Luke smiled at her. "Wrong play, angel," he said. "Try Ferdinand to Miranda, Act Three of *The Tempest*." His voice dropped to a husky murmur. "'I, beyond all limit of what else in the world, do love, prize, honor you.'"

Miranda wiped away a sentimental tear. She'd once played her namesake and recognized the speech he'd quoted. "That's from the scene where Miranda's father has Ferdinand carry all those logs to prove his love for her." She giggled. "It's a little backward, Luke, but very appropriate all the same. And a lovely quote." She pecked him on the lips as a reward. "How nice that you can recite Shakespeare to me. Do you remember the part that goes, 'Admired Miranda! Indeed the top of admiration! Worth what's dearest—'"

Luke cut her off with a burst of laughter. "Darling Miranda, I picked up a copy of the play in Dallas to find one appropriate line to recite to you when we got to London. Which will hopefully be some time Tuesday, if we ever get off this blasted island."

Miranda grinned at him. "Prospero, Act Five of *The Tempest*: 'I'll deliver all, and promise you calm seas, auspicious gales, and sail so expeditious . . .'"

"Oh, shut up," Luke laughed, and pulled her into his arms.

**Silhouette Special Edition**

## August Special Editions
## Available Now

### An Act Of Love by Brooke Hastings

The act of mistaken anger that led Luke Griffin to
"kidnap" Randy Dunne soon gave way to a passion
from which there was no turning back.

### Fast Courting by Billie Douglass

Journalist Nia Phillips' assignment: interview
basketball coach Daniel Strahan—one of five
most eligible bachelors on the East Coast. Soon
Daniel was involved with the most important
game he'd ever play.

### Looking Glass Love by Carolyn Thornton

Winning Isaac Fielding's heart seemed hopeless,
especially when his past was as unhappy as
Chrissa's own. But Chrissa fought to convince
him that their love was special,
and would endure.

## August Special Editions
## Available Now

### Captive Of Fate by Lindsay McKenna

Alanna went to Costa Rica to expose Matt
Breckenridge but in the end she exposed only
her own heart by falling in love with the
arrogant colonel.

### Brand Of Diamonds by Ann Major

Lannie no longer wanted Brandon for what he
was worth . . . but for what he was. She wanted
the man beneath the glitter and this time,
she wanted him forever.

### The Splendoured Sky by Jeanne Stephens

Justin Kane never forgave Amber Rowland for
leaving him to pursue a modelling career. Now
she returned to Montana to run the family ranch
and to convince Justin she was back for good.

# Silhouette Special Edition

## Coming Next Month

**Enchanted Surrender by Patti Beckman**

Haunted by her past, Sandy Carver worked to
build a new life—one with no room for love.
But Carl Van Helmut insisted that she find
a place for love—and for him.

**The Marriage Bonus by Carole Halston**

An unhappy stint as a "country club wife"
had left Charlene longing for real love and
a real man and in Burt, her high school
sweetheart, she found both.

**Jessica: Take Two by Diana Dixon**

As if redoing a scene for one of her films,
actress Jessica Steele had a chance to try
again with the one man who had mattered:
her ex-husband, Grahme Foreman.

## Coming Next Month

### Paradiso by Antonia Saxon

Pat Jessup thought she had found her own
private paradise in Mexico. But it was a paradise
without passion—until she met local mayor
Santos Ribera.

### Sweet Adversity by Kate Meriwether

Probation officer Meredith Jennings gave
her whole heart to her job, until it
led her into the chambers of Judge
Warren Baxter, where a whole new
challenge awaited her.

### Passion's Victory by Jennifer Justin

Five years had passed since Alexandra
O'Neill had been in the arms of Matt Farraday,
but nothing—not time, not space—could
diminish their passion for each other.

# Silhouette Special Edition

## £1.10 each

61 ☐ TENDER DECEPTION
Patti Beckman

62 ☐ DEEP WATERS
Laurey Bright

63 ☐ LOVE WITH A PERFECT STRANGER
Pamela Wallace

64 ☐ MIST OF BLOSSOMS
Jane Converse

65 ☐ HANDFUL OF SKY
Tory Cates

66 ☐ A SPORTING AFFAIR
Jennifer Mikels

67 ☐ AFTER THE RAIN
Linda Shaw

68 ☐ CASTLES IN THE AIR
Tracy Sinclair

69 ☐ SORREL SUNSET
Gena Dalton

70 ☐ TRACES OF DREAMS
Jane Clare

71 ☐ MOONSTRUCK
Christine Skillern

72 ☐ NIGHT MUSIC
Kathryn Belmont

73 ☐ SEASON OF SEDUCTION
Abra Taylor

74 ☐ UNSPOKEN PAST
Linda Wisdom

75 ☐ SUMMER RHAPSODY
Nancy John

76 ☐ TOMORROW'S MEMORY
Margaret Ripy

77 ☐ PRELUDE TO PASSION
Fran Bergan

78 ☐ FORTUNE'S PLAY
Eve Gladstone

79 ☐ AN ACT OF LOVE
Brooke Hastings

80 ☐ FAST COURTING
Billie Douglass

81 ☐ LOOKING GLASS LOVE
Carolyn Thornton

82 ☐ CAPTIVE OF FATE
Lindsay McKenna

83 ☐ BRAND OF DIAMONDS
Ann Major

84 ☐ THE SPLENDOURED SKY
Jeanne Stephens

*All these books are available at your local bookshop or newsagent, or can be ordered direct from the publisher. Just tick the titles you want and fill in the form below.*

Prices and availability subject to change without notice.

SILHOUETTE BOOKS, P.O. Box 11, Falmouth, Cornwall.

Please send cheque or postal order, and allow the following for postage and packing:

U.K. – 45p for one book, plus 20p for the second book, and 14p for each additional book ordered up to a £1.63 maximum.

B.F.P.O. and EIRE – 45p for the first book, plus 20p for the second book, and 14p per copy for the next 7 books, 8p per book thereafter.

OTHER OVERSEAS CUSTOMERS – 75p for the first book, plus 21p per copy for each additional book.

Name ............................................................................................

Address .........................................................................................

.....................................................................................................